A CAPT. CYNDI STAFFORD NOVEL

VANISHED

BEHIND ENEMY LINES

Cover Design and Interior Format

VANISHED

BEHIND ENEMY LINES

DAN STRATMAN

ALSO BY DAN STRATMAN

The Capt. Mark Smith Series
MAYDAY
HURRICANE
BETRAYAL

THE CAPT. MARK SMITH SERIES BOXED SET

The Capt. Cyndi Stafford Series
DEADLY DILEMMA
LETHAL WINGS

DEDICATION

To the brave men and women in the US military who sacrifice so much to keep the rest of us safe, thank you.

PROLOGUE

WITH THE WEIGHT of the mission resting heavily on his shoulders, 1st Lieutenant Lance Garcia flexed his lean, muscular frame and dropped to one knee on the scorching-hot tarmac at Laughlin Air Force Base. Sweat coated his palms. The butterflies in his stomach collided midair in an abdominal demolition derby.

Despite the pain radiating up his leg, Lance's brain barely registered it. He was preoccupied with a far more significant matter. Mission success was too crucial to let anything distract him.

Lance was about to ask the beautiful woman standing in front of him a life-changing question. He reached inside his blue uniform jacket and pulled out a small, red velvet-covered box.

Captain Cyndi Stafford's mesmerizing crystal-blue eyes widened as she gazed down at the box. She cupped her hand over her mouth. "Oh my God, is that for me?"

Lance rolled his eyes. "No, it's for the hot woman behind you. Of course it's for you." Before continuing, Lance did a quick check of his wristwatch. "There's something important I want to ask you. But before I do, I have something to say." He cleared his throat. "Since we've been together, we have been through more"—he looked down and took a deep breath, searching for the right words—"more craziness and danger than most people experience in a hundred lifetimes. If there was ever any two people who were meant to be together, it's us. I think it's obvious. We are soulmates."

He stole another glance at his watch. Cyndi was so overwhelmed she didn't seem to notice.

Lance opened the lid and cradled the small box in the palm of his hand. In it was an antique ring that had been passed down through generations of the Garcia family. A three-carat canary diamond twinkled with an intense yellow hue in the Texas sun.

Lance embraced Cyndi's left hand and slipped the opulent ring onto her slender finger.

Cyndi's chest tightened. She suddenly had trouble taking a full breath. Tears trickled down her beautiful face.

Looking deep into his girlfriend's eyes, he said, "Cyndi Stafford, will you be my wife?"

Dazed by the surprise proposal, she held out her left hand and peered at the enormous gem as it sparkled in the sun. "It's stunning."

"Yes, it is." As he gazed into her eyes, Lance wasn't referring to the ring. "So…will you marry me or not?"

"Oh, sorry." Cyndi forced herself to take a deep breath. "Before I answer that"—she swallowed hard—"I need to tell you something."

Lance's growing level of anticipation suddenly deflated like a balloon dashed against a prickly cactus. His head drooped. *Great, she's going to try to let me down easily and explain why she won't marry me.*

Cyndi put her right hand under his chin and gently lifted Lance's head. "I've dated practically every type of guy there is. Some women want a man who's tall, handsome, smart, funny, and athletic. That's okay—if you're into that sort of thing. Others want a guy who is caring, sensitive, and in tune with what she's feeling." She looked into his brown eyes and let out a long sigh. "Then, there's you."

Lance's face contorted in confusion. "Wait. What are you trying to say?"

"Hang on, I'm getting there. What I'm saying is you aren't either one of those types of guys." A delightful smile crossed her face. "You're the one in a million who's both. There's no question in my mind you are my soulmate. Yes, Lance Garcia, I will marry you."

Cyndi had expected some type of ecstatic reaction to her answer. Instead, Lance casually stood up, stole one more glance at his watch, then just grinned.

Suddenly, the earth shook as a thunderous boom rattled the base.

Cyndi looked around frantically, overwhelmed by uncertainty. Oddly, there wasn't a cloud in the sky. "What in the world was that?"

Lance chuckled and pointed upward. A lone contrail, thirty thousand feet above the base, provided the answer to her question.

Lance's flight instructor had been the lead pilot in the formation flyover marking the end of their graduation ceremony. He'd slipped him $500 to break off after the flyover and go supersonic in the T-8 Arrow at the exact moment he planned on asking Cyndi to marry him.

Lance wanted to be able to boast for the rest of their relationship that popping the question was so momentous for Cyndi that the earth shook at the very moment she said yes.

Of course he'd conveniently leave out the part about the meticulously planned and paid-for sonic boom.

Cyndi glanced upward. "You arranged that?" she said with a wry smile.

"Yes, ma'am," Lance replied, pouring on the Texas twang.

Cyndi laughed and shook her head. "Why am I not surprised. Come here, *soulmate*." She wrapped Lance in a strong embrace and planted a deep, passionate kiss on his grinning lips.

Suddenly, a raucous outburst erupted behind Cyndi. Their entire Air Force pilot training class—including Gump, Barf, Tire, and Princess—had quietly snuck up behind Cyndi while Lance distracted her.

They'd been tipped off that he was going to propose on the tarmac as soon as the graduation ceremony ended.

The group of newly minted Air Force pilots applauded and cheered for their classmates. One by one, they shook the couple's hands and offered their best wishes for a long and happy marriage—even Princess.

The stunning beauty pageant veteran feigned a smile. "Congrats on your engagement, Hollywood. I'm happy for you," Princess said with very little conviction She stepped forward and opened her arms to give Lance a warm farewell hug.

Lance extended his right arm, surprising her by offering a purely platonic greeting. He took Princesses well-manicured hand and shook it in a business-like manner. "Thank you, Lieutenant Richards. Best of luck to you in your next assignment."

"Oh…um…okay. Thanks. Same to you." She turned to Cyndi. "You got yourself a great guy, Captain Stafford. Take good care of him." Her voice was thick with regret and a tinge of envy.

"Oh don't worry about that, I will." Cyndi lifted her newly bejeweled left hand, cupped it slightly, and gave Princess an apropos Beauty Queen wave. "Bye-bye now."

Message clearly delivered, Cyndi watched as Skylar Richards sulked off toward the refreshments table at the edge of the tarmac.

Mopping tears of joy with a handkerchief, Cyndi's mom walked up. "I wish your father could have been here to see this, sweetie. Knowing your dad, he would have given Lance a hard time when he asked for your hand in marriage, but I know he would have approved." She clasped Lance's hand. "Welcome to the family, Lance."

"Thank you, Mrs. Stafford. It would have been an honor to meet Cyndi's dad. She's told me a lot about him."

"He was quite a man." She looked down and slowly pulled her hand away. Her cheerful smile faded. "As you know, Cyndi has been through a lot. Promise me you'll take good care of my daughter."

"I promise. I won't let anything happen to her."

Eager to change the subject, Cyndi searched the tarmac. "Where's Stevie?"

Her mother fumbled out a response. "He…um…He was feeling under the weather yesterday. I thought it would be best if he stayed home and rested."

Cyndi rolled her eyes and nodded knowingly. "Right."

Unlike her older brother, Cyndi had been a model child and student, bringing home stellar report cards throughout her years in school. Her mother always tried to find a way to praise both of her children's academic efforts—Cyndi for getting straight As and Stevie for… well, for "Doing the best he could," as she diplomatically phrased it.

Her dad had a habit of being much blunter. "Shape up and get with the damned program, Steven," he'd bark. As intelligent as her dad was, he couldn't seem to grasp why the sledgehammer approach to child rearing failed to work on Stevie. In high school her brother rebelled by dabbling in every type of delinquent behavior he could think of just to piss off the "old man,"—an insulting title aimed squarely at denigrating their dad.

But Stevie had also resented Cyndi. For years, her brother had tormented her at every opportunity, a much safer target for his pent-up anger than taking on the old man.

That was until she'd become proficient at martial

arts. After delivering a black eye and a bloody nose in response to one particular mistreatment, Stevie did what most cowards do when they're challenged—he moved on in search of a weaker victim.

Her mom quickly wandered away, avoiding the need to make up any more excuses for Cyndi's vagabond brother.

Moments later, Lance's large family swarmed the couple. His four sisters, loads of cousins, and his parents all added their congratulations.

His mother's eyes lit up as she gushed, "I know just the right wedding planner. Fernando did an exquisite job planning the wedding for the Hamptons' daughter. Saint Joseph's Church was so tastefully decorated. And what he did with the ballroom at the country club was amazing. There must have been over five hundred people—"

"Actually, Mrs. Garcia, I've always dreamed of a more simple, intimate affair," Cyndi interrupted. "We could have the ceremony and the reception in my mother's backyard."

At hearing this, Josefina Garcia grimaced in pain. She made the sign of the cross then clutched the silver crucifix dangling from her neck. "Are you saying you don't want a traditional Catholic wedding? In a church?"

As sweet as Lance's mother was, she didn't hesitate to play the guilt card if it meant getting her way.

Before Cyndi could react, Dr. Garcia quickly stepped forward. His meticulously trimmed gray beard, impeccably tailored suit, and piercing brown eyes projected an intimidating air of authority.

The renowned heart surgeon wrapped a comforting arm around his wife's shoulder and wagged his finger. "Nonsense. Of course she's not saying that, *Querida*. Why don't we leave these two alone? I'm sure they'd appreciate a little privacy so they can plan their future."

The Garcia family dutifully followed their patriarch's wishes and walked away.

Cyndi turned to Lance, planted her hands on her hips, and gave him *the look.*

He raised his hands in surrender. "I know, I know. I'll talk to my parents. You know they mean well."

"I know they do." Cyndi pressed her sexy body against Lance and snuggled up to him. "After all the crap we've gone through, I suppose future in-laws who want their son to start off his new life with his adorable and understanding wife in regal style isn't the worst thing that could happen." She wrapped her arms around him and gave his butt a squeeze.

The real strategy for her sensual embrace soon revealed itself.

"As long as the wedding and reception is held in my mom's backyard," Cyndi purred.

In a rare display of wisdom and diplomacy—or more likely a response born of a more carnal explanation—Lance held his tongue and enjoyed the moment.

"Besides," Cyndi continued, "it's time to put the past where it belongs. I'm not a weather expert, but I forecast our future together will be nothing but smooth sailing and blue skies."

CHAPTER 1

Three days later.
Friday, 1100 hours.

CYNDI TURNED OFF Litchfield Avenue and pulled up to the Lightning Gate at the north end of Luke Air Force Base.

She approached the gate guard and rolled down the window of her trusty sky-blue Honda Accord. It felt like Cyndi had just opened the door to a smelting furnace.

Welcome to Arizona.

Sizzling air flooded into her car, instantly overwhelming the air conditioner.

As uncomfortable as Cyndi was, she felt even worse for the security policeman. He was kitted up in full battle gear, including a ballistic vest and helmet.

"ID, ma'am," he barked, as rivulets of sweat dribbled down the back of his neck.

She fished her Common Access Card (CAC) out of her wallet and held it out for the gate guard. He scanned the card with a militarized version of the bar code scanners used in stores, then looked at the built-in screen. The usual message indicating it was safe to let her through didn't pop up. The guard's eyes narrowed as he looked at Cyndi.

"Is there something wrong, Sergeant?"

He tapped the device with the side of his hand and scanned her ID again. After a brief delay there was a sharp beeping sound. A disconcerting message popped up on the screen. The guard waved over his supervisor while surreptitiously unsnapping the retaining strap over his holstered Sig Sauer M18. When the supervisor walked up, the guard tilted the scanner his way and showed him the message.

The master sergeant lifted his eyes from the screen without moving his head and peered out over the top of his reading glasses at Cyndi. He looked back down at the screen and reread the message. The supervisor grunted, nodded his head, then went back to the comfort of the air-conditioned guard shack.

"Have a good day, ma'am," the guard said, followed by a crisp salute.

Cyndi returned the salute then quickly rolled up her window and drove off.

Lance pulled up to the gate in his tricked-out black Ford Raptor pickup truck with the deluxe off-road package. His CAC card scanned successfully on the first try, and he was waved through.

Cyndi cradled the steering wheel with her knees while she scanned the base map she had printed out, searching for the location of the 60th Fighter Squadron. Confident she knew the correct route, she tossed the map onto the passenger seat and took in the scenery of their new base.

The rock, sand, and hard-packed dirt landscaping scheme at Luke AFB mimicked the surrounding Sonoran Desert. Even though it had opened in 1947, the majority of the buildings on the sprawling base appeared to be less than ten years old. The robust budget Luke obviously enjoyed reflected the continuing largesse delivered over the years by a long string of very powerful Arizona senators like Barry Goldwater and John McCain.

Nearly every structure on the base was painted the same coyote-tan color, outlined by trim painted a boring brown. If the unimaginative paint scheme at Luke wasn't bad enough, nearly every Air Force Base in the world replicated it. The tan and brown colors were so universally unpopular that years ago some creative spouses had altered the classic German Christmas song "O Tannenbaum" by substituting the colors for the original words to create a new tune. The modified song started with the refrain, "O Tan and Brown, O Tan and Brown…" then continued on, humorously mocking the lack of aesthetic creativity of the senior leadership.

As they made their way across the base, Cyndi and Lance approached an area known as the Mall. The blocks-long airpark contained pristine examples of the various aircraft that had flown at Luke over the years.

The person who had decided on the placement of the aircraft must have had a pilot's sense of humor. The Air Force's first jet trainer—the slow, stubby T-33 Shooting Star—sat next to its aerodynamic polar opposite. Thirty feet away was the sleek, Mach 2-plus manned missile with wings, the F-104 Starfighter.

At the west end of the Mall was the historic White Chapel. Occasions of great joy and profound sadness had taken place at the chapel over the decades. Neil Armstrong, the first human to step foot on the moon, had gotten married in the chapel.

In stark contrast to that momentous occasion, far too many pilots had had their funeral services held in that same sanctuary.

As they neared the end of the Mall, Cyndi could see hordes of people lining the roads surrounding the chapel. It looked as if everyone on base had shown up. A black hearse parked at the curb in front of the chapel signaled the type of event taking place.

A funeral with full military honors was in progress. Cyndi and Lance stopped and got out of their vehicles to show respect to the fallen service member.

They stood at attention in the blazing heat while the

base chaplain, dressed in ornate white vestments, exited the chapel first. A flag-draped coffin carried by six men in dress blues appeared. Silver pilot wings were pinned to the chests of each of the pallbearers. Dozens more pilots flooded out of the chapel. The pallbearers stopped and paused next to the open door at the rear of the hearse.

A lone bugler raised a trumpet to his lips. "Taps" began to play.

Of all military songs, none was more prone to evoke a powerful emotional reaction than the eloquent and haunting twenty-four notes that made up "Taps." Originally used as a signal to extinguish the lights, the music for "Taps" was revised in 1862 and was now sounded primarily at funerals, wreath-laying ceremonies, and memorial services.

When Cyndi heard it, she recalled the grief that she saw her father go through whenever he lost a fellow pilot.

Cyndi's father was one of the strongest men she'd never known. She'd never seen him cry. With one exception. Movies on the couch was a tradition at the Stafford household practically every Saturday night. Invariably, her dad would pick one from the military genre. But every time he heard the languid, melancholy sound of a bugle playing "Taps" during funeral scenes, her dad would turn away from the screen. Her mom would reach out in a comforting embrace and calm the deep trembling of his shoulders.

As she got older, Cyndi began to understand what was happening.

It was tough for her to watch.

After a career as a fighter pilot and a test pilot, "Taps" wasn't just a song for her father. It was a painful reminder of the close friends he'd lost in the prime of their lives. A pain that never diminished.

The moment the poignant music ended, seven members of the honor guard raised their rifles skyward and fired off a volley, causing Cyndi to flinch. After chambering another round, the guns fired again in perfect unison. A thunderous boom echoed off the surrounding buildings. A third round completed the twenty-one-gun salute.

Before the smoke had cleared, four F-35s in tight formation roared over the top of the chapel. At the exact moment the jets reached the Mall, the third aircraft pulled up sharply, aiming for the heavens in full afterburner.

The missing man formation had been used since the early days of aviation as a final aerial salute for a fallen pilot at their funeral. The lone aircraft soared upward, symbolically pointing the departed aviator toward his final mission.

The pallbearers gently guided the casket onto the rollers of the hearse floor and slid it into place.

Once the somber-faced undertaker had secured the casket in the hearse, Cyndi and Lance drove on, eventually finding the parking lot for the 60th Fighter Squadron.

Before they went in, Cyndi pulled Lance aside. Her brow furrowed. "You know we no longer use our call signs from pilot training, right?"

Lance flashed a thumbs-up. "Got it."

"Okay."

He moved to open the door.

Cyndi held out a hand and stopped him again. "Also, this is our new home for the next few years. Our chance to be at the top of the fighter-pilot pyramid. We only get one opportunity to make a good first impression."

"Of course. I know that."

She continued, biting her lip. "Student pilots going through UPT can be competitive. But a squadron full of fighter pilots is a whole different ball game. Don't let their laid back, outwardly friendly demeanor fool you. Trust me, you've never experienced this level of competitiveness before."

Lance cocked his head. "You sound worried. What are you trying to say?"

"I'm saying play it cool. Fly under the radar. Blend in."

"Don't worry about me," Lance replied. "I can hold my own. Besides, we're all Air Force pilots, remember? It'll be fine."

CHAPTER 2

AS SOON AS they walked through the doors, there was no doubt that Cyndi and Lance were in an Air Force fighter squadron. High on the wall, a sign greeted everyone who entered: "Through These Portals Pass the Best Damned Fighter Pilots in the World!"

Memorabilia such as old unit patches, framed letters of commendation, and historical photographs proudly exhibited the long and distinguished heritage of the 60th Fighter Squadron.

Black-and-white photos of pilots decked out in their leather flying caps and Mae West life preservers, posing proudly on the wings of their P–47s, lined the hallway.

Cyndi and Lance got the message. If you want to be one of us, you're damn well going to earn it.

At the end of the hallway was a large open area. It had a long counter on one side with multiple workstations behind it. This area appeared to be the nerve center of the squadron. On the back wall were three large monitors displaying flight schedules, current weather, and airfield conditions. Above the monitors was the 60th Fighter Squadron slogan: Welcome to the Jungle.

"Hello? Is anyone here?" Cyndi called out.

Her words echoed off the walls. No response came. There wasn't a soul in sight.

"I guess we'll come back later," she said, shrugging her shoulders.

As they turned to leave, they saw that the exit was

blocked. Two dozen melancholy pilots filtered through the front door. Each man was wearing his dress blues. They strode silently into the building and gathered loosely around the counter. In hushed tones, they commiserated with each other and offered consoling pats on the back. Cyndi and Lance stepped aside and tucked themselves into a corner.

A man wearing the rank of lieutenant colonel positioned himself in the middle of the gathering. He was tall, tanned, and had a commanding presence about him. His haircut was high and tight—shaved on the sides and flat on the top—a look more typically seen among humorless grunts in the Marines. Although he was only in his midthirties, the demanding life of the military, and maybe a little too much Jim Beam, had aged him beyond his years. The squadron commander, Cyndi assumed.

A major standing next to him raised his arms and cleared his throat. "Quiet everyone, Tank wants to say a few words!" he yelled out. The deputy squadron commander, no doubt.

The murmuring immediately ceased.

The squadron commander looked around at the young, distraught men he was charged with leading and let out a long sigh. "I know how difficult today is for you. Viking was a good man and a damn good pilot." His piercing blue eyes began to water. "Most of you have never buried a friend and fellow pilot. I have. More than once. I can tell you this: It never gets any easier."

Tank straightened up and drew his shoulders back.

"Don't misunderstand what I'm about to say. Despite what happened to Viking, despite how much you're hurting, we still have a job to do. Every one of you needs to find a way to emotionally deal with what happened and move on. Compartmentalize it, box it up, then stow it somewhere out of the way in the back of your mind. Today we buried Viking. Tomorrow you need to bury your grief. If you can't do that, you're a danger to the man standing next to you and to our mission of total domination of the air."

Lance leaned to the side. "That was harsh," he whispered to Cyndi.

Cyndi cupped her hand next to her mouth. "He's right," she responded quietly. "If you dwell on the dangers of this job, you're dead meat."

"Carry on, men," Tank instructed his charges.

The pilots went back to their subdued conversations. They would never have said it out loud, but it was almost a certainty that each fighter pilot in the room was thinking the same thing—what happened to Viking would have never happened to them. They were a better pilot than he was. If not, he'd still be alive.

Harsh indeed.

The squadron commander grabbed one of his guys and said, "Lurch, I'm taking Captain Thorvald's parents over to his apartment in Glendale this afternoon to help them pack up his belongings. Here's the key. Go over and scrub it before his parents have a chance to go inside."

Lurch furrowed his protruding brow—the facial feature that had earned him his call sign. "But sir, I'm a fighter pilot, not a maid."

The commander let out a frustrated breath. "I'm telling you to cover your squadron mate's six, Lieutenant. Sanitize his apartment. Find and destroy any Playboy magazines, women's panties, any *toys* he might have. Anything that could tarnish the reputation of Viking in the eyes of his grieving parents. Am I making myself perfectly clear?"

Lurch nodded knowingly. "Yes, sir. I understand, sir." He trotted off to carry out his critical new mission, determined not to disappoint his boss.

"Let's give Viking a proper sendoff!" one of the pilots yelled.

"To the bar!" another one shouted.

"It's called the Heritage Room," the commander scolded him.

"Roger that, sir," the chastened pilot murmured.

Following a tradition borne many wars ago, each fighter squadron had its own bar where pilots could go to celebrate the fact that they had survived another day. But recently the Air Force had ordered that they be referred to as Heritage Rooms so as to not provoke the "woke" mob, who seemed to want to drain every last ounce of fun out of military life.

With renewed energy, the pilots migrated down a hallway, eager to drown their sorrows. They had set aside ample space for their Heritage Room. The vibe in the bar screamed frat house—with an aviation twist. One of the custom beer tap handles was an F-16 control stick grip. The walls were lined with aircraft photos and colorful plaques. A large rack held a personalized beer mug for each pilot.

Behind a curved bar was a mirrored wall displaying every type of liquor imaginable on glass shelves. The buttery aroma of a commercial popcorn machine churning out a fresh batch welcomed the group. As was the custom in the Air Force, jalapeño seasoning was liberally sprinkled on the batch. Next to the popcorn machine was a full-size pool table with the squadron patch silk-screened onto the felt.

The dour mood had lightened up considerably. Pilots ditched their stodgy blue uniform coats and ties and bellied up to the bar. Cyndi and Lance huddled around a high-top bar table in the corner trying to look inconspicuous.

They failed miserably.

Being the only two people in the bar wearing sage-green Nomex flight suits, they stuck out as if they had neon signs dangling from their necks, flashing Beware of Strangers.

Although Cyndi's curvaceous and athletic body did make a standard issue flight suit look damn amazing.

Being the only sexy blonde female in the room was nothing new for Cyndi. Neither was having most of the young, virile alpha males she worked with pretend they weren't ogling her from head to toe. Whenever she turned to look their way, they quickly averted their eyes. Ever since puberty she'd accepted the fact that beauty could be a double-edged sword. Besides, she'd used her good looks to her advantage plenty of times in the past, so she didn't waste a lot of time worrying about the fact that males were far from perfect.

Lance made the perfect partner. He was movie-star handsome. Flowing black hair topped his six-foot-two-inch muscular frame. His alluring brown eyes sparkled. That's why the Air Force had tapped him to star in its recruiting commercials a few years ago. At the time, he was a new ICBM missileer who'd spent mind-numbing twenty-four-hour shifts buried sixty feet underground in a launch control center. The Air Force knew the best way to ruin any hope of recruiting new officers would have been to show Lance doing that job. So it filmed him strutting out of a hanger carrying a flight helmet and wearing a G suit.

Because of course, as the movie *Top Gun* had reinforced in the minds of the public, all fighter pilots looked like they'd stepped right out of central casting.

The homely two-star general who'd signed off on the commercials obviously had his own definition of truth in advertising.

A guy at the next table over pointed at a small wooden sign on the opposite wall and asked Cyndi and Lance, "Have you guys read the bar rules yet?"

Having had a fighter pilot for a dad, Cyndi knew the ropes when it came to the quirky rules associated with squadron bars.

Lance, on the other hand, took the bait and walked over to the sign, eager to familiarize himself with the local customs. When he got down to the last rule on the list, his head sagged. He turned around to find everyone in the bar pointing at him and laughing. A small brass bell was affixed to the wall, next to the sign. Someone grabbed the rope attached to the clapper and rattled it back and forth, signaling that a free round was in order. Pilots cupped their empty hands and raised them up, yelling out the names of their favorite libation.

Lance had fallen for one of the oldest tricks in the Air Force. The last rule on the list read: "Anyone caught reading the rules must buy a round." He shuffled over to the bar, turned his wallet upside down, and dumped all the money he had on it. "I guess this round is on me," he mumbled.

A loud cheer erupted as the thirsty pilots swarmed the bar.

After Lance returned to their table, a tall, thin guy with gold oak leaves on each shoulder walked up to the pair and introduced himself. Cyndi recognized him as the deputy squadron commander she'd seen at the counter.

He singled out Cyndi, checking her out from head to toe, ignoring Lance. "You must be the new guy. I'm Major Frey, call sign Zombie. Welcome to the Valley of the Sun, where we have abundant sunshine, great hiking, and endless billboards advertising ambulance-chasing lawyers."

Cyndi noticed that he noticed.

She reached out and shook his hand. "Hey, Zombie, I'm Cyndi Stafford." She gestured toward Lance. "I'd like you to meet my fiancé." She intentionally put extra emphasis on the last word.

"Fiancé?" His grip went limp. The man turned and shrugged. "Oh. Okay. Cool."

Lance enthusiastically shook the man's hand. "Hello, Major…I mean…Zombie, I'm Lance Garcia."

Frey threw his shoulders back and jutted out his chin. "Good recovery, Garcia. In the fighter world, we only use call signs. You'll get yours after you are officially mission ready." Zombie looked around and shrugged. "Hell, to be honest, I hardly know the first names of most of the guys in this room." He pointed at one of the pilots. "For example, that's Weasel over there. Next to him are Bluto, Crisis, and Mad Dog. Crime and Bikini are playing crud at the pool table."

"Crud?" Lance said, his head tilted in confusion.

"Think of it as a mixture of billiards, football, and rugby. But play it at your own risk. It's a good way to get taken off flight status, until your broken bones heal."

As delicately as she could, Cyndi asked, "If you'd rather not talk about it, I understand. What happened to—"

"How did Viking buy the farm?" Zombie said bluntly.

"Yes, sir."

"Captain Thorvald—Viking—died a week ago when he was doing a loop in the SELLS 1 Military Operations Area. He had a midair with a civilian airplane."

Cyndi winced. "A civilian was flying in the MOA? What the hell was the pilot thinking?"

Although technically legal for civilian airplanes to fly through MOA's when they were active, at the speeds fighters flew it was the height of stupidity. By the time the intruder saw him, it was far too late to avoid Viking's jet.

Zombie shook his head. "Talk about ironic. Viking made it through fifty missions over Iraq and Afghanistan without a scratch, and then was killed by an impatient doctor taking a shortcut in his Bonanza."

Even more ironic was the fact that since their debut,

Beechcraft Bonanzas had been given the derisive nick-named Doctor Killers. The high-end, expensive airplanes were known to be a handful to fly. Arrogant doctors, who naturally assumed they were able to handle the plane, had accounted for most of the fatal accidents in it.

Not surprising in this litigious age, his widow had already filed a lawsuit against the government for $3 million. Chump change compared to the $175,983,949 value the Air Force had assigned to the lost aircraft in the preliminary accident report.

And the life of one fighter pilot—value unspecified.

To avoid any more uncomfortable conversations, Cyndi excused herself and drifted over to the other tables to introduce herself.

Lance glanced over at Cyndi and smiled, thinking what a lucky guy he was. Her silky blonde hair was pulled back into a ponytail that ended at her shoulder blades, per the newly revised regs for females. Feeling his hungry eyes on her, Cyndi turned and gave Lance a wink. Then she went back to her conversation.

They made a very handsome couple. The minute they finished their checkout on the F-35 and their lives slowed down to a reasonable pace, he was going to make her his wife. Lance had dated a lot of disappointments over the years. He couldn't believe how fortunate he was to have finally found his one true love. He puffed out his chest, certain that every hotshot fighter pilot in the bar was insanely jealous of him. If he were being honest, his competitive personality was delighted at the thought.

One of the pilots walked up behind him and slapped him on the back, interrupting Lance's train of thought.

"Hey, Bro, welcome to Luke. I'm Toilet."

Lance swiveled around to see a guy built like a fire-plug—if fireplugs had Neanderthal foreheads, greasy black hair, and a porn 'stache—grinning at him with an outstretched hand.

"Oh, hey…um…Toilet. I'm Lance Garcia," he replied, firmly gripping the man's hand.

Undressing her with his eyes, Toilet gawked at Cyndi. "Who's the hot babe? I'd sure like to tap that," he announced, arching his bushy eyebrows.

The lecherous comment instantly shot Lance's blood pressure through the roof. His primal, protective instincts went into overdrive as he balled up his left hand into a fist.

Before he could torpedo his nascent flying career by decking a senior officer in front of a roomful of witnesses, Zombie stepped between the two men. "She's his fiancée, dickhead. That means she's off-limits, Toilet. Got it?" he barked.

Toilet raised his hands in mock surrender and shrugged. "My bad, dude. I was just asking, that's all. No harm, no foul." Toilet might have proffered a weak apology, but he wasn't about to lose face to some new guy in front of the other pilots. He made a show of perusing Cyndi again while licking his lips. "Nice job, Garcia. Let me know if things don't work out between the two of you." He fired off a slimy wink, fully intending to twist the knife even more.

Lance had regained his composure—somewhat. He glanced down at Toilet's left wrist and snorted. "That's a pretty big watch for a guy with such small hands."

Toilet flaunted a large, gaudy Breitling aviator watch on his wrist.

The standard joke in the flying community was the smaller the manhood, the bigger the watch. Zombie hooted out loud at the perfectly delivered verbal right cross.

Lance cranked his Texas twang up to an eleven and lifted his closed fist up to his lips, as if he were speaking into a microphone. "Paging Dr. Sigmund Freud. You're needed in the bar. Stat."

Toilet looked like he was about to detonate. "It's a Heritage Room, smartass!" He stomped off, looking for someone else to annoy.

"Don't mind him; he's from New York," Zombie said. "The only thing holding in his brains is his zipper."

Cyndi wandered back over to the table and asked, "What did I miss?"

"Nothing," Lance said, faking a smile. "I was asking Zombie about the F-35 course."

"I can tell you this," Zombie said. "Prepare for the toughest course in the Air Force. Especially for pilots without any previous fighter experience."

"We're not worried."

Zombie's eyes narrowed. "And why would that be?"

In a cocky gesture, Lance ceremoniously reached up and dusted off each of his shoulders. Something he'd seen brash NFL players do after scoring a touchdown. "We aced UPT," he bragged.

Cyndi's eyes opened wide. She kicked him in the shin and shook her head ever so slightly to send a message.

It was too late.

"I graduated number three in our class, and the lovely and talented Captain Cyndi Stafford graduated number one."

"Number one?" Zombie nodded, appearing impressed. "Wow."

"Damn straight, *wow*," Lance replied, swelling with pride for his future wife.

Zombie turned to the pilots in the bar and banged his beer bottle on the edge of the table. "Can I have everyone's attention? I've been talking to Ken and Barbie here, and I have to say how lucky we are to have these two newbies in our midst. You're not going to believe this, but these FNGs graduated at the top of their pilot training class."

Chortles spread through the crowd.

"Anyone else here graduate number one in their pilot training class?"

Every man in the bar, including Zombie, raised their hand.

Cyndi shook her head and let out a long sigh.

Zombie slapped Lance on the back. "Welcome to the jungle, Garcia." He turned and walked away. Before getting very far, he turned back to deliver one more painful jab. "Great first impression, by the way."

In the mind of a fighter pilot, everyone was considered a competitor to be vanquished. The only discriminator was what weapon to employ—a 25 mm GAU-22/A Gatling gun, an AIM-120 AMRAAM, or piercing words.

The cheeks on Cyndi's beautiful face turned crimson with embarrassment. "Don't worry about me, you said. I can hold my own, you said."

"What? What did I say?" Lance asked, arms extended, palms up. "You *did* graduate number one."

Cyndi closed her eyes and buried her head in her hands.

CHAPTER 3

TANK, THE SQUADRON commander, caught everyone's attention by ringing the bell. "Bartender, a bottle of Jeremiah Weed, please."

A hush fell over the room.

The pilot tending bar unlocked a small door under the counter and pulled out a bottle wrapped in a tall blue velvet bag. In it was a smoky brown bottle of 100-proof bourbon liqueur distilled in Kentucky.

The brew had earned an almost cult-like following in the fighter pilot community as a way to toast a fallen comrade.

The bartender lined up rows of shot glasses and dispensed a gulp of Jeremiah Weed into each one. Cyndi and Lance tried to hang back and observe but were swept up in the crowd moving toward the bar. Everyone grabbed a glass.

Tank lifted his and said, "To Viking. And may his final flight west be a smooth one."

"To Viking!" everyone shouted in unison, lifting their glasses.

The pilots tipped their heads back, pressed their glasses to their lips, and snapped their wrists, downing the ceremonial bourbon.

Cyndi pinched her nose, turned toward the wall, took a deep breath, and tipped her head back.

Lance opened wide and poured the ceremonial libation down his throat. One second later he doubled over, gagging violently. "It tastes like friggin' kerosene," he coughed.

Cyndi giggled. "I know. That's why I poured mine into this plant." She pointed at a tiny cactus in a small pot sitting on a shelf.

In less than a day the innocent cactus would be dead and flopped over.

"Why didn't you warn me?" Lance croaked, his throat on fire.

"I figured since you graduated number three from UPT you were way too intelligent to not know about Jeremiah Weed," Cyndi said with obvious relish.

It was now time to conclude the tradition. The shot glasses were shattered as they were forcefully hurled into the trash can, never to be used again.

With the salute to Viking complete, the squadron commander approached Lance and Cyndi. He was even bigger and more imposing up close. His square jaw and buzz-cut projected a decidedly threatening demeaner. "Welcome to the 60th. I'm Lt. Col. Tank Abrams," he announced with little enthusiasm. "You two must be part of the new class."

"Yes, sir." Lance extended his hand.

Tank practically crushed Lance's hand when he shook it. He eased up only slightly when he shook Cyndi's.

Their new boss wasn't one for idle small talk. He got right down to business. "On Monday, you'll catch a commercial flight to Spokane, Washington. Fairchild Air Force Base is where you'll go through SERE training. After you get back from survival school, you'll go through local orientation then start ground school. I'd spend this weekend finding a place to live. If you want to impress me, keep your nose clean, and hit the books hard."

"Understood, sir," Cyndi said.

"In pilot training, you got your top-secret clearance. In

order to fly the F-35, you'll need to add an SCI to it," Tank informed them.

"What's that?" Lance quietly asked Cyndi.

"It means Sensitive Compartmented Information," Cyndi whispered.

"And as your commander, I'll also need to certify that you meet the standards of the PRP."

"Sorry sir, what's a PRP?" Lance asked sheepishly, realizing his second impression was likely going off the rails just like the first.

"Personnel Reliability Program," Tank said, impatiently exhaling. "The F-35 is certified to carry the B61 tactical nuclear bomb. No one gets anywhere near a nuke if they have any black marks on their record."

Lance cleared his throat as he stole a sideways glance at Cyndi.

Tank's eyes narrowed. "That's not going to be a problem, is it?"

Cyndi jumped in before Lance could respond. "Not at all, sir. Nothing in our past to worry about."

Lance nodded, trying his best to look innocent.

"We better start packing for SERE school. Isn't that right, Lieutenant Garcia?" Cyndi said. She pulled him away before Lance could slip up and accidentally set off the "ticking time bomb" loaded with the details of their past.

CHAPTER 4

Saturday morning.

CYNDI AND LANCE walked out of their cozy air-conditioned room at the Fighter Country Inn temporary officer's quarters and straight into a furnace. It was only 9 a.m., and the temperature had already topped one hundred degrees.

"Damn, it's so hot in this town even the devil would complain," Lance moaned.

"You have such a clever way with words, *sweetheart,*" Cyndi purred as she hooked her arm through Lance's.

He shot a sideways glance at her. "Um…thanks."

Approaching his pricey pickup truck, Cyndi skipped in front of Lance and walked backward. She flashed a coy smile and held out her hand. "Can I have the keys? I want to drive."

"You want to drive my truck?" Lance replied, disbelief blanketing his face. "Sorry, that's not gonna happen. Ever. *Sweetheart.*"

"How about this: I'll drive it straight to a Western Wear shop and buy a pair of cowboy boots if that helps," she said playfully.

"Still no."

Cyndi stuck her bottom lip out and curled it down into a wounded, sad pout. "If the Air Force trusts me to fly its supersonic, multimillion-dollar aircraft, I can't *believe* you wouldn't trust me to drive your pretty little pickup truck."

Normally, Lance was putty in her hands when Cyndi gave him that pouty face.

But this was about his truck.

And she had just called it pretty.

Worse than that, she'd called it *little*.

"Darlin', let me explain something to you. In Texas, a man's house is his castle. His truck, on the other hand, is his—"

"Phallic symbol?" Cyndi shot back, teasing his Latin machismo, and simultaneously skewering a Texas cliché.

Lance's blood pressure shot up a few millimeters of mercury, but he pretended to ignore her as he pulled out his keys.

Arriving at the black Ford F-150, Cyndi noticed that the mammoth truck was manspread across the entire parking space, touching both white lines. She glanced sideways at Lance as if to say "See what I mean?" but held her tongue.

Lance pressed his key fob twice. The doors unlocked with a clunk. Electrically operated running boards swooped down from the undercarriage.

Cyndi grabbed a bar mounted behind the passenger door and stepped up onto the running board, beginning her trek up the mountain and into the seat. After settling in, she twisted, reached back to grab her seatbelt, and promptly learned the hard way to never touch the metal tab. It had been baking in the Phoenix sun and felt like it was only a few degrees below the melting point of steel.

Lance didn't say a word as he cruised down Camelback Road, en route to a rental he'd found online. Traffic was light for a Saturday, which he was glad to see, but he was still miffed about the slight to his truck.

"How about putting on some music?" Cyndi suggested, trying to lighten the mood.

He leaned her way and held a finger to his ear. "Did you say put my *little* truck in afterburner?" Lance asked with a wicked smirk.

"What?" she replied, totally confused.

Lance stomped on the gas pedal.

The truck lurched forward so fast Cyndi actually clutched her chest. "Okay! Okay! I'll never ask to drive your truck again," Cyndi promised. "Now please slow down!" she pleaded.

Lance lifted his foot off the accelerator slightly. "Country music it is." He tuned in KMLE 107.9 FM, a local country station, knowing full well that Cyndi hated that genre of music.

Then Lance cranked up the volume.

Kacey Musgraves was singing something about making a lot of noise and kissing a lot of boys.

Lance sank triumphantly back into his buttery-soft leather seat and smiled.

"Texans…" Cyndi moaned, rolling her eyes at him. "No sense of humor."

———◆———

A few miles from their first stop of the morning, Lance said, "I can't believe the cost of living in Phoenix. Rundown cracker boxes in the bad parts of town start at $1,700 per month."

"How are we going to afford to live off base?" Cyndi asked. "We're in the military, not overpaid Silicon Valley code jockeys."

"We'll figure something out," Lance assured her. "I don't want to live in a high-crime area, though. If that means we have to pay a little more, that's fine with me."

"Where are we going first?"

"Glendale. I checked it out. It got good reviews on Zillow."

Cyndi looked askance at Lance. "I don't suppose the Cardinals stadium being in Glendale had anything to do with it."

"It is?" Lance said, feigning surprise. "What a coincidence."

As he slowly circled the cul-de-sac, Lance looked down at Google Maps on his phone to confirm he had the right house. He steered his four-wheeled land barge along the curb and stopped short of the driveway. They jumped out and checked the house number on the mailbox.

"Yep, this is the right place," Lance stated, pointing his key fob back over his shoulder and locking his truck.

"Hmm…" Cyndi said, nodding slowly. "Okay. This could work."

The house was a modest two-story, nestled on a pie-shaped lot. The design was noticeably different from the cookie-cutter houses seemingly everywhere in Arizona. Rather than desert tan-colored stucco exterior walls under a terra-cotta tile roof, it had a rugged, timber frame style more commonly seen in the mountain states.

Lance rang the doorbell and waited on the front porch, Cyndi at his side.

Rusty hinges creaked as the door opened as far as the security chain would allow.

A scowling face, belonging to a robustly proportioned woman in her early eighties, glared out at Lance. "What do you want?" she growled.

Lance's Adam's apple bobbed up and down as he swallowed hard. "Are you Marge Thompson?"

"Who's asking?"

"I'm Lance." He jabbed a thumb to his left. "This is

Cyndi. We've been transferred to Luke Air Force Base, and we're here about renting the second floor."

"You're in the military?" Her suspicious expression softened ever so slightly.

"Yes, we are."

"Well, why the hell didn't you say so?" The chain came off, and the door opened wide. Her scowl reversed to a warm, welcoming smile that reminded Cyndi of her dearly departed nana.

Marge Thompson weighed more than Lance. Was a foot shorter than Cyndi. And wore a kitschy flower-print muumuu that ended right above her fuzzy pink house slippers. "I always prefer renting to you military folks. You're clean, don't cause a ruckus, and always pay your rent on time." She waved them into the foyer. "Come in, come in. Where are you folks coming from?"

"Del Rio, Texas, ma'am." Cyndi threw in the "ma'am," hoping to ingratiate themselves to a member of the Greatest Generation. "We just graduated from pilot training and now we're here to fly the F-35 Lightning II."

Marge just shrugged, wholly unimpressed. "Planes from the base fly over my house all the time, but I don't know one from the other. You look like a sweet couple. Let me show you the second floor." She grabbed her cane with its tripod foot, which enabled it to stand upright on its own—unlike its owner.

She led them through the first floor to a set of stairs at the back of the house. Each room they passed was decorated in the same retro-country style. Elvis Presley was belting out "Jailhouse Rock" from a dusty wooden hi-fi stereo cabinet the size of a small couch. Passing through the kitchen, a freshly baked pie was cooling on the avocado-green Formica countertop.

Marge took the stairs one step at a time, ignoring the constant pain in her hip from advanced rheumatoid arthritis. "Okay, here we are," she said, panting from all the exertion. She swung open the door to the bedroom. A handmade quilt was draped across the mattress. Round white doilies covered the tops of each nightstand. "The bathroom is down the hall. You two will have the run of the second floor."

Lance nodded approvingly.

Perceiving an unfamiliar accent, Cyndi inquired, "If you don't mind me asking, where are you from, Mrs. Thompson?"

"No need for formalities, dearie. Call me Marge. I hale from Bozeman, Montana."

"That's quite a change. Did you move here to be near your kids or grandkids, Marge?"

Her warm smile melted away. "Don't have any kids. My husband and I always wanted a big family, but I guess the good Lord had other ideas."

"Sorry to hear that."

"Don't go feeling sorry for this old gal. I'm not lonely. No siree. I've got my quilting ladies and my bridge club that I go to once a month."

"How do you like Glendale?"

"It's a nice little town. Far enough away from the hustle and bustle of Phoenix to suit me. Hotter than the blazes during the summer, though. Still not used to it myself. The first winter after my beloved Ralph kicked the bucket, I said the hell with this blasted cold weather. So I figured I'd fly south with the rest of the snowbirds and plant my butt in Arizona for the winter. That was fifteen years ago, and I ain't been back since."

Marge hobbled out of the bedroom and showed them the rest of the second floor. When her back was turned, Cyndi flashed Lance a thumbs-up sign, their agreed upon signal.

They patiently waited as Marge descended the stairs,

one hand on her cane and a death grip on the handrail with her other.

Back where they started, at the front door, Marge announced, "Rent is $1,000 a month."

"A thousand a month!" Lance loudly gasped.

"That's what I said, sonny. Take it or leave it."

Lance's outburst wasn't part of a strategy to negotiate a lower rent. Given the going rates around town, he was astonished at how low the amount was.

"Now don't get your panties in a wad, junior," Marge said, her free hand planted on her hip. "I know it might seem like a lot, but that includes utilities and meals."

"Utilities and *meals*?" Lance seized the opportunity to tease his fiancée about her problematic cooking skills. "You mean I won't have to eat Cyndi's cooking? Where do I sign?" Lance said as fast as he could get the words out of his mouth.

Cyndi elbowed him in the ribs.

Marge limped over to a dusty rolltop desk in the family room and pulled a rental agreement out of the top drawer. "First month's rent is due before moving in, plus a security deposit equal to one month of rent. By signing, you hereby agree to hold me harmless for any and all claims for accidents or injuries sustained on said property in perpetuity, regardless of the cause. Also, no pets, no parties. Sign here." She held up a pen and flashed that warm, grandmotherly smile.

Ol' Marge Thompson was a little savvier than she'd let on.

Lance scrawled his signature on the first line at the bottom of the rental agreement.

With the pen in her left hand, Cyndi added hers below.

Marge tilted her head, noticing there was no wedding ring on Cyndi's finger. "I thought you two were married?"

"Engaged," Lance quickly responded, hoping the issue wouldn't be a deal killer.

"I see," Marge said, casting a disapproving look his way. "Why buy the cow when you can get the milk for free?" she mumbled under her breath. "Back in my day, a girl didn't put out until the wedding ring was officially slipped on her finger." She straightened up and wagged her cane in Lance's direction. "I assume you're going to make an honest woman out of this pretty little thing soon, young man?"

"As soon as we're checked out on the F-35 and get some leave, a wedding is our first priority. Scout's honor." Lance held up the Boy Scout three-finger sign.

Marge wrapped her arm around Cyndi's shoulder. "Darlin', I know a thing or two about men. If you don't grab 'em by the ear and lead them down the aisle, they're likely to never get hitched. You hold him to that promise, you hear?"

Cyndi gave her a wink. "Marge, I think you and I are going to get along just fine."

As they were saying goodbye on the front porch, Marge looked out at the horizon and froze. "Oh Lordy, here comes another one."

Lance and Cyndi turned around to a terrifying sight.

"What in the world is that?" Cyndi asked.

"It's a haboob."

"A what?"

"It's what the locals call a terrible dust storm. Happens around these parts during the monsoon season when dust and sand is stirred up by winds from a passing thunderstorm."

Dust and sand being in plentiful supply in the northern Sonoran Desert, haboobs were a common occurrence in Phoenix. And a leviathan wall of it was rapidly headed their way.

"You kids ought to hurry on back to the base before this thing hits. You don't want to get caught in the middle of it."

———

If Cyndi thought Lance was driving fast before, he was now trying to set a new land speed record trying to outrun the storm. God forbid he got dust or a scratch on his immaculate truck.

Bumper-to-bumper traffic had choked every lane of Camelback Road as the locals scrambled to get their vehicles tucked safely back into their garages. Suddenly, a wave of brake lights rushed toward the Raptor like falling red dominos. Lance was left with no other choice. He slowed to a crawl and joined the four-mile-long metal conga line headed west.

A few minutes later, the apocalyptic storm had overtaken them, transforming the streets into a scene ripped straight from a Mad Max movie. The sky turned black as midnight. Sixty-mile-per-hour winds hauled tons of dust and sand up into the atmosphere, cutting the visibility to mere feet. A demolition derby featuring minivans and pickups played itself out right before Lance's eyes. He considered trying to weave his way through the tangled jumble of metal, but the minuscule chances of coming out the other end unscathed tipped the scales in favor of pulling over and letting the haboob pass.

———

At Luke AFB, two hours later, Cyndi got out and looked back at the truck. She winced. "Sorry, babe," was all she could muster in way of a condolence. She glanced at Lance and thought she saw tears welling up in his eyes.

His once-pristine truck looked like it had been run through a car wash. Except in this Arizona version of a car wash, the spinning brushes that were supposed to polish a vehicle had been made from sandpaper. The windstorm had scraped nearly all of the paint from the Raptor's body.

CHAPTER 5

Monday morning.

CYNDI AND LANCE bounded down the stairs, suit-cases in hand, late for their flight to Spokane.

Marge was waiting for them at the bottom.

"See ya, Marge. We're headed to eastern Washington to spend a week out in the woods with no food," Lance said.

"Well then you're gonna want these." She handed them each a brown paper lunch sack with their names printed on the front in pencil. "This should help tide you over until you get there."

Lance opened his bag and peered in. "Oh…um…wow…carrot sticks, a juice box, and more of the fried bologna casserole from last night."

Marge beamed with pride. "Don't forget about my rhubarb pie. Didn't want a growing boy like you to go hungry, so I put an extra big slice in your bag."

Lance took a second peek. He nodded slowly and groaned. "You sure did. How about that." He held up his sack. "And look, Cyndi, she even put our names on the bags so we wouldn't get them mixed up."

Before he had a chance to lay on the sarcasm any thicker, Cyndi put her hand in the small of his back and pushed Lance toward the front door. "That was very thoughtful of you, Marge. Lance loves your pie. We have to go. See you soon." They scampered out the door.

The notorious rush hour traffic in Phoenix rivaled that of any freeway in Los Angeles. Lance merged into the flow and inched along Interstate 10 as he drove east toward Sky Harbor airport in his sandblasted F-150. At this time of day it could take twenty minutes to reach the airport, or it could take forty-five. With Phoenix traffic, you never knew. He looked down at the brown paper bags between them, then up at Cyndi. "We have to find another place to live."

"Are you serious? We just moved in yesterday. We'll never find another place with so much room for that price."

"I hate to mess up a good deal, but Marge's cooking is…?"

Cyndi turned and glared at him. "Worse than mine? Is that what you were about to say?"

Lance had inadvertently planted himself in the middle of a relational mine field. One false move and it was all over. Before he could answer and seal his fate, Cyndi burst out laughing.

"You're right. I didn't think it was possible, but her cooking is worse than mine. It's awful."

Lance let out a relief laugh. "I'm glad you agree."

Just when he thought he'd survived the mine field, Cyndi wagged a scolding finger his way.

"Don't even think about telling Marge we don't like her cooking. She's a sweet old lady, and she's obviously lonely. Why do you think she gave us such a great deal on the rent? And threw in meals. We can't move now. We're like the kids she never had."

CHAPTER 6

Fairchild AFB, Spokane, Washington.

"WELCOME TO SURVIVAL, Evasion, Resistance, and Escape training. I'm Staff Sergeant Nichols, SERE specialist with the 22nd TRS, Delta Section."

Nichols had the sturdy outdoorsman physique you'd expect from a guy who'd spent most of his life rigorously avoiding being trapped in a cubical. A mop of sandy blond hair complimented a face that exuded a laid-back attitude about life and anything that smacked of bureaucracy.

Imparting the knowledge needed to survive after ejecting was an entirely different matter. That he took very seriously.

"If you need to use the skills we teach you at SERE school, then you are having a really bad day. Whether you live or die depends entirely on you, so listen up."

The four dozen officers and enlisted personnel in the class sat up a little straighter. The group was made up of an eclectic mix of pilots, navigators, electronic warfare officers, tanker boom operators, and E-3 AWACS sensor operators.

In the perplexing world of military speak, they were called personnel who were at a high risk of isolation. Translation: people whose "office" had wings, engines, and a cockpit.

"Beginning tomorrow, you will spend a week in the

woods learning how to live off the land," Nichols continued. "You'll need to think outside the box about what is
considered edible. Practically everything you come across
is fair game. Being a picky eater is not an option when
your life is on the line.

"This course used to be ten days long, but since we
are no longer engaged in active combat in Trashcani-
stan, desert survival training has been eliminated from
the program to save money." He paused for dramatic
effect. "The most important tool you have to increase
your chances of surviving a bad day isn't a knife, matches,
or even water. It's the unbreakable will to live. You need
a mindset that says, 'No way in hell am I not going to
make it through this.' A handy trick we teach is to pick
someone or something that's important to you. Use it as
a device to motivate you to make it back alive."

The rest of the morning was filled with a hectic barrage
of information. Nichols briefly touched on the basics of
survival medicine, food procurement, land navigation,
evasion travel, camouflage techniques, ground-to-air
signals, aircraft vectoring procedures, and shelter construction. After all that, each student was given a few
minutes to learn how to operate the Combat Survivor
Evader Locator (CSEL) radio that was used by aircrew to
"phone home" after an ejection or survivable crash.

⎯◆⎯

At lunch, Cyndi unzipped a pocket on her flight suit
and pulled out two silver pieces of metal. If welded
together, they would've made up a complete—although
mismatched—set of Air Force pilot wings. "These are my
motivation to make it back alive."

When Lance saw them, a look of delight filled his face.
"The broken wings. I didn't know you brought those
with you to work."

To bring good fortune during their aviation career, a

pilot's first set of wings were broken in half at their UPT graduation ceremony. One-half was kept by the pilot and the other was given to someone significant in their life. Cyndi and Lance had exchanged halves of their broken wings.

Lance lifted the two pieces from Cyndi's hand and began to join them together.

"No!" Cyndi snatched them back. "Never do that. It's bad luck."

Tradition dictated that the two halves should only be brought back together in the next life, to ensure a successful flight through eternity.

"I didn't know you were superstitious."

"I'm not." She held a piece in each hand. "It's just that being a pilot means a lot to me. You mean a lot to me. I can't think of anything that would symbolize those two priorities in my life better than these." Cyndi's eyes sparkled as she gazed at Lance.

"I'm touched. I didn't realize you were so sentimental."

Cyndi quickly stuffed the broken wings back into her pocket. "You tell anyone that, and I'll—"

Lance chuckled and raised his hands in surrender. "Don't worry. I won't tell anyone what a softie you really are. Your secret is safe with me."

◆

After a bumpy two-hour ride the next morning, the blue Air Force bus came to a stop at the end of a narrow dirt road. The students filed off and found themselves standing in the middle of a lush forest in Northern Idaho. The large group was split up into groups of eight and assigned an instructor.

SERE specialist Nichols was assigned to Cyndi's group. "Welcome to the Kaniksu National Forest," he began. "It gets its name from a Kalispel word meaning 'black robe.' They were referring to the Jesuit missionaries who brought their faith to this area. But don't count on any help from the padres while you're out here. You are stuck with me for the next week."

"Our base camp is five miles from here," Nichols said, pointing to a peak on the far side of the valley. "Once we arrive, we will prioritize needs like food, water, shelter, and fire." He handed Cyndi a map and a compass. When she opened it, he tapped a spot on the map. "Your turn to run the show today, Captain. Take the group to base camp."

"Piece of cake," Cyndi replied with confidence. She sat down, laid the map out, and opened the compass. After flailing for twenty minutes trying to figure out her location and a course to base camp, Nichols knelt down and rotated the map 180 degrees. "It's easier if you orient the map with the top edge facing north."

"I knew that," Cyndi said sheepishly. She started plotting their course again.

As they trudged through the thicket carrying heavy rucksacks, Lance tapped the SERE instructor on the shoulder. "Hey, Sarge, what kind of animals roam these woods? Any that would make a good meal?"

"I've run across elk, moose, mountain goats, big horned sheep, cougar, lynx, bobcats. And my personal favorite, grizzly bears."

Lance did a quick check of his six, then tightened up the gap between himself and Nichols for the rest of the hike.

A chilly, drenching rain seemed to stalk the group. Mud and hypothermia had become relentless, irritating companions as the students spent each day learning valuable skills for surviving in the wilderness in enemy territory.

Lesson number one was how to build a fire deep in a hole to prevent it from being seen by the enemy. Lesson number two was a no-brainer: Use the fire to dry out their soaking wet clothing before the rain began again.

They only ate what they could forage. Reluctantly, a variety of live bugs were on the menu. Ripe berries were eagerly plucked from surrounding bushes. One small rabbit was finally trapped and roasted on a spit. Split eight ways, the morsel of meat each person received only amplified their hunger.

The paucity of food combined with exhausting hikes up and down the mountain eventually drained everyone's energy levels. Cyndi understood why this course had such a high washout rate.

As the sun set on the last night in the woods, the clouds finally parted. The instructors took pity on the bedraggled students and gave them the rest of the evening off. Cyndi and Lance seized the opportunity and snuck off together. Together, they forced their weary bodies up a steep incline until they reached a small clearing at the top of Scotchman Peak. Their efforts were rewarded with a stunning view.

Cyndi gazed up at the sparkling canopy of lights above them. "Aren't the stars beautiful?"

Lance looked up and just shrugged. "I guess. You know what I would rather see? A double cheeseburger with a side of fries. Now *that* would be beautiful."

"Please, don't mention food," she chuckled, snuggling up next to Lance.

He wrapped his strong arms around her slender body, enveloping Cyndi in his warmth. Lance checked their surroundings then said, "Looks like we're all alone. Lights out isn't for a couple more hours."

Cyndi let out a contented sigh. "Isn't this wonderful?"

"Are you thinking what I'm thinking?" he said in his bedroom voice.

"I'll bet it's the same thing I'm thinking," Cyndi whispered in his ear.

"I thought so." He leaned in for a kiss.

"This is the perfect opportunity to talk about our future."

"Talk?" Lance released Cyndi. His eyes opened wide. "Oh boy. My guy-dar is flashing warning signals. Bandits inbound at twelve o'clock and closing fast. Where's this headed?"

"Don't worry, I'm not trying to rope you into a deep discussion about your innermost feelings. I've been around guys long enough to know what a waste of time that is. It's like shoving kryptonite down their throat then expecting a guy not to gag.

"Now that we're engaged, our futures are intertwined. We've never talked about our long-term career goals."

Lance switched his guy-dar into standby mode. Temporarily. He lay back in the grass and combed his brain for an answer. "I remember visiting the cockpit on a flight to Mexico City as a kid. Ever since then, I've wanted to be an airline pilot. Layovers in Paris, Rome, Tokyo. Wearing a sharp uniform. And the pay sure beats what we're making. How about you?"

Cyndi lay next to Lance. "I want to be a test pilot, like my dad."

"Test pilot would be cool," Lance said, nodding approvingly. "You'd be perfect for the job."

"After that, I want to go there." Cyndi pointed up at the vast cosmos.

"Mars?"

"Yep. I never knew women could be astronauts until I watched shuttle launches back in the day on NASA TV. I made up my mind that if they could do it, then I could do it."

Lance's head slowly bobbed up and down as he pondered her revelation. "Hmm, astronaut. Interesting."

"Many of them were test pilots first. After a few years at Edwards I'll put in my application with NASA."

Lance traced a huge arc in front of himself with both hands while staring out into space. "Cyndi Stafford. Galaxy Girl." He rolled on his side and enveloped her in his arms again. "Has a nice ring to it, don't you think?"

"Speaking of rings…" Cyndi dug out the exquisite engagement ring from a small pocket on the arm of her flight suit that she'd hidden it in and twirled it on her left ring finger. "I think it would be best if we got married by a justice of the peace and avoided all the hassles and expense of a big wedding."

"You obviously don't know my mom very well. Trust me, you don't want the guilt trip she'd lay on us if we don't have a big Catholic wedding and an extravagant reception at their country club in Dallas."

Cyndi clamped her arms tightly across her chest. "Fine, we can talk about it later."

Lance had a long way to go, but he was making progress on what to say in these situations. "Whatever you want. I'll back you up 100 percent."

It worked.

Cyndi looked over at Lance with a sparkle in her beautiful blue eyes. "Really?"

"Absolutely," Lance wisely replied. He leaped at the chance to quickly divert the conversation. "Any thoughts on where you want to go on our honeymoon?"

"I've always wanted to go to New York City."

"Why the Big Apple?"

"My dad's grandparents immigrated from Ireland and were processed through Ellis Island. When he was a little kid, they told him stories about how overjoyed they were when they first saw the Statue of Liberty, or as they always called it, Lady Liberty. The chance to actually walk in the same building and see where my family got its start in America would be epic."

"Whatever you want," Lance repeated. He sat up, extended his hand, and said, "Let's head back to my shelter. I snuck something into my pack before we left Fairchild that I think we'll both enjoy," he said, suggestively arching his eyebrows.

When they got back, Lance looked around to see if anyone was watching them. He scooted into the crude lean-to he'd constructed out of western white pine boughs then motioned for Cyndi to join him.

She crouched down and joined Lance on the bed of straw he'd laid down. He rolled down the tarp that served as the door then dug into his pack.

"Look what I have," he whispered.

"You waited until the last night?"

He'd pulled out a Bic lighter.

"Why didn't you tell me you had that before I spent thirty minutes rubbing that stupid stick between my hands trying to light a fire?"

"Because it would have been confiscated. Then I wouldn't have anything to roast these over."

He reached into his pack again and pulled out a big bag of marshmallows.

Cyndi shielded her mouth with a cupped hand. "We could get in big trouble. Sergeant Nichols specifically said bringing food was prohibited."

"You're such a rule follower," Lance teased.

"So I like structure; there's nothing wrong with that."

"He also said to think outside the box. Be creative when you find yourself in a survival situation. Do whatever it takes." He opened the flap on his pack and dangled the bag over it. "But if you don't want any…"

The growling in her empty stomach won the contest over her need to follow arbitrary rules. Cyndi grabbed the bag from his hand and ripped it open. "Fire up the lighter."

As famished as they were, the mere thought of feasting

on the gooey, lightly toasted morsels had both of them salivating.

Cyndi speared marshmallows on thin twigs she found nearby. Lance flicked his Bic and lovingly roasted each one to golden perfection.

It didn't take long.

The sweet smell of toasted marshmallows wafted through the pine trees, igniting pleasantly odiferous childhood memories in their fellow campers.

Soon, the lean-to was swamped with SERE students begging for a taste. Lance and Cyndi happily shared their bounty.

———◆———

An hour later, everyone had drifted off to their shelters and turned in for the night with huge smiles on their faces.

Lance scooped up Cyndi in his arms and gave her a long, passionate kiss. "I'm going to hit the hay. I guess I'll see you in the morning."

"If I remember correctly," she replied, "you were thinking about more than just talking earlier." Cyndi rolled the tarp down over the entrance to the lean-to, giving them complete privacy. "So was I."

———◆———

By the final day in the field, the survival students were starving, exhausted, and miserable. Now came the ultimate test of their newfound skills. With instructors who were intimately familiar with the area posing as heavily armed adversaries, the students were to pair up and try to evade the enemy while traversing the woods to the pickup point.

Get captured, and you'd spend an extra day in the woods.

Get separated from your partner, and you'd spend an extra day in the woods.

Get to the finish line successfully, and the reward was a ride back to the base.

Cyndi and Lance felt confident they would avoid capture after concocting a circuitous route to the pickup point. They smeared meandering streaks of green and black camouflage paint across their faces then disappeared into the forest.

Lance snatched a fallen branch off the ground and used it as a walking stick, leading the way. When his energy level began to wane Cyndi assumed the lead. Determined to cross the finish line and get back to their warm and dry quarters on base, they prodded and encouraged each other to continue despite being near total exhaustion.

With only a mile to go, they crested a small rise.

Cyndi's shoulders sagged. "Crap."

A SERE instructor was waiting. He leveled his M4 at them and yelled: "On the ground! Hands on your heads!"

They obeyed and lay on their stomachs, interlacing their fingers on the backs of their heads.

The instructor performed a quick body search for weapons then stood the two up. "Join the party."

Twenty other students were sitting in a line on the damp grass with their hands on their heads.

As dejected as Cyndi was, knowing that the intricate plan they'd concocted had failed, she took solace in the fact that they weren't the only ones.

"Everyone up!" the instructor shouted.

The captives rose. Cyndi and Lance joined them at the back of the line.

The instructor went to the front and ordered, "Follow me, prisoners. March in single file, and keep the line tight. No talking."

The students complied, their spirits flagging in defeat.

As the group marched through the thick forest, the space between each person expanded like the bellows of an accordion.

Recognizing an opportunity, Lance whispered, "I'm not about to spend one more day in this friggin' five-star resort. See that big tree up ahead? When we reach it, duck behind it."

Cyndi had a split-second decision to make. She could color within the lines like she always had and willingly follow her armed captor, or risk his ire and make a break for it.

She decided it was long past time to release the abstract artist inside of her and splatter a few gallons of paint on the canvas. "I'm in."

As they reached the tree, the pair quietly broke from the formation and hid behind the wide trunk.

The last man in line turned and saw what they were doing.

Cyndi held one finger to her lips, requesting his silence.

He winked, gave her a thumbs-up, and continued to march forward.

As soon as the group was out of sight, Cyndi and Lance double-timed through the woods toward the pickup point. Their scheme worked. A group of students who had succeeded in evading the enemy were standing in a clearing. They approached them from behind and quietly blended in without the instructors noticing.

Or so they thought.

The line of captured students marched into the clearing a few minutes later. They were kept separated from the others.

"Captain Stafford and Lieutenant Garcia, front and center!" Sergeant Nichols yelled.

Cyndi glanced at Lance and shrugged. "Busted."

They separated from the group.

Nichols walked up to them. "Did you two disobey

your captor and leave the formation as it marched back to the pickup point?"

Lance stepped forward. "It was my idea, Sergeant. Captain Stafford was just following along so we wouldn't get split up."

"I don't give a shit whose idea it was!" He stomped over to the group that had been captured. "What these two did is exactly what you should have done! American fighting men and women never surrender! They never go willingly! If there is ever any reasonable opportunity for escape from the enemy, you will take it!"

Nichols went back to the other group. "Board the bus. You fine folks are going back to Fairchild. The chow hall opens at 1700 hours." Before Cyndi and Lance turned to leave, he whispered, "Well done."

Back at Fairchild, a carload of SERE students decided to pass on the gourmet food served at the base chow hall and headed downtown for pizza at Gaetano's. They'd been warned of the consequences of overeating after a week in the woods without much food. One of the guys ignored the advice and wolfed down as much pizza as he could stuff into his pie hole. Fifteen minutes later he was in the bathroom, praying to the porcelain god.

CHAPTER 7

The next morning.

A DIFFERENT CADRE OF trainers, aptly nicknamed the goon squad, ran the next phase of SERE school.

A dozen instructors made a show of marching into the classroom and standing at parade rest in a laser straight line. They wore the unfamiliar uniforms of some foreign country, complete with a mysterious rank insignia.

A mountain of a man with a graying crew cut and a chin chiseled from granite stepped up to the podium. "Knock off the chatter," he barked in a gruff voice. "I'm Master Sergeant Gagliardi. I hope you maggots enjoyed your little vacation in the mountains. Today you start course SV98, formerly known as POW training. Now it's the resistance and escape part of the SERE acronym. My job is to test your resilience and fortitude like never before." A wicked smile crossed his face. "And I do love my job."

The students were about to find out the hard way he wasn't joking.

"We will teach you the proper conduct expected of all members of the military and how to stay alive if you're captured by the enemy. The school has incorporated lessons learned from service people who have actually been held hostage to make our training as accurate and realistic as possible. Some of them have even volunteered to come to Fairchild in the past and bravely share their experiences with students.

"Because of the regrettable behavior of a few during their captivity in the Korean war, six articles of the Code of Conduct were created to use as your guide on how to return home with dignity and honor. Before you leave today, you will be expected to recite them from memory.

"During class I'll cover three scenarios: being captured during wartime, peacetime detention by a hostile foreign government, and being held hostage by a terrorist organization. For American military members, each one has its own legal and political technicalities concerning your status.

"That type of bureaucratic crap is above your pay grade and something you can't control anyway. The thing to focus on if captured is that the enemy might control every aspect of your environment, but they can't control what you think or how you feel. Only you can. Use that to your advantage.

"Remember, eventually, everyone reaches their limit. Don't be ashamed when you do. The goal is to return with your dignity and honor intact."

The instructors opened a box and grabbed stacks of pamphlets to hand out.

During the pause, Cyndi leaned toward Lance and said, "These clowns aren't going to get me to crack."

"What makes you so sure?" Lance responded.

"Bruno."

"Who?"

"My tae kwon do instructor during high school. He was a tough Italian named Bruno. He retired from the *Gruppo di Intervento Speciale* and wanted to live without constantly looking over his shoulder for bad guys who still held a grudge. So he emigrated to America. Anyway, he nicknamed me *testa dura*."

"Sorry, *no hablo* Italian," Lance said with a straight face.

"It means hard head. Bruno said I was the most stubborn student he'd ever taught."

Lance knew Cyndi too well to let this opportunity pass. He stifled a laugh, saying, "Bruno had it all wrong; you're not stubborn at all."

Gagliardi's disgust with the next topic was evident in his voice. "Ever since that *ridiculous* lawsuit a few years back, the spineless JAG lawyers have required me to forewarn you snowflakes that physical abuse and enhanced interrogation techniques are authorized during this phase of training. Expect treatment similar to what you would experience in a real-world situation." He flashed a malevolent grin and fist-bumped the instructor next to him. "That ought to satisfy those pansy barristers."

"Hell yes, it does, Master Sergeant!" his comrade shouted with an equally wicked grin.

He nodded Cyndi's way. "I see we have a female in the group. You might as well know this up front, the harsh realities of what the enemy does to females in captivity is anything but pretty. Oh, and one more thing. Everything you students encounter is classified."

"How convenient," Cyndi grumbled. "Abuse the women then ship us off to Leavenworth if we complain about it."

Gagliardi's glare bore into Cyndi's chest like a diamond-tipped drill bit. "Something on your mind, Captain Stafford?"

Cyndi sat at attention and shouted, "Hell no, there isn't, Master Sergeant!"

The veins in Gagliardi's thick neck began to throb. He took a slow, calming breath. "I was about to say that during your time as a captive, find ways to win small victories over the enemy. Something that will improve your spirits but not get you killed or injured. It appears the lovely captain here doesn't quite understand the subtleties on how to go about that." He grabbed the edges of the podium and leaned forward. His eyes narrowed. "She will by the time we get done with her."

———◆———

The students were taken to a SCIF, or a sensitive compartmented information facility, in the building and logged into a highly classified, compartmentalized DOD website. Each person entered a question that only they would know the answer to, and then the answer.

In case of capture, during any communications the US might have with a soldier, they would be asked the secret question. The response would be compared with the answer they had entered today in order to verify their identity.

———◆———

After spending eight sobering hours in the classroom learning various cruelties to expect during captivity, Gagliardi dismissed them. "Enjoy your time off. Go have a good meal at the chow hall. Tomorrow you'll learn more techniques for surviving as a prisoner of war."

The instructors lined up and paraded out of the classroom.

Students milled about, trading opinions on what they had learned. The consensus was that the best strategy to prevent becoming a captive was to not get shot down over enemy territory.

As the saying went, hope springs eternal.

The group formed up in columns outside the building and began marching in formation, eager to get back to their warm and comfortable quarters.

Suddenly, shots rang out. Chunks of bark splintered off nearby trees.

"Jesus! Someone is firing real bullets!" Lance yelled.

Masked instructors playing the part of enemy soldiers swarmed the group. They fired their weapons wildly into the air while screaming commands. The students were forced to the ground. One by one, their heads were covered with black hoods and their hands tied behind their backs.

Once the group was secured, one of them yelled, "On your feet, you maggots!"

Gagliardi.

The instructors forced the students back into a loose formation and pushed them forward.

After marching for about thirty minutes, the small amount of sunlight filtering through the hood had disappeared. Cyndi sensed that they had entered a large structure. She could hear their footsteps echoing off the walls.

The group was led down two flights of damp concrete stairs into a dank, musty underground bunker. The repulsive stench of stale body odor hung in the air.

A guard grabbed Cyndi's arm and led her away from the group. Rusty hinges creaked, indicating that a makeshift door was opening. Cyndi was pushed forward. Then the guard untied her hands and ripped the hood off.

She was standing in a tiny cell with plywood walls. The claustrophobic space was approximately six feet tall and only half as wide. Before she could turn around, the door was slammed shut and locked.

"Well, this sucks," Cyndi mumbled, alone in the damp, icy darkness.

CHAPTER 8

AFTER EVERYONE HAD been locked up, a guard began barking out instructions. The captives were ordered to stand at attention in their cells the entire night. Failure to obey the rules would result in severe punishment.

These clowns are taking their roles as prison guards seriously. Cyndi couldn't prevent her brain from agonizing about what might come next.

Contrary to the plots of most spy movies, Cyndi had heard that physical torture rarely yielded any meaningful intelligence. She took some solace in that.

Years of experience at black sites around the world had proved sleep deprivation to be a much better tool for extracting information. The human brain needed sleep to keep it functioning on a rational level. In extreme cases, depriving the brain of restorative sleep long enough had caused psychiatric disorders in prisoners. Rather than dealing with the bad publicity that would surely come from destroying a person's mind, clandestine agencies typically found convenient ways for the unlucky individual to quietly *disappear* instead.

What seemed like hours—but who could tell—passed. Rather than submit and stand at attention all night, Cyndi thought she would outsmart her captors to win a small victory. She approached her cell door and listened. Not hearing any footsteps, she sat down in the corner and loosened the laces on one of her boots. If the door opened, she would claim that she had just sat down to tie her boot.

She massaged her left calf, working out the knot that had formed. Her knee, thigh, and ankle were next. After finishing her left leg, Cyndi began working on the right.

The door suddenly burst open, slamming against the wall with a deafening bang.

A guard stormed into her cell, brandishing a black hood and a pair of flex cuffs.

Cyndi jumped to her feet, but it was too late.

"So you think you're too good to follow the rules, huh. We'll see about that," he sneered. "The commandant has ordered us to make an example of you, so the others don't get any bright ideas. Lay on your stomach, and put your hands behind your back."

Cyndi lifted her chin defiantly and glared at the guard, sending a clear message.

"I said get on the ground, Stafford!" he ordered in a booming voice.

She held her position.

"Be a good little girl now. Lay down, and nobody will get hurt."

If he thought that misogynistic taunt would convince Cyndi to cooperate, he had grossly misjudged her. "Oh, I'm not worried about getting hurt. You should be, though," she threatened.

The guard snorted at her threat, dismissing it as typical military pilot bluster.

That was a mistake.

The man turned and yelled, "Boys!" Three more guards rushed into the cell, packing the small space. The lead guard said, "Last chance, Stafford. Lay down, and put your hands behind your back. Now!"

Something inside her snapped. Cyndi just couldn't meekly surrender like a compliant lamb. She'd been that way as long as she could remember. Call it stubbornness, call it pride, hell, call it foolishness. Cyndi had spent her whole life refusing to back down from bullies. Even though she was badly outnumbered, this time would be no different.

"I don't surrender. Ever."

The four men stood shoulder to shoulder and advanced on Cyndi. She backed up against the wall and set up in a defensive position. She launched a fist at the man in front of her, but he easily deflected her blow. Before she knew it, he had her in a headlock. Another man grabbed her left arm and twisted it behind her back.

She had badly underestimated the close-quarter combat skills of her opponents.

Before being subdued, Cyndi managed to catch the third man in the groin with her foot. He doubled over, in the type of overwhelming agony only a male could understand.

The last guard helped his comrades slam Cyndi to the floor, face-first. He knelt on her back to immobilize Cyndi while her hands were secured in the flex cuffs. A black bag was forced over her head. The drawstring was tightened like a noose around her neck.

The four men, two on each side, yanked Cyndi off the floor by her arms and stood her up.

Still, she struggled.

"Goddammit, Stafford, *stop!*" the lead guard yelled. "We teach you to resist, but that was stupid! You need to learn when to battle and when to go with the flow. In a real POW situation, doing that would've gotten you killed!"

This was the only time since the ambush that Cyndi had seen a guard go out of character and revert to being a survival instructor. Her actions had obviously hit a raw nerve in the guy. Of course she wouldn't admit it out loud, but she knew he was right. That was dumb. Retribution when you were an actual POW could be fatal.

Cyndi took a deep breath, let her muscles relax, and

stopped resisting. If she thought that would placate the guards, she was fooling herself.

The lead guard had other ideas. He nodded at the man Cyndi had kicked in the groin. The guard balled up his fist and delivered a powerful punch to Cyndi's kidney. She doubled over coughing, trying desperately to catch her breath. Cyndi's temper immediately flared up again.

"Well, Stafford, what are you going to do, just let him sucker punch you like that?" the lead guard said, goading Cyndi, hoping she'd retaliate. "Come on, kick his ass, Stafford! Don't let him get away with a cheap shot like that!"

Testa dura.

Hard head.

It was decision time. Was she going to lash out and get revenge for the cheap shot or not? With her martial arts skills, Cyndi knew she could do some serious damage before the men could respond. Just as she was about to launch a kick, the guard's earlier words popped into her head. *Learn how to pick your battles.*

She'd been in many battles before. On the mat at tournaments. In bars with guys who wouldn't take no for an answer. A punch to the kidney was nothing compared with the blows she'd taken in those situations. This was her opportunity to get in a small win. Ignore the taunts from the guard and prove that she wasn't as dumb as he thought.

Through the black fabric Cyndi replied, "What shot? I didn't feel anything."

"You coward," the lead guard scoffed, shaking his head.

Cyndi let out an exasperated sigh. *Damn, this guy just won't let up. I guess he's back in character again.*

CHAPTER 9

WHEN THE COMMANDANT said to make an example of Cyndi, he was deadly serious.

A dozen prisoners were taken from their cells and marched to a different building. Once inside, they were funneled into a long, narrow space. Then their hoods were yanked off.

They were standing in front of a bulletproof glass partition wall that separated them from a small, dimly lit room. Security cameras were mounted in each corner. In the middle of the room was a low table that had been modified with thick leather wrist and ankle restraints.

The guards marched Cyndi into the murky room and held her down on the table. They forced her wrists and ankles into the restraints, buckling them tightly. Then the table was tilted back so that her hooded head was lower than her feet.

"Stay strong, Cyndi," Lance blurted out.

The door opened and the commandant walked in.

He was a short, chubby man with a round, balding head. The unnerving eyes of a psychotic peered at the group through thick, round glasses. He went up to the glass wall and said, "Prisoners, pick up a sheet of paper and a pen."

They shrugged indifferently and complied.

"You will write your full name, the aircraft you fly, your base, and your classified mission objectives on the paper. After providing the information, you will sign your name."

The men just laughed at the absurd request. One of the pilots folded his sheet into a paper airplane and sailed it over the top of the partition.

The commandant sneered at the men. "Have it your way." He walked over to Cyndi. "I hear you've been giving my men a difficult time, prisoner Stafford." He grabbed a bucket and filled it with water in a nearby utility sink.

"What the hell are you doing?" Cyndi yelled, jerking her head left and right, hoping to get a glimpse under the hood of her surroundings.

He carried the bucket over to Cyndi, water sloshing over the edge and spilling onto the floor. Hovering the bucket over her, he tipped it, dribbling water onto her hood.

Cyndi forcefully coughed, trying to expel the water that had gone up her nose.

The commandant slammed the bucket down next to Cyndi's head. "That was one cup of water, Stafford. The bucket I just put next to you has five *gallons* in it!"

On hearing this, her body stiffened as she strained against the restraints. "No! You can't do this!"

"What are you going to do about it, prisoner Stafford, go running to the JAG office?" With his hands clasped behind his back, the commandant slowly strolled down the length of the glass wall. "If you maggots think SERE training is some kind of joke, I assure you that you are mistaken. My job is to prepare you to survive one of the worst possible situations imaginable, being taken prisoner of war by a savage enemy who doesn't give a shit about the Geneva Convention. Now, pick up your paper, and write down the information!"

Lance was livid but he recognized the true reason for the maltreatment of his fiancée. "It's a trick!" he shouted to the others. "The cameras will record us giving up classified information then signing the paper without any type of coercion or torture. Don't do it."

The commandant scurried over and stood in front of Lance.

Despite knowing there was a wall of bulletproof glass between them, the commandant lurched back in fear after seeing the fury raging in Lance's eyes. Confident he was safe, the commandant's eyes narrowed as he glared at Lance. Without breaking his stare, he said, "Turn off the cameras."

"Say again, sir?" one of the guards said with disbelief.

"You heard me, turn off the video cameras."

"Sir, I'm not sure that's such a good—"

"Now, dammit!"

The guard's head sagged. He opened the door to a circuit breaker box mounted on the wall then tripped one of the breakers. "Cameras are off, sir."

The commandant walked back over to Cyndi and picked up the bucket.

CHAPTER 10

"I THINK YOU'VE MADE your point, sir," Lance blurted out, slapping his palms against the glass. "We definitely understand the importance of why we are here."

He ignored Lance's comment and dumped two gallons of water on Cyndi's hooded face.

Without any way of knowing that the water was coming, Cyndi had drawn in a breath at that same moment. The torrent of water filled her lungs, triggering an immediate gag reflex. Panic set in as Cyndi was overcome with the sensation that she was drowning. She convulsed violently against the restraints, trying to scream.

But the water just kept coming.

Lance and the others pounded their fists on the glass, demanding that the commandant stop this barbaric demonstration. Some men grabbed their papers and began frantically writing.

A demonic glee washed over his face as the commandant continued to pour water from the bucket. The sick bastard was actually enjoying this.

No amount of mental toughness could prepare a person to successfully withstand the terrorizing interrogation technique. The body's natural response to being asphyxiated—gulping down as much oxygen as possible—only made the predicament worse.

Two of his guards finally stepped in and grabbed the

bucket from their bosses hand. "I think you've made your point, sir," one of them said.

He shrugged as if he'd just been told lunch was ready. The commandant went back over to the glass. Prisoners screamed profanities at the man while trying to shatter the glass and get to him.

He held up his hands to quiet them. "You fools. You just witnessed an interrogation tactic called coercion pressure. Why do you think I chose a woman for my little demonstration? The enemy will use every tactic at its disposal to get information from you—including manipulating your sense of chivalry. In our culture, a real man would never stand by and watch a woman be tortured. You'd do practically anything to stop it." He thumbed back toward Cyndi. She had been unstrapped from the board and was being administered oxygen. "If you think what you just witnessed was difficult, imagine being forced to watch female prisoners being gang-raped daily in front of you and being powerless to stop it. Sad to say our enemies have done just that. How much information would you be willing to divulge in order to save someone you cared about from suffering from such inhumane treatment?" A nauseating, victorious smirk formed on his face. "I'm afraid I have some bad news. Those of you who wrote anything on your papers will be shipped back to your base at once. You just failed the course."

One of the men who'd been duped by the cunning exhibition fired his pen at the glass wall, leaving a long black scar across it.

Hatred for the commandant burned like a blast furnace inside Lance's gut. At that moment he vowed to strangle the man on sight if he ever got the chance.

CHAPTER 11

THE GUARDS FORCED the black hoods over the prisoners' heads once again and led them to a different building. Screeching loud music interspersed with strange animal sounds was playing over the speakers.

"I hope you maggots aren't afraid of confined spaces," a guard said as their hoods were yanked off.

Wooden boxes no bigger than old steamer trunks lined the wall.

Lance looked down the line of fellow students. Cyndi was at the end. Her damp blonde hair was plastered against her head. He silently mouthed, "You okay?"

She winked back. Her full lips turned up slightly at the ends.

"Listen up, maggots, this is how it's going to work. Because of the disgraceful behavior of the men who were just sent home, you're going to be punished in their absence. You will spend the rest of the night in these tiny little boxes."

Lance gazed at the crate and swallowed hard. "Shit."

"What's the matter, Garcia, claustrophobic?" the guard asked.

"Not at all. Nothing to worry about," Lance replied as he took a deep breath, trying to calm his nerves.

"If you maggots can't handle being crammed into the box all night long, I completely understand. Very few people could. Say the safe words *flight surgeon* twice, and you will be let out."

Lance felt a wave of relief at the out being given to them.

"Of course, if you can't stand a few minutes in the box, you obviously couldn't make it through an entire flight in the claustrophobic cockpit of an F-16."

He had chosen the Fighting Falcon because of its incredibly tight cockpit.

"The Air Force can't risk having one of its pilots freak out during combat because they can't handle a little claustrophobia. Say the safe words, and you're through. You will lose your wings and never fly again."

Harsh but logical, Lance thought.

"Let's go! Everyone in your box!" yelled a guard.

The students sat on the floor and slid feet first into their cage. Lance curled up into the fetal position, but with his long legs he couldn't quite fit. One of the guards sat on the floor and used his feet to force the door to close. Then a padlock was installed.

Within seconds, Lance felt like he was suffocating. His diaphragm was compressed to the point he couldn't draw in a full breath. Lance's heart pounded like a bass drum in his chest. Then he started to overheat. Sweat dampened his flight suit. To stave off a panic attack, Lance hurriedly came up with ideas to occupy his mind. He measured the width of the cage by positioning his arm across his chest. It was no wider than the distance from his elbow to his balled-up fist—only sixteen inches.

The diversionary tactic helped some, but his heart rate continued to spike.

Next he estimated the length of the box. Maybe thirty inches. Lance compared the measurement to his closet back at Marge's house, or anything else that would take his mind off his predicament. The mental tricks began to work. His heart rate slowed. His breathing returned to normal.

Cyndi came up with a more meaningful and personal solution to calm her nerves. She twisted and squirmed until she could reach the pocket on her flight suit that held the two broken wing halves. Laying her hand over the pocket and gently caressing its contents did the trick. A sense of calm washed over her.

It wasn't long before the first man had reached his breaking point.

A pilot in a nearby box started banging on his cage, freaking out from a severe claustrophobia attack. "Let me out of here! Please, let me out!" His anguished cries echoed off the concrete walls.

Those around him offered words of encouragement to the poor guy. "You can do it, man," one said. "Sing a song or imagine building a skyscraper floor by floor," another suggested.

Cyndi was unable to tell if the unnerving tumult was just the guards playing a cruel game by banging on a box and faking a panic attack or an actual student begging for mercy. Regardless, she had gone through too much crap in her Air Force career to have it all taken away now. Cyndi clamped her hands over her ears and sang to herself to prevent the cries from causing her frayed nerves to cascade into a full-blown panic attack of her own.

"Say flight surgeon if you want to be let out," the guards demanded, snickering at the desperate man.

"No! I'm not giving up my wings!"

"Then you stay in the box!"

"Please, you don't understand. I'm suffocating! I just need a few minutes, then I'll go back in, I promise."

"Say flight surgeon!"

The dreadful back and forth continued for a few more minutes then abruptly stopped. Cyndi lowered her hands and strained to hear what was going on.

The psychological trauma had proved too overwhelming to conquer. The man finally capitulated. "Flight surgeon…flight surgeon," he whimpered, his resolve shattered.

The mind can be your greatest ally, or your own worst enemy.

Cyndi heard a padlock click open. The rusty hinges on the door squeaked. The prisoner was led away, sobbing from the realization that his nascent flying career had abruptly ended.

After only thirty minutes, they were let out and taken back to their plywood cells. The threat of spending the entire night in the box had been a hoax designed to heighten their already considerable anxiety.

It was still early. The mind games had only just begun.

CHAPTER 12

IN THE MIDDLE of the night Cyndi was roughly escorted by six guards to another building in the compound.

She had learned her lesson and put up no resistance.

The guards led Cyndi to a small office and told her to take a seat in front of a shabby metal desk. Then they left her.

Cyndi looked around, unsure why she was there. The square of glass on the wall was almost certainly a one-way mirror, she assumed.

The door suddenly burst open. A guard stomped in and planted his massive frame behind the desk. Cyndi's head drooped.

Gagliardi.

"Well if it isn't Captain Stafford. How's it going so far, tough guy?"

Cyndi drew in a calming breath and ignored his taunt.

Gagliardi slapped a manila folder on the desk. "My first prisoner interrogation tonight. This ought to be fun." He picked up a handful of papers and scanned each one. "You Americans are such fools. You post every nauseating detail about your pampered lives on the internet for everyone to see. It's like you *want* your enemies to win."

His acting, as an enemy interrogator, wasn't nearly convincing enough to win Gagliardi an Emmy or an Oscar. But he did deserve an award for effort. As an enlisted man, he relished the opportunity to stick it to cocky pilots without any repercussions. He'd be loath to admit it, but losing his chance to go to pilot training, after a drunk driving arrest in college, was the fire motivating his acting.

Gagliardi stuffed the pages back into the folder. "So, Stafford, are you excited to fly the F-35?"

"I hear it's a cool plane," Cyndi replied, cleverly avoiding confirming or denying that she would soon fly it.

"You think this is a damned game!" Gagliardi yelled, pounding his fist on the desk. "Answer my question. Do you fly the F-35 or not!"

Cyndi looked him right in the eyes. "Like I already said, I hear it's—"

Before she could finish her sentence, Gagliardi had pounced on Cyndi and lifted her out of her chair. He slammed her into the corner and spun Cyndi around to face him.

His flushed face was mere inches from hers. "I'm going to break you, Stafford," he growled.

"Like *hell* you will," Cyndi hissed, in the most venomous tone of voice she could muster.

"We'll see about that." The master sergeant grabbed a large chunk of plywood leaning against the wall. "You will hold this at arm's length until I say drop it. Understood?"

Cyndi refused to respond. She grasped the sides of the heavy piece of plywood and held her arms straight out, glaring at her interrogator. Gagliardi went back to the desk and sat on the edge, waiting to pounce again when the inevitable came.

Testa dura.

Hard head.

Stubborn.

Take your pick. Cyndi was not going to let Gagliardi win. She was going to embarrass him no matter how long it took or how badly her body hurt. She rolled her head in circles, trying to loosen the knots forming in her neck. Within minutes the muscles in her arms began to shake uncontrollably. To take her mind off the pain, Cyndi scanned the office, taking in every detail.

Her eyes suddenly stopped moving. A small hole had been cut in the top of the corner on the opposite side of the room. She focused on the round, black object poking out from the hole.

It was a small camera lens.

Cyndi's heart sank. She turned the piece of plywood around. It was actually a sign. On the opposite side were the words: *I am a war criminal. I have murdered innocent women and children.*

Gagliardi stood and crossed his massive arms. A victorious grin crossed his face. He walked over to Cyndi. "By tomorrow morning, every news outlet and blog in America will have received a photo of you voluntarily holding this sign. And no one but you will be in the picture."

Cyndi dropped the plywood and crumpled to the floor, mortified at being so easily deceived.

———◆———

Back in her plywood cell, Cyndi sat on the damp concrete floor, too humiliated and too despondent to care if she was caught not standing at attention.

CHAPTER 13

"EVERYBODY UP! LET'S go!"

Mentally exhausted, Cyndi had drifted off to sleep. Guards shouting commands and pounding on cell doors jolted her back to reality. She reluctantly stood, dreading the next humiliating lesson in store for her.

A small slot on her door slid open. A black hood was tossed through the opening.

"Prisoners, put on your hoods, and stand at attention at the front of your cell," a guard yelled.

Cyndi complied, too drained to bother resisting.

After donning their hoods, each prisoner was released from their cells. Unable to see, they were instructed to line up by placing their hands on the shoulders of the person in front of them. After marching up the stairs, Cyndi realized she was outside when she drew in the sweet smell of fresh air.

"Halt! Remove your hoods!" a guard ordered.

Cyndi immediately recognized the gruff voice.

Gagliardi.

The prisoners stopped and removed their hoods. Cyndi instinctively raised her hand to her eyes to shield them from the glare of the bright sun.

It was morning in eastern Washington state.

When her vision had adapted to the light, Cyndi almost began to cry. In front of her was one of the most beautiful sights she'd ever seen. A rusty and dented blue

Air Force bus was parked only fifty feet away. The crucial but challenging ordeal of SERE training was over. Cyndi, Lance, and the rest of the group were going home.

The guards/instructors were lined up at the open bus door. They were wearing standard Air Force-issue OCP utility uniforms with easily recognizable rank insignia.

Students whooped and cheered as they bounded up the stairs into the bus.

Cyndi paused to take in her surroundings. This was the first time she'd actually seen the POW compound she had been imprisoned in. The innocuous cluster of bland-looking buildings betrayed their true purpose. Cyndi couldn't wait to shake the dust from this hellhole off her combat boots.

She rushed over to board the bus. As luck would have it, Gagliardi was positioned at the door. A vengeful smirk formed on her face.

Gagliardi snapped to attention and saluted. "Enjoy the F-35, ma'am. I have it on good authority that it's a very cool jet."

This was her chance to settle the score and pull rank on the E-7 for the untold amounts of misery he'd inflicted on her.

"I refuse to confirm nor deny that information, Master Sergeant Gagliardi."

"Okay, tough guy, have it your way." He held his salute and waited.

In the ultimate insult to a lower ranking member of the military, Cyndi boarded the bus without returning the salute. She plopped down in a seat and tightly folded her arms, staring straight ahead.

As the bus pulled away, something in the distance caught Cyndi's eye. The Stars and Stripes were fluttering gently in the wind.

The real reason that the Survival, Evade, Resist, and

Escape instructors were so dedicated to their jobs suddenly crystallized in Cyndi's mind. They did it to give every student who went through their program the tools needed to make it back alive from captivity with their honor intact. They did it for the flag and the noble principles it represented.

Cyndi and Lance had wandered into a convenience store in the Spokane airport, killing time before their flight back to Phoenix. Lance grabbed a bag of peanut M&Ms. Cyndi picked up the local newspaper. CNN was playing on a flatscreen TV on the wall.

After paying the cashier, Cyndi stepped in front of the TV to catch up on what she had missed during SERE school.

A distinguished looking silver-haired anchorman was reading his lines from the teleprompter. "In world news, the nasty spat between President Horatio Ashford and Mexican President Ortega continues to escalate. With both men running for reelection, the diplomatic rhetoric heated up again this past week. President Ashford's reputation as a bare-knuckled brawler was on full display again when he accused Mexico of causing the illegal drug problems America faces. He was quoted as saying, 'The Mexican drug cartels are flooding the streets with tons of fentanyl, poisoning millions of Americans while Ortega vacations on his yacht with his reality TV star wife.'

"Political analysts say the Mexican president is barely hanging on to his office by a thread. He is fighting a civil war with the drug cartels for control of his country, severely handicapped by corruption in every level of law enforcement and the military. In a recent interview, Ortega told CNN en Español, 'We live next to the world's largest drug consumer, and other countries want to sell them drugs through our door and our window.

If that isn't bad enough, we also live next to the world's largest arms seller. Criminals in America are supplying all the weapons they can find to the barbaric savages in the drug cartels.'"

Cyndi shook her head, disgusted at the untold misery a few egotistical politicians could unleash upon millions of civilians and soldiers.

They left the store and settled into two seats at their departure gate, relieved to have checked off the SERE school box on the list of prerequisites before beginning F-35 ground school. Lance sat back and watched workers scramble around the ramp readying airliners for their next flights.

Cyndi opened her paper. Of course the spat between the two presidents was front page news.

Conflict sells.

Below the headline article was a long piece that went in depth on how Mexico had gotten itself into the present quagmire.

The article began with an overview of the carnage, noting that over four hundred thousand people had been killed during Mexico's wars with the drug cartels since its start in 2006. The deaths were attributed to the government's crackdown on the violent cartels as well as battles between cartels for territory and the billions that came with it. In addition to the people who'd been killed, another eighty-five thousand people had "disappeared."

The government's main foes were powerful gangs like the Omega Cartel that controlled large swaths of Mexico. It had been started by traitorous former elite members of the Mexican military. Initially, they'd worked as hit men for the Gulf Cartel, before becoming independent. The group had a reputation for being particularly savage and was known for massacres, killing civilians, leaving body parts in public places, and posting killings on the internet.

The group's main asset wasn't drugs but organized violence, including theft, extortion, human smuggling, and kidnapping, according to a government report.

The report carried the grisly title *Bodies for Billions*.

CHAPTER 14

SHOCKED BY HOW much weight they'd lost during SERE school, Marge had been preparing banquet-sized meals for Cyndi and Lance since they returned. After relying on bugs and berries for sustenance for an entire week, Lance had gladly gobbled up anything she heaped on his plate.

The two were spending a lazy Sunday afternoon snuggled up on the couch, recovering from their latest food coma before embarking on the exhausting nine-month marathon called F-35 training.

Cyndi wore a cut-off white T-shirt that exposed her taut midriff and a pair of comfortable old sweatpants. Ruby-red nail polish made her bare feet dazzle.

Marge emerged from the kitchen and said, "Well aren't you two just the picture of contentment. There's nothin' on God's green earth quite as charming as young love. Warms my heart."

"That's sweet, Marge," Cyndi replied with a smile. She gave Lance a peck on the cheek. "I had to go through a lot of frogs, but I finally found my Prince Charming."

"Prince? If he's a Prince then ol' Romeo here shouldn't have any trouble springing for a wedding. And soon."

Lance had grown accustomed to her good-natured motherly nagging and had no hesitation teasing Marge in return. "If Cyndi gets tired of waiting, maybe you and I could get hitched."

Marge's face turned bright red with embarrassment.

"Sonny, you couldn't handle a spry young heartbreaker like Marge Thompson. No siree."

"You tell him, Marge," Cyndi chimed in. "I guess I'll just have to wait to get married..." She poked Lance in the ribs and made a croaking sound. "To my frog."

Lance held up both hands. "Okay, I know when I'm beaten. I don't stand a chance against formidable females like you two."

Marge wiped her hands on her apron and said, "Now that that nonsense is settled, how about I get you two something to eat?"

"Please don't go to any trouble, Marge. We're fine. *Really*," Cyndi quickly replied, still hurting from the last meal.

"Fiddlesticks, you two are skin and bones. Let me see what I can whip up." With all the vigor a person of her age could muster, Marge rushed to the kitchen like a woman on a mission. The sound of cabinets opening and pans clanging soon followed.

Luke AFB, Monday morning

The big day had finally arrived.

Cyndi and Lance walked briskly into the classroom in the 60th Fighter Squadron with big smiles on their faces, eager to get started.

The table in the first row had been taken by three broad-shouldered, handsome pilots in flight suits. They were talking among themselves—which in the Air Force meant their hands were imitating airplanes, swooping up and down recreating their last flights.

"Hey, guys, what's up?" Lance asked in a friendly, bubbly tone.

In an intentional attempt to project superiority, they ignored him.

Cyndi and Lance glanced at each other and rolled their eyes. They grabbed seats at the table in the second row and settled in for a long day.

A few minutes later their instructor strutted into the classroom. When Lance spotted him, his head sank.

The instructor had a Neanderthal forehead and sported a porn 'stache.

"Well, well, well, if it isn't Ken and Barbie," Toilet said with obvious delight. "This ought to be entertaining." He looked away and pointed at the first table. "Before I get started, everyone introduce yourselves and tell us your prior flying experience."

The first man leaned back in his chair and plopped his feet on the desk. "I'm Riddler. Before this, I flew the badass A-10 Warthog. I did one combat tour in Iraq, and I've got 1,800 flight hours."

"Call sign's Fudge," the second man announced. "I did two tours in Afghanistan. I've flown the F-16 and F-15 and have over two thousand hours."

"Boozer. Over 2,700 hours. I flew the B-1 in the Gulf War. I'm coming from Edwards where I was a test pilot on the awesome F-22. Now I'm stuck flying its little sister."

"Little sister?" Toilet growled, his nostrils flaring and his complexion reddening.

Boozer leaned back in his chair and crossed his arms. A smarmy grin crossed his face. "No offense. Of course."

"Of course not. None taken," Toilet replied coolly. "If a Chinese surveillance balloon attacks Luke Air Force Base, it's comforting to know the *awesome* F-22 will protect us."

Boozer's smug grin evaporated.

"How about you two lovebirds in the second row?" Toilet asked before Boozer could fire off a return verbal jab.

"Cyndi Stafford. One hundred eighty military flight hours in the T-6 and T-8. I've also got my fixed wing, rotary wing, multi-engine, commercial, instructor, and instrument tickets and around four thousand civilian hours."

The experienced fighter jocks didn't want to acknowledge that Cyndi had more flight hours than any of the men in the room, but their bobbing heads betrayed that they were impressed with her aviation experience.

Lance sat at attention in his seat and flashed a toothy smile. "Lance Garcia. One hundred eighty hours in the T-6 and T-8 trainers."

Boozer turned and shot Lance a withering glare. "That's it?" he scoffed.

Lance's cheeks flushed as he sank back down. "Well… yeah." Hoping to beef up his unimpressive resume, Lance added, "But I did play a fighter pilot in some Air Force commercials a few years ago."

"Play?" Boozer questioned incredulously.

"I had the lead role in *Our Town* in high school," Riddler announced, "but that sure as hell doesn't mean I'm Thornton Wilder."

"I've been an instructor on the F-35 for six years," Toilet said. "If you ask me, virgin pilots right out of UPT have no business flying such a complicated fighter. But surprisingly, the Air Force neglected to ask for my opinion on the matter. So, I follow orders and teach whoever shows up." He opened the door to the classroom. "Let's get this party started. First stop is a visit to the life support shop."

The life support technician excitedly rubbed his hands together as he addressed the class of new F-35 students. "Good morning, future Panther pilots. My job is to get you fitted for your new gear." He held up a piece of equipment belonging to one of the pilots in the squadron. "We'll start with this."

The students crowded around him to get a closer look.

Lance cocked his head. "What is that thing?"

"This is the future," the proud tech boasted. "Your helmet."

Rockwell Collins and an Israeli company, Elbit Systems had teamed up to create a helmet worthy of a starring role in the next Star Wars movie.

"Each of you will get a carbon fiber flight helmet custom fitted to your head. It takes two days of measurements, scans, and tweaking to get the perfect fit," the tech continued. "You won't find one of these bad boys on the shelves at Walmart."

Cyndi grabbed the helmet and closely examined it.

The life support tech snatched it back from her hands. "Please don't touch that, ma'am. They cost $450,000 a pop. That's more than a Ferrari F8. Plus a new Corvette Z06. Plus a Tesla Model Y for getting groceries. I can't afford to let you drop it."

Cyndi was glad to transfer financial responsibility for the astronomically priced piece of equipment back to the technician.

"What are these for?" she asked, pointing at two round lenses mounted across the brow at the front of the helmet.

"Those are miniature projectors, part of the helmet-mounted display system." The tech sensed the confusion in the room. "Okay, let me back up. Starting today, you need to wrap you heads around the fact that you will be flying a fifth-generation fighter. Every piece of your equipment is fifth generation as well."

He plugged the helmet into a test stand. The miniature projectors lit up. Then the tech lowered the clear helmet visor.

Airspeed, altitude, and a myriad of other simulated mission-critical information magically appeared on the visor.

"Looking straight ahead at a HUD is so two-thousand-yesterday. The jet doesn't even have a heads-up display. No matter where you look, the information you need is always right in front of your eyes."

Lance nodded his approval and smiled. "Awesome."

The tech enjoyed lording his knowledge of the helmet and jet over the newbies. "But wait, there's more. Six high-resolution infrared sensors are embedded around the F-35, part of the AN/AAQ-37 Electro-optical Distributed Aperture System. Imagery from the DAS sensors is fused together and projected onto your helmet visor, giving you a 360-degree view of the battlefield. For example, you can look down at the floor and see what's below your aircraft."

"Just like Wonder Woman's glass airplane!" Lance proclaimed.

Everyone in the room groaned, including Cyndi.

By the end of the second day, the pilots had perfectly fitting helmets. They customized them with their name and graphics that expressed their unique personalities.

Next, the optics in their helmets were aligned using a pupilometer. The contraption measured the distance between their pupils within two millimeters of its center, assuring they would see a single, focused image on the helmet-mounted display.

Satisfied with the final product, the tech gave the pilots one last piece of advice. "If you cut your hair or gain more than a few pounds, you'll need to come back in and see me to recalibrate your helmet."

"And don't drop it!"

The next day, the class received detailed briefings specific to flying out of Luke AFB.

"My dad flew the F-4 at Luke back in the Stone Age," Toilet said with a laugh. "Back then it was out in the boondocks. Now there are thirty-seven airports in the area, ranging from small airports with no control tower to Sky Harbor, the main hub for Southwest Airlines. With three hundred sunny days a year, it's easy to understand why Phoenix has become a mecca for aviation. Keep your head on a swivel, and constantly be on the lookout for traffic. You know what happened to Viking. Don't let it happen to you.

"The sky isn't the only dangerous place. We're in the Sonoran Desert. It covers over one hundred thousand square miles and stretches from the Southwest United States to northwest Mexico. If you go hiking, realize that there are scorpions, rattlesnakes, coyotes, and mountain lions out there. Remember, you're in their world, not yours. The law of the jungle rules. They might not be toting an AK-47, but they can kill you just the same. Treat the desert as enemy territory. And always have water with you wherever you go. Dehydration can set in faster than you think."

Toilet escorted the students from the classroom and deep into the interior of the building. At the entrance to a dimly lit hallway warning signs threatened incarceration for any unauthorized personnel, indicating they were about to enter a high-security restricted area.

Lieutenant Colonel Tank Abrams met the group. "You folks are being trusted with classified details on how to operate the newest fighter in the sky. I expect you to take that responsibility seriously. The Air Force learned a hard lesson about protecting sensitive aircraft data after the Chinese debuted their J-31—a clone of our F-22. Follow me."

He opened a thick steel door and led the group inside a moderately sized room bristling with workstations. Aviation maps were spread out on tables. Flatscreen monitors displayed classified intel from hot spots around the world.

"This is our SCIF. The spooks call it the Sensitive Compartmented Information Facility, but that's way too long. We call it the vault. Anytime you discuss sensitive or classified information, you'll do it in the vault."

Random nature sounds and strange music were always playing in the vault to prevent eavesdropping equipment from getting a clear recording.

Abrams stepped to the front of the room. "Cyber warfare is now the weapon of choice among our adversaries. State-sanctioned operations like the Lazarus Group in North Korea and the Russian group Fancy Bear have targeted the F-35 program since its inception. Buying a bunch of hackers unlimited pizza and a subscription to an internet porn site is a drop in the bucket compared to fielding an entire anti-aircraft missile system. If that isn't bad enough, ever since that damned article in *Popular Mechanics*, every pimple-faced loser living in his mom's basement now thinks they have what it takes to hack the F-35.

"Last month the DIA discovered a Trojan horse virus planted on one of our pilot's phones. They believe the phone could have been used as a cyber warfare tool to compromise the flight control computers. The source of the virus couldn't be determined, but the pilot was warned of the potential dangers of consorting with female foreign nationals with dubious…morals."

Tank's body language clearly indicated he was referring to a certain nearby F-35 instructor pilot sporting a porn 'stache.

"As of now, no cell phones, smartwatches, Apple Air-Pods, or any other device with Bluetooth or Wi-Fi connectivity are allowed in briefings, the sims, or the airplane. They are to be secured inside a Faraday bag anytime you are in the vault or flying."

Toilet handed out black pouches that blocked RF signals from being received or transmitted by electronic devices. The students deposited all the devices that could be used as a weapon against them into their bag.

Not having her cell phone surgically attached to her side was no big deal for Cyndi. Despite her young age, she wasn't a slave to social media, messaging, or gaming. She never quite understood the need of others in her generation to manufacture staged photos claiming to be "living their best life" when they could just go out and actually live an interesting one.

Of course that would mean getting up off the couch and interacting with real human beings. Cyndi let out a chuckle tinged with embarrassment. *Oh great, I'm beginning to sound like my dad,* she thought.

CHAPTER 15

"THE ROOM IS yours, Toilet," Tank said. "I expect you to turn these pilots into the most formidable human weapon systems on the planet. Don't disappoint me."

Toilet looked directly at Cyndi and Lance. "I've got my work cut out for me, but I'll do my best, sir."

After Tank left the SCIF, Toilet dimmed the lights and fired up a PowerPoint presentation. "Welcome to the F-35 B-Course. Before it's over, you'll be intimately familiar with every nut and bolt on the jet. But don't expect me to spoon-feed your asses. The Air Force can't afford it. The F-35 is the most expensive weapons system in American history. By the time you are fully combat ready, the Air Force will have invested over $12 million in you.

"Screw the money. Let the bean counters worry about that. Soon, you will be flying the most advanced fifth-generation fighter ever built. You'll be at the top of the fighter pilot food chain. In an F-35 you don't share the sky; you own it!"

Testosterone was practically oozing from Toilet's pores.

He looked right at Cyndi and Lance again. "As of today, I expect you two rookies to start acting like it. Self-doubt has no place in the cockpit. It could cripple your chances of surviving, even when going up against lesser pilots flying crappy Soviet or Chinese jets. Whether it's true or false, you have to *believe* that you are invincible.

"Those folks over in Fort Worth have built us one hell of a sweet ride. For such a complicated aircraft, the F-35 is actually very easy to fly. Unless you're maneuvering, the fly-by-wire flight control system automatically trims the plane to maintain one G. As long as you don't move the stick, the plane will just keep on doing whatever it's doing at the time.

"The voice recognition system also helps reduce your workload. Just say the keyword for the system you want to change, then the command. And just like a good wife, the plane does what it's told."

Cyndi didn't take the bait. She pretended to take notes, ignoring the jab.

"Exceptional stick-and-rudder skills aren't really crucial in this job. What is crucial is learning to understand and process the tsunami of information that is coming at you. That's the most challenging part of flying the Panther. Some people think being a floor trader on Wall Street is a high-pressure job. Try doing it at nine Gs and nine hundred knots with SAMs flying up your ass. Then you can talk to me about pressure."

Toilet advanced to the next PowerPoint slide of the cockpit. "The panoramic touch screen will become the center of your universe."

The huge screen dominated the cockpit. Contrary to most jets, only a few switches and knobs were sprinkled around.

"The screen has four portals or windows, plus the ability to display any information anywhere on it. We've nicknamed the F-35 the Burger King jet because you can have it your way. And no, before you ask, Garcia, you can't get Monday Night Football on it."

"Or your damned commercials," Riddler grumbled.

Toilet rolled out an F-35 screen mounted on a cart to demonstrate its capabilities. When he powered it up, an astonishing amount of information flooded the screen.

"With all this information available to you, your job is to be the battle manager. That includes wingmen. As number two, you might be positioned twenty miles off lead's wing."

"Did you say twenty miles?" Fudge asked. "Number two could never see his leader at that distance."

"You are going to have to wrap your mind around a completely new paradigm, Fudge. Every pilot in the formation has to think for himself. The jet helps. It fuses information coming from every source imaginable then displays it on your screen. Your job is to process what you see and then call the play. Think of yourself as Tom Brady—except if you read the defense wrong, you die. No pressure there."

"If I'm expected to be Tom Brady, then where's Gisele?" Riddler asked.

"The same place all the other women in your life are," Cyndi retorted. "In your dreams."

Far from making a new enemy, the experienced fighter jock laughed out loud at Cyndi's jab. His respect for her had just jumped up a notch.

In this high-speed, high-altitude fraternity, being able to throw a punch was just as admired as being able to take one.

"What about going stealth?" Lance asked. "How do I keep the bad guys from seeing me?"

Toilet did his best to keep a straight face. "If you want to make your plane disappear, just press the big red button in the cockpit."

CHAPTER 16

SIX WEEKS LATER, ground school wrapped up. The class rankings were pinned to a bulletin board in the hallway. Students gathered around it to see where they'd finished. Cyndi and Lance had earned the top two spots, followed by Boozer, Fudge, and Riddler.

Lance couldn't resist the opportunity. "How about that. We aced the systems tests, local airspace test, and the emergency procedures boldface tests," he bragged. "Not bad for a couple of virgins."

Cyndi gladly piled on. "But who's keeping score. Certainly not us. I'm sure our hotshot fighter jock classmates will do better going forward."

They bumped fists as they strutted triumphantly down the hallway.

Simulator training was next on the agenda. Like everything else associated with the F-35, the simulator was next generation. Gone was the huge box on hydraulic legs. Instead, a replica of the cockpit slid on rails into an enclosure with a wraparound projection screen. Only a small amount of motion, combined with IMAX-quality graphics, was needed to make the pilots feel like they were actually airborne.

By the end of the month, Cyndi and Lance had been put through every conceivable flight and emergency scenario an F-35 pilot would ever face in the jet—many that were far too dangerous to risk doing in the outrageously expensive airplane.

Now it was time for the real thing.

After briefing their first sortie in the SCIF and then suiting up, Cyndi and Lance met back at the briefing desk with their air instructors, eager to step out to their jets. Since this was their very first flight—and all flights were solo—the pilot behind the desk assigned to brief crews before they took to the Arizona skies went into excruciating detail covering weather, field conditions, and alternate airports in the vicinity in case of an emergency.

When finished, he warned them, "Don't bend any metal out there, rookies."

———◆———

Lance and Cyndi walked across the sweltering ramp and up to his jet. Seeing pictures of the F-35 and flying the simulator had familiarized Lance with the plane. But seeing it up close and personal for the first time gave him pause.

Lance tilted his head. "Hmm, looks like the Panther could stand to lose a few pounds. Either that or she's pregnant."

"I see what you mean," Cyndi agreed, nodding.

The engineers had envisioned a jet with the same slender profile as current fourth-generation fighters. But the overriding mandate to maximize its stealthy characteristics had tied their hands. Rather than being mounted under the wings, its bombs and missiles were concealed in two cavernous bomb bays on the underside of the F-35. Above them was the largest jet engine ever installed in a fighter. Throw in a few gas tanks in the barrel-shaped fuselage, and the end result was anything but svelte.

Lance shrugged. "At least it's in the shade."

For years, pilots at Luke had complained about how hot it was in the cockpit when they first jumped into their jets. Assuming the pilots were acting like prima donnas, the Air Force decided to put an end to their whining by measuring the cockpit temperatures of aircraft on the tarmac. The pilots were right. During the hottest part of the year the temperature inside an F-16 cockpit was recorded at 210 degrees Fahrenheit. A line item was added to the budget the following fiscal year for shelters similar to carports over every aircraft. The big difference being that a carport over your minivan didn't cost $1.2 million each.

Lance moved to hug Cyndi before they parted and to wish her good luck. Knowing that a display of affection on the flight line would unleash a torrent of ribbing from the guys, instead he pulled back and blurted out, "Don't die out there."

Cyndi winked. "That's the plan."

Lance strapped into his ejection seat then fired up the big screen and logged in to the jet. As he set up the cockpit, he hunted for the red stealth button. He searched every corner of the cockpit but came up empty-handed. Cyndi's jet was parked in the shelter next to him. "Hey, where's the stealth button?" Lance yelled.

"It's right next to the flux capacitor switch!" she yelled back, trying to conceal her amusement.

As she waited for the radio call to start their engines, Cyndi noticed tall, scattered rain clouds dotting the area. Occasional flashes of lightning could be seen in the buildups.

During the monsoon season, isolated storm cells teased southern Arizona as they drifted by, dropping soaking rains long enough to wet the ground but not long enough to quench the thirst of the bone-dry desert.

"Ambush One-One, this is Ambush One-Two. Looks like we're going to have to stand down," Cyndi transmitted over the radio to her instructor. "Lightning is in the vicinity. We can't risk the OBIGGS failing."

She was referring to safety regulations specific to the F-35. The Air Force required their outrageously expensive supercomputer with wings to avoid any lightning by at least twenty-five miles. The restriction wasn't instituted to protect the advanced avionics, which were attached to a fuselage made from composite material. The faulty Onboard Inert Gas Generation System was the culprit. When it was working correctly, the system injected nitrogen-enriched air into the fuel tanks—so they wouldn't explode when struck by lightning.

How ironic, Cyndi thought. If late-night comedians cared about such things, they'd do an entire bit pointing out that the nickname for the F-35 was the Lightning II, but the intimidating war machine was prohibited from flying anywhere near any actual lightning.

After the bad weather had passed, the formation taxied out to the runway. Cyndi lined up on her instructor's left wing. The two Pratt & Whitney F135 jet engines roared as each pilot selected afterburner. With forty thousand pounds of thrust at her command, Cyndi was airborne in the blink of an eye. Her entire existence was focused on staying in the perfect formation position. Thirty seconds later, Lance did the same with his instructor.

At an eyewatering cost of $67,000 per flight hour there was no time to waste on a leisurely familiarization flight. Their instructors led Lance and Cyndi through every aerobatic maneuver in the book. After that they were tested on each emergency and boldface procedure.

Two hours later, Cyndi and Lance trudged across the sweltering tarmac back to the squadron building. They were drenched in sweat and exhausted from the mental and physical strain.

And they'd never been happier.

CHAPTER 17

THE PACE OF training had only intensified after their first flights.

Time off to enjoy the bountiful recreational opportunities Arizona had to offer was nonexistent. Cyndi and Lance spent nearly every waking hour studying for the next flight, briefing it, flying it, or debriefing the flight. The fact that they were new to the fighter world earn them no slack from the instructors. Every mistake was examined under a microscope. Criticism replaced conversation. A thick skin and an unquenchable desire to fly the perfect sortie became the best antidotes for the pain.

As the months wore on, they continued to build hours by flying routine, repetitive training sorties. With no hot war going on, they struggled to make a connection with the training and any battlefield application.

One night Cyndi and Lance were up well past midnight, studying in the family room. Marge shuffled in wearing a pink terry cloth robe. She yawned and said, "Are you kids still at it? Haven't you hit the books enough for one night?"

"I hope we didn't wake you, Marge," Cyndi replied.

"No, of course not. Why would I be asleep at this godawful hour."

"Sorry about that. Once I get a handle on how the screen in the cockpit displays the hydraulics available to the flight controls when the jet is powered by the standby electrical system, I'll turn in, promise."

"I don't have the foggiest notion what you just said, but it sounds complicated."

"Yeah, a little bit," Cyndi admitted.

"I got just what you need to get your brain firing on all cylinders. Wait here; I'll get you a slice of pie."

Cyndi started to object but didn't have the heart to disappoint Marge. She was offering to help in the only way she knew how.

Marge waddled off to the kitchen.

"Give yourself a break," Lance said. "If you don't get it figured out tonight, there's always tomorrow."

Cyndi had always been her own worst critic. Her need for perfection often led to exasperation. "Easy for you to say. You're not one of the 3 percent of fighter pilots who are female."

"In this job it's not about what's between your legs; it's about how well you can fly and fight," Lance said.

"Tell that to the guys in the fighter community still living in the Dark Ages—like Toilet."

"Forget Toilet. For that matter, forget studying." Lance leaned back and laced his fingers behind his head. "*Tarta*."

"Excuse me," Cyndi said, looking up from her F-35 manual.

"I said tarta." Lance had a suspicious grin on his handsome face. "It means pie. Now that we live in Phoenix, it's about time you learn some Spanish." He grabbed her manual and closed it. "I'll teach you a few words while we eat a slice of Marge's delicious tarta."

Cyndi grabbed the manual back and angrily flipped through the pages, searching for her lost place. "I'm a little busy right now learning to fly the F-35. Besides, you don't even like Marge's—"

"Oh boy, mincemeat!" Lance said loudly, preventing Marge from hearing Cyndi's criticism of her cooking as she emerged from the kitchen. He jumped up off the couch and took the two plates from Marge. "My favorite. Cyndi's too. Isn't that right, Cyndi?"

"Sure, of course," Cyndi sighed in resignation.

"I thought you kids might like it. That's why I went ahead and baked two of them," Marge said, beaming with pride. "Enjoy your pie. And don't forget to turn off the lights before you go upstairs." She shuffled off to her bedroom and closed the door.

"Enjoy your tarta, *sweetheart*," Lance said with a grin, holding up a fork full of mincemeat pie.

Cyndi glared at her fiancé. "There are a few words of Spanish you can teach me. How do you say, 'You're sleeping on the couch'?"

CHAPTER 18

A week later.

CYNDI MET HER instructor, Snake, at the squadron briefing counter. "Ready for your first dogfight training sortie, Stafford?"

"Yes, sir. Locked and loaded."

"Good to hear. Four F-16 pilots are waiting for us in the vault. Let's go kick some ass."

"There's four of them against only two of us?"

"Don't worry; just follow my lead." As they walked toward the vault, Snake's phone rang. When he saw the caller ID, his stomach began to churn. "Hey, babe. I'm about to brief a flight, what's up?" His suspicions were correct. "Okay, I'll leave for the hospital immediately. Tell the baby to wait until I get there."

"What's going on?" Cyndi asked.

"That was my wife. She's at the hospital. She just went into labor. I hate to do this to you on your first dog fighting sortie, but I really need to be there this time. I missed the births of our first two kids because I was TDY. And there won't be a fourth."

"How can you be so sure?"

"After my wife showed me the plus symbol on her pregnancy test, I went and got snipped the very next week."

"I did not need to know that. TMI, sir." Cyndi said.

"But I completely understand. Go be with your wife. She needs you."

"You'll be okay?"

"I…um…" Cyndi bit her lower lip. "I guess so."

Snake was torn. He needed to be with his wife, but he also wanted to lead the "battle" against their opponents. He decided to do what good leaders do: step back and let his subordinate take the wheel so that someday she, too, would be qualified to lead. It was time to kick Cyndi out of the nest and let her learn how to think, fly, fight, and win without someone holding her hand.

"Look at it this way: If you go up against the Russians or the Chinese, you'll always be outnumbered. Do what you'd do in a real dogfight. Find a way to win."

Cyndi understood what Snake was doing—and why. "No problem. I got this. Go be with your wife. It's time for me to go kick some Viper ass."

"Thanks, Stafford, I owe you one."

As Snake sprinted down the hallway Cyndi yelled, "Congratulations!"

She put all her electronic devices in a Faraday bag then walked into the vault. The same weird music was playing.

Four veteran F-16 pilots—a lieutenant colonel, a major, and two captains—were waiting for her.

She took a deep breath before beginning the life-and-death version of chess and announced, "Hey, guys. I'm Cyndi Stafford."

The LC puffed out his chest and said, "I'm Jekyll, flight lead. You must be the Fat Amy pilot."

Cyndi didn't let the derogatory nickname other fighter pilots had given the F-35 bother her. "Cute, but we prefer the nickname Panther."

"Okay, Fat Amy it is then. Where's your husband, Stafford?" Jekyll said with an annoying smirk.

"Say again?" Cyndi replied, confusion blanketing her face.

"Your flight lead. The guy who's supposed to take care of you and run the show while you're out there."

Okay, let the combat begin, Cyndi thought. "I have a suggestion. Why don't we bring the conversation back to the current century? Snake had to rush to the hospital. His wife is having their third baby."

"What a novel concept. A female who knows her place, popping out kids then raising them. At home."

That left a mark.

Cyndi glared at the man. *Now the fight's really on, you SOB.*

"Let's get started," the flight leader said. "Since you're new at this, I'll speak slowly. Rule number one is that there is no rank in the briefing or debriefing. This is serious shit. Say what needs to be said."

We'll see about that.

"For today's mission our radio call sign will be Satan 26 Flight, you'll be Hunter 13. I don't want to be responsible for starting an international incident, so don't cross the border. With their ancient equipment, it's not like Mexican Air Space will be able to tell if you accidentally strayed into their ADIZ anyway, but just don't do it."

The official name of Mexico's air traffic control authority was Mexican Air Space. It had been in turmoil for years because of underfunding, deteriorating infrastructure, and poorly trained controllers. Their ability to detect aircraft coming from the US that strayed into the Mexican Air Defense Identification Zone was spotty at best.

"I'll start with the big picture. We will launch out to the SELLS 1 MOA for multiple one versus four, high aspect BFM engagements. The first engagement will be BVR with fifty-mile separation, head to head, north to south. At the merge—"

Cyndi touched her hands together, forming a capital letter T. "Timeout, sir."

"What is it, Stafford? Am I speaking too fast for you?"

"Is this some kind of hazing ritual? How about starting over but this time in English."

The flight leader shook his head. "You should already know the lingo. It's Fighter Pilot 101, Stafford. If you'd done your homework before showing up today, you would have understood everything I just said." Jekyll's eyes narrowed. "Wait, don't tell me. You're fresh out of UPT."

"Yes, sir."

"That's such bullshit. Fifteen years as a fighter pilot, and I'm stuck flying a plane that came out forty fucking years ago while the Air Force lets wet-behind-the-ears chicks like you fly the F-35."

"I'm so sorry to hear you feel that way, sir. Hang tight. I'll get your mommy on the phone." Cyndi pantomimed pulling out her iPhone and placing it against her ear. "Mrs. Jekyll, would you mind coming down to the squadron and giving your baby a hug? His feelings got a little bruised today."

The other F-16 pilots practically fell out of their chairs, convulsing in laughter.

Jekyll was livid. But the only outward sign that Cyndi had scored a direct hit to his ego was a slight twitch of his jaw muscles. After her insubordinate retort to his whiny rant, the light colonel wished he hadn't said that rank wasn't allowed in the briefing. He'd have pulled rank on the spot and threatened Cyndi with a court-martial for such an insult. Without that option at his disposal, he ramped up the hostility instead.

"The winner—who will obviously be me—conducts the debrief. Got it?"

"Got it. Of course, it's not exactly a fair fight. Four F-16s against only one F-35."

Like the saying goes, all's fair in love and—"

"Never really cared for that saying."

"Hey, if chicks want to run with the big dogs, then they have to earn it, just like a dude.

"Tell you what, *Jekyll*, since this is my first lesson in big dog fighting, I'll go easy on you guys. Is that fair enough?"

The veteran fighter jock looked like he was about to have a stroke. The veins in his neck were throbbing. "Easy on us!"

One of the other pilots jumped up and stepped into the fray. "Don't worry, little lady, seeing as how it's your first time, we'll be gentle." He gave Cyndi a slimy wink.

"Like hell we will," Jekyll barked. "Second place in a dogfight is dead!"

Hard to believe that it was possible, but the frosty atmosphere in the vault went downhill from there.

CHAPTER 19

AN HOUR LATER the pilots suited up and stepped to their jets.

Once the opposing sides were in position out in the SELLS 1 MOA, the F-16 flight leader keyed his mic and announced, "Satan 26 Flight, assume combat spread formation."

The formation loosened up, with a comfortable distance between each plane.

"One bandit twelve o'clock, fifty miles. Fight's on."

With the perfunctory radio call out of the way, Jekyll's fangs came out. Like knights of old, mounted on their trusty steeds, the fearless fighter pilot lowered his lance and charged at Cyndi.

"Hunter 13 copies. Fight's on," Cyndi casually replied. Forty miles apart, far outside of missile range, Cyndi turned off her transponder. Her plane vanished from the F-16's AN/APG-68 earlier-generation pulse-doppler radars.

"Shit, were did she go?" Jekyll said, frantically tweaking the controls on his radar trying to reacquire her.

Cyndi advanced her throttle to military power, careful to avoid using afterburner to reduce her IR signature, and soared up to fifty thousand feet.

All four of the F-16 pilots were heads down in their cockpits when Cyndi looked through the floor of the jet using DAS. "Suckers." She rolled inverted, pulled back on the stick, and performed a split S. Cyndi's airspeed had doubled by the time she leveled off.

Unfortunately, her momentum had placed her directly in front of the formation of F-16s, with less than a mile between them.

"Four bandits headed north at my twelve o'clock. Ten miles until the merge. Arming AMRAAMs," Cyndi called out over the radio.

The F-16 flight leader was absolutely dumbfounded. Cyndi appeared to be completely clueless as to her location in the fight. He was laughing so hard he had to lower his oxygen mask to keep his visor from fogging up. Jekyll looked to his left at his wingman, shook his head, and threw up his hands as if to say, *Can you believe this chick? What an idiot.*

The wingman did the same to the man on his left.

Cyndi calmly motored along. The four portals on her screen displayed various bits of information. She tapped the screen and pulled up the tactical situation display on the left half. Four white squares in loose formation were displayed. Enemy fighters.

In air-to-air mode, the F-35 AN/APG-81 radar could detect and track twenty-three targets simultaneously. Finding and locking on to four bandits wouldn't even cause the radar to break a sweat.

But Cyndi wasn't using only the radar. It was operating as part of a tag team with the passive infrared, electro-optical Distributed Aperture System. Adhering to the mandate that all hardware on the F-35 contribute to its stealth, the DAS system tracked and locked on to her targets but didn't emit any detectible energy.

Her cocky adversaries had no way of knowing they were about to die.

On her throttle, Cyndi worked the cursor slew controller button to hover the cursor on her screen over the F-16s. On her stick, Cyndi clicked the target designation switch. The four Vipers instantly became targets. Each simulated AMRAAM in the weapons bay was automatically assigned an F-16 to obliterate.

The mock dogfight felt so real that Cyndi's pupils dilated as adrenaline began to course through her body. With her heart racing, Cyndi squeezed the trigger on her stick. The weapons bay doors snapped open. In rapid succession, AIM-120s simulated dropping from their racks, igniting their rocket motors, and locking on to their targets.

Then the missiles did something truly revolutionary. Something fighter pilots have dreamed of since the Sopwith Camel trolled the Western Front in 1917. The missiles violently pitched up, pulling thirty Gs, and did a 180.

If the launch had been real, the AIM-120Ds would have streaked over the top of Cyndi's canopy in the opposite direction, focused on their prey. She watched the impact countdown timer on her screen and waited. With the missiles going Mach 4 and the F-16s flying toward the AMRAAMs at five hundred knots, the simulated impact happened before the pilots could even comprehend what was happening.

After the simulated missiles had demolished the F-16s, Cyndi gleefully announced over the radio, "Hunter 13 is calling four Fox Threes from right in front of your face!"

The F-16 pilots snapped forward in their seats. Cyndi gave them a friendly wave—although four of the five fingers on her hand were folded back.

She keyed her mic and said, "Knock it off. Bad news, gentlemen. Fat Amy just blew your skinny asses out of the sky. Let's RTB and talk about it on the ground. Hunter 13 has the lead."

She selected full afterburner and blasted away from the formation of humiliated Viper pilots.

CHAPTER 20

CYNDI STOWED HER helmet and G suit in her locker then strutted into the vault. She plugged the solid-state flight recorder she'd pulled from her jet into the debriefing computer and brought up the engagement on the monitor. The software in the F-35 had automatically recorded every parameter of the engagement for replay on the ground.

Jekyll and his wingmen slinked in and plopped down in chairs.

"If I remember the rules correctly, the winner conducts the debriefing." Cyndi could hardly contain herself. "That would be me. Of course there's no rank in the debriefing. This is serious shit. Say what needs to be said."

"Just get on with it, Stafford," Jekyll groused. "We have more important things to do."

"Yes, sir." Cyndi reviewed the dogfight in excruciating detail. "As you gentlemen so kindly pointed out, the F-35 fuselage is not particularly svelte. That causes it to bleed energy like crazy in high-G turns. A turn-and-burn dogfight with F-16s would be suicide. That's your strength, not ours. So I chose a different tactic. I'm talking about Fighter Pilot 101, boys. Avoid the enemies' strong points and exploit your own.

"Once you shit-hot fighter pilots made it obvious that your egos—to put it politely—did your thinking for you, coming up with a winning strategy for our little game of testosterone tag today was easy. I intentionally insulted your manhood. I doubted your competency. Then I pretended I had superior knowledge and flying skills. In other words, I created the perfect targets."

Cyndi knew that bravado—a synonym for stupid—was an easy thing to manipulate to your advantage if you played your cards correctly.

She looked the formation leader in the eyes. "You let your egos get in the way of practicing sound ACM fundamentals out there, Jekyll. And it got you and your wingmen killed."

Jekyll shifted in his seat and didn't react. But his eyes bore through Cyndi's.

"When I intentionally dropped in right in front of you, you should have blown me out of the sky within seconds. Instead, you wasted time celebrating how superior you were. How could you not know the DAS system could see you and track you at my six? And that my AMRAAMs could flip a U-turn?"

Jekyll jumped up. "That's bullshit. We don't have access to your plane's classified tracking and weapons capabilities."

"Come on, boys, by now it's certainly no mystery. There's at least a dozen YouTube videos out there on how the DAS system works. If you electric lawn dart pilots had done *your homework*, you would have known that.

"Look, all the high-tech equipment in the world won't save a pilot's ass as long as their head is firmly planted up inside it. Get your egos out of the cockpit. Stealth technology might provide a cloak of invisibility during combat, but you can't spoof or jam eyeballs. They always work."

In an attempt to save face with his wingmen, Jekyll shouted, "You lied to us in the briefing! This wasn't your first BFM training mission!"

"This was my first BFM ride, honest. But not my first

rodeo." Cyndi did a deep bow. "And the Oscar goes to Cyndi Stafford. You guys really bought into my rookie act during the briefing, didn't you? Feign madness but keep your balance. Worked like a charm."

Apparently, Jekyll's ego hadn't gotten the memo warning him that he wasn't the smartest person on the planet. "What the hell are you talking about?"

"It's one of the Thirty-Six Stratagems. Ever heard of them?"

"Of course," the flight leader said with dubious conviction. "It's some of that crap from Sun Tzu's *The Art of War*."

Cyndi was enjoying this immensely. "Swing and a miss, batter. It's from a collection of Chinese military strategy lessons. My dad was a legendary fighter pilot. He would bore me to tears when I was a kid, telling stories at the dinner table about strategy, high-aspect, basic fighter maneuvers, missile envelopes, and radar limitations. And how to get inside your enemy's head. I guess some of it must have stuck." Cyndi flashed a lethal smile. "Lesson learned, boys: *Never underestimate your enemy!*"

"What's that from, more of that Chinese stratagem bullshit?"

"Nope. That's from Captain Cyndi Stafford. Fat Amy pilot."

She walked out of the vault with the biggest smile on her face since starting F-35 training.

◆

Cyndi pulled up to the house and strutted confidently through the front door. Lance jumped up off the couch and gave her a peck on the cheek. "How did your first BFM sortie against the F-16 guys go?"

Cyndi faked a breath of exasperation. "Geez, fighter pilots can be so competitive. They'll do anything to keep from losing." She had to look away to keep Lance from noticing the guilty grin on her face.

"Don't let it bother you. You can't win them all. Better luck next time."

"Yep, better luck next time. I'm starving. What did Marge make for dinner?" Cyndi asked, deftly avoiding any further probing.

CHAPTER 21

NOW THAT FLIGHT training was going well and the pilots had mastered the basics, it was time to move to the next level. They were ordered to report to Building 2132, the Human Performance Lab—jokingly nicknamed Dr. Frankenstein's lab.

The new top-secret facility was located at the far west end of the base at the intersection of Super Saber Street and West Strike Eagle Street. For obvious reasons, the building was not shown on any official Luke AFB map. Companies like Google that sold satellite photos had been politely asked by the Air Force to Photoshop any pictures of the base to remove the building. Google politely complied, not wanting to endanger its lucrative military contracts.

Massive arrays of solar panels surrounded the building on three sides like encroaching desert weeds. The official explanation for the large number of solar panels was to reduce the cost and dependency of the base on the Arizona Public Service electric utility. The close proximity of the shadowy facility to the abundant power source had caused the rumor mill to run wild with alternative explanations.

Armed guards in full battle dress were stationed at the front door. ID cards were scrutinized closely before anyone was allowed to enter the building. The class found their assigned room and got settled in. The space was laid out more like a university biology laboratory than a workout facility.

Two men walked into the classroom. "Good morning. I am Colonel Sam Baker," the taller of the two announced. "Prior to coming to Luke, I managed the 711th Human Performance Wing at Wright-Patterson Air Force Base, one of the technology directorates of the Air Force Research Lab." Baker gestured to his left. "We are fortunate to have one of the world's preeminent experts in human performance engineering joining the team here at Luke. Doctor Herman Eisenstein has PhDs from both Harvard and MIT."

The slightly built doctor wore thick black plastic-framed glasses with overly thick lenses. Despite living in America for over thirty years, Eisenstein still spoke with a German accent. "You people are fortunate to be able to participate in this groundbreaking experiment."

Baker quickly jumped in. "The Air Force prefers the term *program*, Doctor Eisenstein."

"*Ja, ja*, program. That is what I meant to say. The goal of our *program* is to optimize the lethality of the human weapon system, otherwise known as the pilot. Your mental and physical capabilities will be tested like never before. We intend to push you to your limits!"

"But we don't want to break you," Baker assured the crowd. "An injured pilot is as useless to the Air Force as a broken airplane. That's where the *human* engineering part comes in. To make sure that doesn't happen, each of you will be issued one of these." He held up a thin band of black plastic. "This wearable device measures your heart rate, core body temperature, fatigue level, sleep patterns, hydration, perspiration, metabolic rate, and energy expenditure efficiency. This ain't no Fitbit," Baker said with pride.

Eisenstein opened a tiny metal box and lifted out something barely bigger than a grain of rice. "You will swallow this small transmitter. Your wearable device picks up and stores the data. Then we download it, analyze it, and compare it to your peers. Based on what we find, we will dictate changes you must make in order to become more lethal."

Lance let out a chuckle. "Doc, you've obviously never worked with fighter pilots before. As soon as you use the word *dictate* to a pilot, you are screwed. The last thing you'll ever get is cooperation."

Doctor Eisenstein had spent his entire esteemed career in academia. He was new to the fighter pilot world and apparently didn't realize that everything he said and did would be questioned.

Annoyed by the brash behavior of his subjects—correction, willing participants—Eisenstein continued. "We will be observing you while you are going through the exercises, looking for any asymmetries in musculoskeletal performance."

Lance raised his hand. "Say again, Doc?"

"What part did you not understand?"

"All of it. Once more if you don't mind, but this time leave out the geek speak."

Eisenstein brought his hand to his chin. Stroking his gray goatee, he said, "Let's see. How can I dumb this down enough so even a fighter pilot could understand it. Ah yes, I have it. We're trying to prevent you from getting a boo-boo."

Baker redirected the conversation before the pilots could organize a mutiny. "The strength training and cognitive performance concepts you were introduced to in UPT were just the first phase. Now my colleagues and I are going to introduce you to the next level. Let me give you an example. To simulate the strenuous conditions of a high-G dogfight, you will suit up in all of your flight gear. Then you will perform ten repetitions as fast as possible at each of the eight stations on the weight machine at your personal maximum weight.

"This will tax your large muscle groups and test your gross motor skills. The throttle and stick in the F-35 are covered with buttons, knobs, and switches that control target cursor slewing, threat designation, weapons release, and so on.

"All of these are very important tasks that require the pilots to do them quickly and correctly the first time. To test your hand-eye coordination and fine motor skills, we use this."

Doctor Eisenstein reached under the table and pulled out the high-tech apparatus.

Lance's eyes narrowed. His mouth was agape. He turned to Cyndi with a bewildered expression. "Is he serious?"

CHAPTER 22

THE ESTEEMED DOCTOR with PhDs from over-rated Ivy League schools laid the training device on the table.

It was the classic children's game Operation.

Eisenstein spoke like he was addressing a lecture hall-full of medical students. "After stressing your large muscle groups, you will be tasked with removing each body part from the patient with tweezers without setting off the buzzer by touching the sides of the body cavity."

"I'm pretty sure we all know how this game works, Doc," Cyndi said sarcastically. "I had one as a kid. Are you trying to tell us this game is a scientifically accurate test of our fine motor skills?"

"We have other methods of testing, of course," the doctor responded defensively. His arrogant demeanor tempered a bit. "But our research shows that none of them are as effective. That's none of your concern. Leave the science to the experts. Why don't you take over, Colonel Baker."

Baker nodded. "Of course. After establishing a baseline for each of you, we will administer various experimental chemical compounds then run you through the tests again. Exploiting what we've learned from the burgeoning field of synthetic biology, we've discovered ways of manipulating biological processes that will improve your performance. One of my favorite compounds is ZX-191, a human gut microorganism we engineered that produces a beneficial metabolite when a stress biomarker is sensed, like when a pilot sees a surface-to-air missile being launched at his aircraft. Unfortunately, we've discovered that it needs a little more tweaking and testing. That's where you folks enter the picture. Thank you for volunteering, by the way."

"Volunteering? Yeah, right," Lance said with disgust. "We were ordered to show up here today. Sounds to me like you're trying to turn us into Skyborgs."

Doctor Herman Eisenstein peered over the top of his reading glasses in a way that signaled Lance's observation was too evident to bother justifying. "The Air Force should promote this one. Then it would be official, *Captain Obvious*."

It didn't take much effort to figure out where his acidic, dictatorial personality originated. The man was a textbook case of a Napoleon complex. Lucky if he topped out at five feet tall with his thick-soled shoes on, the doctor was overcompensating for his short stature by belittling the pilots, who all hovered near six feet tall, give or take a few inches.

"We're all big boys. Let's move on," Eisenstein said.

Lance turned to Cyndi and snickered. "At least some of us are."

"I assure you there's no need for concern," Baker said. "The military would never subject its own people to questionable or unethical medical experiments."

CHAPTER 23

AFTER ALL THE students had proved themselves competent and safe, the reins were loosened up a bit. They were allowed to venture beyond the Luke AFB traffic pattern solo without an instructor watching their every move. The Gila Bend auxiliary field was only a short flight from Luke but was far removed from the overcrowded skies of Phoenix.

Although unnecessary for such a short flight, Cyndi had meticulously calculated the fuel burn to fly to Gila Bend, shoot multiple touch-and-goes, then fly back to Luke before the heat became unbearable. She walked up to her plane and found the young crew chief napping in the shade, leaning comfortably back against the nose wheel. Cyndi silently snuck up behind the crew chief and yelled, "Fire!"

He jumped up and promptly slammed his head into the bottom of the nose gear door. "You son of a bitch!" He spun around, screwdriver in hand, ready to stab whoever had startled him. When the young man saw Cyndi, his eyes widened. He quickly stuffed the screwdriver back into his tool belt. "Sorry, ma'am."

"Who are you? And where is my crew chief, Sergeant Jones?" Cyndi demanded.

He gingerly felt the top of his head then checked his hand for blood. "Jones shipped out yesterday to Eglin. Lucky bastard got transferred to Florida. I'm your new crew chief, Senior Airman Torres." He had a scrawny build and was barely out of his teens. Greasy coal-black hair and an acne-pocked face were paired with a snarling expression.

Cyndi was close enough to see that Torres's eyes were bloodshot. His breath smelled like cheap whiskey. "The party run a little late last night, Airman?"

"I'm fine. Just tired, that's all," he grumbled, his throbbing headache now even worse after his run-in with the gear door.

"I see. Don't ever let me catch you sleeping on the job again, Airman Torres."

"No, ma'am. Won't happen again."

"Is my jet ready?"

"Yes, ma'am. Inspected it myself."

Trust but verify. Pilots lived by the same philosophy that President Ronald Reagan made famous after the signing of the INF Treaty with Mikhail Gorbachev in 1987. Regardless of who had inspected their plane, pilots always did a quick visual check before getting airborne and risking their lives by defying gravity.

Cyndi walked around her airplane, looking for any flaws. Torres trailed behind her. She stopped and shook her head. An access panel was open at the back of the plane near the tail. At the speed the F-35 flew, it would have easily been ripped off the plane, potentially striking the horizontal stabilizer. "What the hell is this, Airman Torres? I thought you said my jet was ready to fly."

"Oh shit, I forgot about that. I'm waiting for a new battery for the emergency locator transmitter. It's at its five-year time limit and has to be swapped out. Should be here any minute." To his credit, Torres took full responsibility. "There's no excuse for missing that, ma'am. Won't happen again."

"See that it doesn't." Cyndi couldn't tell if the exasperated expression on his face was a byproduct of his pounding hangover, embarrassment at screwing up, or a combination of both. She recalled how devastated she felt after falling for the sign trick during her interrogation by Gagliardi. An open access panel door was nothing to be blasé about, but it paled in comparison to admitting to being a war criminal.

While they waited for the battery, Cyndi decided to take pity on Torres. "How do you like Phoenix?"

"It sucks. Got no friends. None of the guys in my squadron want to hang out. And it's too damn hot around here. Compton weather is more my style."

"You're from SoCal?"

"Lived there my whole life."

"Me too. Well at least after my dad left the Air Force. Why did you decide to enlist?"

"Judge didn't give me any other choice. It was either give up gangbanging and join the Air Force or be sent to Pelican Bay. That ain't no choice. Go to prison and be locked up 24/7 with the same cholos I've been fighting my whole life? Next thing you know, you're minding your own business and you get jumped in the shower. Hell no. I'll take the dry heat any day."

"Sounds like you made the smart decision."

"Sometimes I gotta wonder," Torres said. "I made more cash on the streets than Uncle Sam is paying me. Then my girlfriend went and got herself knocked up, so now I got three mouths to feed."

"You have a baby?"

His dower expression lit up with pride. "Angelina. She's one. Just started to walk. My mom says she's got my eyes." Then his head drooped. The pride on his face evaporated. "Hope she didn't get my brain."

As an officer and a leader, Cyndi felt compelled to impart some wisdom—as much *wisdom* as a person in their late twenties could acquire during their short time on this earth. "Angelina is counting on you to be a man. It's time to step up."

Torres didn't respond. A look of regret and sadness filled his face.

A white van from the parts shop pulled up and honked its horn. The driver held a new ELT battery out of his window. "Special delivery for Senior Airman Dipshit!"

After installing the battery and closing the access panel, Torres used a hex wrench to secure each of the twelve screws on the small panel. The head of every screw had a white line painted across it. The line had to match up exactly with the line painted on each side of the fastener. This ensured that the panel was cinched up tight against the skin on the fuselage.

When designing the F-35, the engineers had gone to obsessive levels to eliminate even the most minuscule gaps or panel misalignments anywhere on the plane to decrease its radar signature. Panels on the plane had twice as many fasteners as those on fourth-generation fighters. This obsession had made the company's fastener supplier very rich, while pissing off every grunt that had to work on the F-35.

CHAPTER 24

"HI, SWEETIE. IT'S your mother."
Despite reminding her mother numerous times that caller ID spelled it out, Cyndi's mother always felt the need to announce who she was.

Because of her insanely busy schedule, Cyndi preferred texting or emailing family members to catch up. Neither alternative appealed to her tech-challenged mother. After hours of frustrating coaching, Cyndi had finally taught her mom how to use Zoom for video chats. The tenth time she'd forgotten to unmute her computer before telling her daughter about her week, Cyndi had hastily grabbed a sharpie and an index card to create a sign she could hold up in front of the camera to catch her mother's attention. When that didn't work, Cyndi finally surrendered. Chatting with her mom happened by phone—and only by phone.

"Hi, Mom. I can't talk for very long. I'm way behind on my studying."

"But it's Saturday. The Air Force certainly doesn't expect you to work on a weekend, does it?"

"Of course not, Mom. Our enemies want us to be well rested, so they've agreed to only attack us Monday through Friday."

"There's no need to be snippy," her mother replied. "Why so grumpy?"

Cyndi rubbed her tight forehead. "Sorry, Mom. I'm a little stressed, that's all. Besides flying, now we have to go to the Human Performance Lab every day and let Doctor Frankenstein run his experiments on us."

Cyndi's attempt at humor sailed over her mother's head.

"Speaking of doctors, that's why I called."

Cyndi sat up straight. "Is there something wrong? Are you okay?"

"I'm okay for now," she replied in a tone that implied there was more to the story. "You know I have diabetes and have to give myself a shot every week. I went to the pharmacy, and my pharmacist told me that they were out of my drug. He said it had something to do with the supply chain delays. It won't be available anywhere in California for weeks."

"Weeks! That's not going to work."

"I told him that. The nice young man got on his computer and found some at a small pharmacy in your area. He sent my prescription over to them. Would you mind picking it up for me?"

"Of course not, what's the name of the drug?"

"Semaglutide. How in the world do they come up with these drug names?"

"You better spell that for me." After Cyndi wrote down the name, she pulled up the FDA's drug shortage database on her laptop. Her mother was correct. The drug was listed as currently in shortage.

"The nice young man said all kinds of bad things could happen if I don't get my medicine. But don't worry about me. I understand if you're too busy. I'll manage somehow."

Cyndi might have had a black belt in tae kwon do, but her mother was a world champ at laying on a guilt trip.

Cyndi let out a long sigh. "What's the name of the pharmacy?"

"Hernandez Drugstore. It's close by, in Maryvale. And don't let them substitute the brand name; it's too expensive. I want the generic version."

"I got it, Mom. I'll get the generic version."

"That would be wonderful. Here's the address."

Cyndi scribbled down the address.

"You'll take care of this today, right?"

"Yes, Mom, I'll do it today. I'll overnight it to you."

"Thank you, sweetie. I haven't been able to sleep a wink lately, thinking I might die alone and nobody I care about would even know."

She was a world champion all right.

———◆———

The streets of Maryvale were teeming with weekend traffic. A few blocks from the pharmacy Cyndi noticed a minivan pull away from the curb. She swooped in and claimed the parking spot before anyone else could take it. With her Honda Accord securely locked, Cyndi walked the last few blocks.

The blue-collar town was many decades past its previously underwhelming prime. Liquor stores and payday loan centers had flooded into the city. Trash littered the potholed streets. Loud music blared from the lowriders cruising the area.

At the address she'd written down was a small mom-and-pop grocery store called Viva Mercado. Fresh fruit was displayed in orderly rows in angled wooden bins out on the sidewalk. Signs in the windows advertising the weekly specials were written in Spanish.

Either Cyndi had made a mistake when writing it down, or her mother had given her the wrong address. She approached an elderly Latina woman who was sweeping the sidewalk in front of the market. "Excuse me, do you know where the Hernandez Drugstore is?"

The woman gave Cyndi a shrug of non-comprehension and went back to sweeping.

Cyndi regretted not taking Lance up on his offer to

teach her Spanish. She wandered the streets of Maryvale for thirty minutes but couldn't locate the store.

In a hurry to get back to her studies, Cyndi decided to approach a man at a bus stop and ask for directions. He had all his belongings crammed into a Walmart shopping cart and was glaring up at the heavens. The man suddenly began cursing the universe for every conceivable wrong done throughout history. She wisely decided to move on and ask an elderly woman sitting at the other end of the bench.

The woman was clutching a faded and worn tote bag stuffed full of who knew what. She looked over at Cyndi and said, "Do you need help, dearie?"

"Yes, thank you. I'm lost. Do you know where the Hernandez Drugstore is?"

"Of course I do. I was just there getting my prescription."

Cyndi waited for the woman to continue. She just looked up at her with an endearing smile. "Would you mind giving me directions?"

"I'd be happy to, dearie."

Cyndi waited again for the woman to continue. "Is it nearby?"

The sweet old lady pursed her lips and shook her head in frustration. "Isn't it just outrageous how expensive bus fare has gotten these days? Almost as bad as my pills. I should write to my congressman and tell him to do something to help us impoverished elderly folks."

Cyndi nodded in understanding. She fished out a five-dollar bill and handed it to the lady. Lady being a generous term for someone who would extort a stranger for providing directions.

"Oh my, that certainly wasn't necessary. How thoughtful of you." She quickly stuffed the bill into her pocket. "You're on the wrong street. It's one block over." She pointed to the north with a boney, arthritic finger. "Cut through there, and it's on the right."

The previous endearing smile and moniker of *dearie* were nowhere to be found.

"Thank you, ma'am."

Cyndi took the suggested shortcut through a trash-strewn alley. Slowly, her eyes adapted to the dim lighting. Haphazardly placed dumpsters created an urban obstacle course. The rancid stench of rotting garbage that had been cooking in the Arizona heat for a week assaulted her nostrils. Beady-eyed rats scurried about, feasting on the mounds of decaying garbage.

Halfway up the shadowy alley, Cyndi heard a woman crying out in anguish. A man was kicking and stomping on the woman as she lay curled up in the fetal position. Despite the fact that the woman was unable to fight back, his vicious attack only intensified.

Cyndi momentarily froze.

Her innate tendency was to be the lion and never the sheep when danger presented itself. To run toward a threat to innocent people rather than away from it. Instinct took over.

Without any hesitation, Cyndi screamed "Leave her alone!" and raced toward the melee. With her long legs, she reached the scene in only six quick strides.

CHAPTER 25

AN ENORMOUS MAN, wearing a black suit, black shirt, and black tie was guarding the opposite entrance to the alley. His slicked back hair was gathered in a short ponytail, and he was built like an inside linebacker for the Cardinals. Acne scars pitted his puffy cheeks.

Cyndi rushed up, yelling for the attacker to stop his assault.

The bodyguard spun around and positioned himself between Cyndi and the man attacking the woman. He thrust out his hand to block her. "Mind your own fucking business and turn around."

"I beg you, please help me! He's going to kill me!" the woman wailed as she tried to shield her body from the assailant's powerful kicks.

Cyndi tried to force her way around the imposing man.

"Get rid of her, Barboza!" the attacker yelled, barking out an order to his bodyguard.

The bodyguard held Cyndi back with his left hand while he reached under the flap of his unbuttoned jacket with his right.

Out of the corner of her eye Cyndi noticed a glint of light as the man's hand reemerged. He'd whipped out a stainless-steel object the size of a small cannon. The man straightened his arm, aimed at Cyndi, and began to tighten his finger on the trigger of his Smith & Wesson Model 29.44-cal. Magnum revolver.

The area of Cyndi's brain called the amygdala abruptly activated. In yet another example of the many marvels of how the human brain functions, as this extremely dangerous situation unfolded, Cyndi's sensation of time seemed to slow down. The fields of neuroscience and psychology referred to it as *tachypsychia*, the distorted perception of time during a traumatic moment.

Cyndi thought of it in a decidedly less academic framework. She called it death-a-phobia.

As if watching a video in slow motion, Cyndi saw the hammer on the gun arch backward.

In that instant, she flung her left hand upward. It caught the meaty area under the man's forearm.

His arm moved upward at an agonizingly slow speed as she snapped her head to the left.

A bright white flash exploded from the muzzle. An ear-splitting shot rang out.

As it passed by her right temple, the shockwave from the bullet blew a tuft of her blonde hair.

Cyndi drew back her left foot while she grabbed the hot barrel and forced it upward. The revolver was now pointed up at a 45-degree angle.

She smashed the side of her left foot down against the outside of the man's right knee. A cracking sound almost as loud as the gunshot confirmed that she had broken the knee joint in half.

The man yelped like a wounded animal. He began to topple over like an enormous, felled redwood tree.

Another shot fired.

The large bullet ricocheted off the dilapidated red brick walls that formed the narrow alley. Shrapnel peppered the attacker, forcing him to stop his assault and shield his face with his hands.

As gravity drove the bodyguard down to the slimy pavement, Cyndi took advantage of his momentum and twisted the barrel of his gun down toward the man. His index finger snapped like a dry twig at the same moment another shot fired. Then his grip went limp.

The heavy gun made a dull thudding noise as it tumbled to the ground. The man collapsed, writhing in pain. A small rivulet of crimson fluid snaked its way across the pavement, seeping from under the bodyguard.

Cyndi snatched the revolver off the asphalt, spun around, and pointed it at the center mass of the attacker.

"Freeze!" she yelled at the top of her lungs.

Before the sensation of time had fully returned to normal speed, Cyndi had the fleeting thought that her command to the assailant could have come straight from any of the cheesy cop dramas she'd watched on TV as a kid. The only thing missing was the addition of the cliched words *dirt bag* after the word freeze.

Cyndi wagged the gun. "Move away from her."

The attacker lifted his hands to chest level and took a step back.

When she felt there was a safe distance between herself and the man, Cyndi helped the woman up. The tall, slightly built attacker wore an expensive bespoke suit. His black eyes were flat and dead, like a snake. He had a prominent scar that slashed across his left eye and face. A pencil-thin black mustache over thin lips jutted down both sides of his mouth, ending into a neatly shaped triangular goatee.

"Real tough guy, aren't you," Cyndi said in a belittling voice. She propped the woman against the wall then moved back to the center of the alley, maximizing her options in the event he attacked. "Not so tough now without your bodyguard, are you?"

She noticed that no matter where she moved, only the right eye of the attacker followed her. The man had a glass left eye.

The attacker was surprisingly calm for having a miniature cannon pointed right at him. A broad smile formed on his thin face. "Gringa, you can't fathom the enormity of the mistake you're making right now. You have no idea who you're messing with." His arrogant smirk exuded an aura of invincibility. It was almost as if he thought he was immortal. The man extended his right arm. "Hand me the gun. I promise I won't hurt you."

With blood gushing from her battered nose, the woman reached out toward Cyndi and pleaded, "Don't believe him. Kill him before it's too late!"

The man calmly advanced on Cyndi. She couldn't believe his arrogance. "Why don't I move to your right so you can see the situation you're in a little better? In case you haven't noticed, I'm the one with the gun. You might think you're bulletproof, but if you take one more step, my friend's Smith & Wesson will prove you wrong."

"Like I said, you have no idea who you're dealing with." A diabolical expression accompanied his warning.

CHAPTER 26

SUDDENLY, CYNDI'S LEFT ankle felt like it was caught in the jaws of a ravenous lion. She shrieked in pain. The bodyguard's massive, powerful hands had clamped onto Cyndi's lower leg. He was trying to take her down, hoping to regain control of his weapon. If that happened, her chances of surviving would evaporate.

Every fiber in Cyndi's body was directed toward preventing that from happening. The gun remained trained on the attacker while her vision focused on the muscular bodyguard. Her sense of hearing narrowed as well, something known as auditory exclusion. Cyndi used her free foot to kick at the man's forearms, but no matter how hard she kicked she couldn't loosen his crushing grip.

Starting to lose her balance, she pointed the gun at the man's face and yelled, "Let go or I'll shoot!"

Cyndi was so intent on surviving that she hadn't noticed the patrol car that screeched to a stop at the entrance to the alley. Only after hearing the policemen yelling did she realize she had company. Cyndi looked to her left. Two cops were crouched safely behind their open car doors. She was staring down the barrel of a 12-gauge Remington 870 police magnum shotgun.

"Drop the gun!" the driver ordered, adrenaline coursing through his rigid body. Cyndi could see his finger twitching as it hovered over the trigger. "Get down on the ground!"

Cyndi held up her hands at shoulder height. "Wait, calm

down, officers, you've got this all wrong," she pleaded. "I'm not the criminal; he is."

He racked his shotgun. "This is your last warning. Drop the weapon. Now!"

With two very amped-up cops pointing guns at her, Cyndi wisely decided to save the debate over who was in the right for a more appropriate time. She let the Smith & Wesson dangle from her finger by its trigger guard then let it fall to the ground.

In case the situation took a horrible turn for the worse she had dropped the pistol within an arm's reach. She dropped to her knees and put her hands in the air.

"Down! Lay facedown on the ground," the driver ordered.

Cyndi reluctantly lay facedown on the grimy pavement.

"Hands on your head!"

She interlaced her fingers behind her head.

The officer on the passenger side of the patrol car came out from behind his door while his partner kept her in the sights of his shotgun. In a crouching walk, he cautiously approached Cyndi with his Glock 17 in the low ready position.

When he reached her, the officer barked, "Move one muscle, and I'll blow your head off! Are we clear?"

"I'm not a threat, Officer. I'm complying," Cyndi said in the calmest voice she could muster, given the extremely volatile situation.

He kicked the gun away, holstered his Glock, then planted one knee in the middle of Cyndi's back to restrain her. Each wrist was wrenched back behind her back and cuffed. His partner approached, still aiming his shotgun at Cyndi. The men each grabbed an arm and lifted Cyndi to her feet.

Even an untrained eye could tell that the situation didn't look good for Cyndi. She was in a bad part of town, in a dark alley, holding a gun over an injured man who was bleeding.

The driver turned his head and keyed the microphone attached near his shoulder. "Clear the air. Car three-seventeen has one party in custody. Send a code-one ambulance for a male shooting victim."

Moaning in pain, the bodyguard cranked up the drama meter to a ten and said, "Thank God you got here so quickly, Officers. This crazy woman attacked me when I refused to buy drugs from her. She pointed her gun at me and said she was going to kill me."

"He's lying! That's not my gun. It's his!"

"Of course she's going to say that. Bitch is crazy."

One of the cops pulled rubber gloves out of his back pocket and slid them on. He picked up the revolver and examined it. "The serial number has been ground off," he said.

"Check it for fingerprints," the bodyguard said. "It's hers."

Cyndi suddenly recalled that the bodyguard had been wearing gloves during the fight. Now they were hidden behind a trash can a few feet away from him.

The officers had never encountered such a bizarre crime scene. Cyndi was claiming innocence, while holding a small cannon. A burly guy twice her size was on the ground injured and bleeding.

Without much expectation of getting at the truth, the driver asked Cyndi, "What happened, ma'am?"

"I was taking a shortcut through the alley when I heard a woman screaming. A man wearing a gray suit was assaulting her. I rushed up and tried to stop his boss from killing the defenseless woman." She thumbed back over her shoulder.

The two cops looked at each other then back at Cyndi. "What man? What woman?" one asked with confusion in his voice.

When she turned around, no one was there. Except for a few rats scurrying about, the alley was empty.

Cyndi closed her eyes and shook her head. Under her breath she mumbled, "I am so screwed."

CHAPTER 27

WITH HER HANDS cuffed behind her, Cyndi was shoved into the back seat of the patrol car and buckled into a prisoner cage that doubled as a seat. A metal wall split the backseat space in half. Steel bars isolated Cyndi from the officers. The side windows had bars over them as well. Molded plastic covered the prisoner's seat and floorboard, making cleanup easier if they decided to relieve themselves on the way to the station.

Being a cop wasn't quite as glamorous as Hollywood portrayed it.

In what some of the more jaded members of society might label as naïve, the police department hoped to discourage a life of crime by taping inspirational signs on the partition in each squad car. In this one the sign read: You can do better than this.

As the bodyguard rolled past Cyndi on the gurney, he turned and glared at her. With his fingers he made a shooting gesture in her direction, baring his discolored teeth in a menacing smirk.

———◆———

The police cruiser turned off Encanto Boulevard and into the parking lot of the Maryvale police station. The nondescript building had a baby-blue metal roof situated over a faded white block-and-stucco facade.

The driver pulled around to the back of the station and

waved his ID badge over the card reader. A metal garage door leading into the sally port retracted up into the ceiling. After pulling in and putting the vehicle in park, the door closed. With all avenues of escape eliminated, Cyndi was escorted from the back seat by both officers. They secured their firearms in lock boxes then took her into the booking area.

"Who do we have here?" the gruff desk sergeant growled, putting his sandwich down.

"This is the aggravated assault suspect we apprehended in the alley," one of the arresting officers said.

"All right, Miss, what's your full name?"

He entered Cyndi's information into the computer.

The desk sergeant scanned the screen. "Okay, here you are. California driver's license." He looked up. "Yep, face matches the picture on your ID. Captain in the Air Force. No priors in Maricopa County. I'll get the booking paperwork started."

"Wait, I'm innocent. I didn't attack that man. He attacked me!"

The desk sergeant folded his arms across his chest and peered over the top of his reading glasses. "Miss, you don't know how happy I am to hear that. I just sent Detective Barnes to the hospital to talk to the victim and start an investigation into this matter. I'll call him and tell him not to bother. According to you, the other guy started it, you're innocent, case closed. I'm sure the taxpayers of Maricopa County will thank you for not wasting a bunch of their money on a real investigation."

Cyndi's eyes narrowed as she gave him the death glare. "Has anyone ever told you that you have a cynical and acerbic sense of humor?"

He tapped his left temple. "Hmm, now that you mention it, yes, she has. Many times. And now every month she gets half my paycheck and will get half of my retirement. That is if I can ever afford to retire." He waved over a stern-looking policewoman. "Matron, finish the booking process then escort Miss Stafford to her luxury accommodations."

Cyndi was handcuffed to a steel bench while waiting to be booked. She didn't exactly fit the profile of their usual customers. Her case was unusual to say the least, but in a department that was perennially understaffed and overworked, it wasn't enough to float to the top of the heap of human detritus who streamed in while she waited.

After an hour, it was finally her turn. Each finger was placed on the glass surface of a small device and electronically scanned for fingerprints. Mug shots were taken in front of a height chart with Cyndi facing forward, left, and right.

"You get one phone call, so make it count," the surly matron told Cyndi.

With her wrists shackled, Cyndi lifted the handset from the wall-mounted phone. As she went to dial, Cyndi paused. She didn't recall Lance's cell phone number. She'd always just swiped his name on the screen to place calls, never having to actually dial the number.

"Hurry up, I don't have all night," the matron barked, looking impatiently at the long line of "customers" shackled to the bench, waiting their turn.

With the matron impatiently drumming her fingers on the counter, Cyndi closed her eyes and tried to envision Lance's entry in her contact list. Finally, a mental picture of his phone number floated out of her subconscious. She dialed Lance's cell phone, but it went straight to voice mail.

"You've reached aviator extraordinaire Lance Garcia. You know what to do at the beep."

Cyndi swallowed hard, searching for the right words. "Umm, hey it's me. Something has happened. I'm in jail." She cleared her throat. "I didn't do…It's all a big mistake.

You need to come down to the Maryvale police station on Encanto Boulevard and bail me out as soon as you get this message." She cupped her hand next to the mouthpiece. "Do *not* tell anyone," Cyndi whispered. "We can figure out how to notify the Air Force after I get home."

———◆———

The matron had passed Cyndi off to the jailer. He removed her handcuffs and shoved Cyndi into the jail cell. Nowhere on earth was there a sound as frightening and suffocating as the sound of a cell door slamming shut.

Cyndi grabbed the bars and said, "You have to believe me, Officer, this is all a big mistake. I'm innocent."

The jailer just snickered. "Miss, if I had a dollar for every time I heard that line, I sure as hell wouldn't be wasting the best years of my life babysitting a bunch of lowlifes."

Cyndi turned to find herself imprisoned in a ten-by-ten holding cell that smelled like urine, vomit, and hopelessness. The caustic commercial cleaning solution used weekly to mop the cell floor left a sticky, oily film behind and made being trapped among the nauseating smells immeasurably worse.

Steel benches were bolted to each side wall and the back wall. Sitting on the bench on the left side of the cell were two women. One was a hooker wearing a blonde wig, stiletto heels, and a miniskirt that left absolutely nothing to the imagination. Next to her was an emaciated woman with sunken, glassy eyes. Her nonstop trembling and the needle tracks on the insides of both arms advertised the magnitude of her chemical enslavement.

Standing in front of the bench on the back wall was a woman who towered six feet two inches tall and weighed 320 pounds. Three of her teeth were missing. The rest were crooked and tobacco stained.

The large woman thought she could intimidate Cyndi. "Lookie here, ladies. It's Miss U-S-fucking-A. Ain't you a fine one. What are you in for? Got caught trying to fix the beauty pageant by banging one of the judges?"

Cyndi ignored her, turned around, and stared out through the cell door bars.

"Hey, I'm talking to you!" The woman stomped up behind Cyndi and shoved her shoulder. "I *said* I'm talking to you."

Cyndi turned around and stood toe to toe with the much larger woman. "I was arrested for killing people who bothered me. Now back up and get the hell out of my face."

The woman's eyes narrowed as her nostrils flared. She'd lived most of her life by the law of the jungle. And Cyndi had just challenged her in front of other members of the pack.

She grabbed a fist full of Cyndi's shirt. "Last night I sent my punk-ass, cheatin' boyfriend to the hospital. Now it's your turn."

With 100 percent confidence that her cellmate hadn't studied krav maga in Israel like she had, Cyndi decided to send her tormentor a clear message. She clamped on to the woman's wrist and rotated her arm in a large circle while simultaneously placing her free hand behind the woman's elbow. Then Cyndi yanked down and pushed up on the woman's elbow. A loud yelp, followed by the woman crashing to her knees, confirmed that she had dislocated the woman's shoulder.

Cyndi bent down and calmly whispered in her ear. "I asked you politely to get out of my face. Now, are we good?"

"Yes, yes, we're good!" the woman cried out. "I'm sorry to bother you, ma'am."

Cyndi released the woman's wrist and strutted across

the cell. She plopped down on the bench next to her other cellmates and casually nodded. "How's it going?"

They jumped up and darted over to the opposite side of the cell.

———◆———

Later that night the jailer unlocked the cell door and waved Cyndi forward. "Stafford, someone is here to get you. Let's go."

Before she walked out of her cell, Cyndi turned to the two inmates huddled together as far as possible from her and said, "It was a pleasure meeting you ladies." To her defeated tormentor, Cyndi smirked and said, "You might want to get that shoulder looked at."

Safe in the knowledge that Cyndi wouldn't be coming back, the large woman suddenly developed a modicum of courage. "If I ever see you again, you're dead, bitch."

Cyndi was led to a small room to change. Then she was taken to a counter next to the booking area to reclaim her personal items. The contents of a large envelope were dumped out on the counter.

"Check that everything is here, then sign the form," the jailer said.

Once that was complete, the jailer waved his ID badge across the scanner and opened the door to the booking area.

Cyndi's eyes widened when she saw who was waiting for her. "Oh crap." She looked back at the jailer and begged, "Can't I stay here tonight?"

The jailer jerked back in surprise. He'd never heard that one before. "Enough with the jokes." He pushed Cyndi forward.

Standing at the counter was her squadron commander, Lt. Col. Tank Abrams.

CHAPTER 28

Three minutes earlier.

AS TANK WAITED for Cyndi, the desk sergeant waved him over to the counter. "Sir. I need to speak with you." His usual bored, blasé expression had been replaced with a mixture of confusion and concern. "Who the hell is this woman?"

"Stafford? She's one of my new pilots. Why? Is there something…?"

The sergeant leaned forward and looked in both directions. In a hushed voice he said, "I did a complete background check on her in the FBI NCIC database. Stafford's record is…" he searched for the right word. "Clean."

"Okay…" Tank cocked his head and waited for the sergeant to explain.

"I mean completely spotless. There's nothing there. No parking tickets. No speeding tickets. Not so much as a citation for jaywalking. I've been a cop for thirty years, and I've never seen anything like this. It's as if her record has intentionally been sanitized by someone way above my pay grade." He slid the manila folder toward Tank. "Take a look."

Just as Abrams was about to open the folder, the electric lock on the door leading to the holding cells buzzed open with a loud click. The sergeant grabbed the folder and pulled it back.

With an embarrassed and chastened look on her face, Cyndi shuffled up to her squadron commander.

"Sorry to disturb your weekend, sir. If you don't mind me asking, how did you hear about this?"

"Once or twice a year I get a call from the desk sergeant telling me to come and get one of my people. He's ex-Air Force and is good enough to cut personnel at Luke some slack when they screw up." Tank planted his hands on his hips. "What in God's name were you doing in Maryvale?"

"I'm here to buy drugs."

"Drugs?"

"Not for me. They're for my mother."

"Your *mother*?"

"Yes, sir, but this is all a huge mistake."

Tank's face turned crimson. "You were arrested in a city notorious for drug dealing. You send a guy to the hospital who says you tried to sell him drugs. And you were the one with the gun!"

"Sir, if you'd just listen, I can explain everything."

"What are you going to tell me next? That this wasn't a drug deal gone bad? No, of course not. You were just in the wrong dark alley at the wrong time. To buy drugs, for your *mother*. Not exactly the most imaginative story I've ever heard in all my years of bailing my people out of jail.

"You can kiss your SCI and PRP certifications goodbye. Without those, you won't fly the F-35 or any other Air Force fighter."

Cyndi was devastated. Her lifelong dream had just turned into a nightmare. Tears began to well up in her eyes.

"Let's go, Stafford. I'll drive you back to your car." Before leaving, the squadron commander turned to the desk sergeant and said, "Thanks, Bill, I owe you one. I'll make sure Captain Stafford shows up for her arraignment. How much will her bail be?"

"It won't be cheap. Aggravated assault is a serious—" The phone rang, interrupting his response. He lifted a finger and said, "Hang on." After picking up, the sergeant listened intently. As the phone conversation progressed, his expression went from boredom to furious. "Are you serious?" The desk sergeant slammed down the phone. "Dammit!" With an incredulous look he barked, "The sky gods must be smiling down on your pilot today. The victim, Mr. Barboza, seems to have had a sudden change of heart. He's refusing to press any charges. He claims he was so traumatized by a thug who mugged him in the alley that he got confused and accidentally blamed Captain Stafford." The desk sergeant flashed a cynical look that had been honed over thirty years of dealing with his share of less than honorable people. "Now he says she actually *saved* his life. Captain Stafford, I don't have any choice, I have to cut you loose. You are free to go." The sergeant tossed the file folder into the wastebasket and waved a threatening finger toward Cyndi. "I don't ever want to see you in my town again. Understood, Stafford?"

"Yes, sir. Understood, sir."

CHAPTER 29

TANK STARED STRAIGHT ahead and refused to talk to Cyndi as he drove. The awkward silence was worse than being waterboarded.

Cyndi badly wanted to explain that this was all just a huge misunderstanding. But every time her lips parted, no words came out. After Tank pulled up behind her Accord, Cyndi opened the car door then turned back. "Sir, I need to—"

Abrams raised his hand to silence her. "I have a reputation of being very funny."

"Oh...I...I didn't know that about you, sir."

"But this is no laughing matter. I fully intended to pull your SCI and your PRP until the victim mysteriously changed his story. I don't know whether to believe your version of events or not, Stafford. But what I do know is that you've made a terrible early impression."

———◆———

Cyndi spent the next day camped out on the couch doing some serious damage to an entire blueberry pie.

Lance plopped down next to her, hoping to console his dejected fiancée. "Cheer up, things aren't that bad. I hear McDonald's is hiring."

Cyndi elbowed Lance in the ribs. "This isn't funny. Training is going great, and now this happens. Colonel

Abrams is sure to find a way to eliminate me from the program."

"He can't. The guy in the hospital said it himself: You were the victim."

Cyndi rolled her eyes. "Please, you and I have been through enough to know better than to trust the system. If Tank wants me gone, I'm history."

Lance put his arm around Cyndi and drew her close. "I'm just glad that you're safe. If the Air Force wants to mess with your career, we'll deal with it. Together. Until that happens, we just keep doing our jobs." He picked up the TV remote and clicked the power button. "It's Sunday. Let's take the day off and watch some TV. After that, we can go for a run." Lance nuzzled her ear and whispered. "Maybe after our run, we can take a shower together."

Cyndi stroked her chin, deep in thought. "Hmm, a shower together." She shrugged and said, "Why not. Beats being locked up in jail."

"Very funny." Lance knew she was very ticklish. He grabbed her ribs and got his revenge for Cyndi's joke.

After the score had been evened, they settled in and watched the local news.

"A woman's dismembered body was found early this morning in south Phoenix," the anchorman stated matter-of-factly.

The newscaster continued, all too eager to convey every gory, lurid detail about the torture the poor woman had suffered. As was all too common in the warped world of *if-it-bleeds-it-leads* TV news, he read the teleprompter without showing any hint of humanity or emotion.

A picture of the dead woman obtained from the DMV flashed up on the screen.

Cyndi jumped up. "That's her! That's the woman in the alley yesterday."

"Although the driver's license found with the body

listed her name as Juanita Salazar, police were not able to make a positive match due to the injuries the severed head had sustained. DNA samples have been sent to the state crime lab for verification."

Cyndi fell back onto the couch. She bent over and put her hand on her stomach. "I think I'm going to be sick. I need some air."

"Let's go outside," Lance said as he helped Cyndi up. He guided her out to the front porch.

The anchorman continued his report. "Salazar was rumored to be the American mistress of Jesus Galindo-Diaz, a.k.a. El Diablo, leader of the vicious *Descendientes del Diablo* cartel just south of the border."

A picture of Diaz came up on the screen. He was glaring at the camera lens with black, snake-like eyes. A long scar slashed across his left eye.

"Two years ago, Diaz was designated as a kingpin under the Foreign Narcotics Kingpin Designation Act by the Department of the Treasury. The DDD is the same cartel suspected of the barbaric torture and murder of DEA agent Ernesto Flores last year. They are also alleged to be responsible for the murders of hundreds of rivals and innocent civilians.

"In national news, the diplomatic row between President Ashford and President Ortega of Mexico intensified last week over who is responsible for the debacle at the border. Each man vows to hold the other one responsible."

Marge walked by the family room and saw that the TV was on. She picked up the remote control and announced to the empty room, "Hey, you two, electricity ain't free, you know."

CHAPTER 30

Monday, 1630 hours, Mountain Standard Time.

CYNDI AND LANCE stepped up to the briefing counter in the 60th Fighter Squadron before going out on a formation low-level mission.

Next to the counter was a table covered with bottles of Gatorade of every flavor and small bags of trail mix. Proper hydration was a big deal at Luke AFB. She grabbed a bottle of the Cool Blue flavor.

"One more flight," Cyndi said. "After today, we will officially be Panther pilots."

"Speak for yourself," Lance bragged. "I had my final ride yesterday. I'm just going along today to keep you out of trouble."

Cyndi just rolled her eyes.

"Have a blast out there, guys," the pilot behind the counter said. "I'm jealous. The SELLS 1 MOA is like a three-million-acre playground for fighter jets. It's got SAM sites, tanks, flatlands, valleys, hills, peaks, and mountains."

The briefer pulled out a checklist and covered NOTAMS and the weather. "It'll be clear and a million for your sorties today. There is a one-hundred-knot jet stream out of the north. It won't take long to reach the MOA with that kind of tailwind. Don't forget to flip the light switch, Stafford."

Cyndi flashed a thumbs-up. "Roger that."

"Sunset is at 1930 hours. You'll need to vacate the MOA no less than thirty minutes before then. A huge joint strike package of Buffs, B-1s, and B-2s is already airborne and headed for the SELLS MOA. It will hit the range for bombing practice precisely at sunset plus thirty minutes. They'll be dropping GBU-10s."

"Two-thousand-pounders? Damn, that ought to wake up the neighbors," Lance said.

"You guys are the last sorties for the day, so I won't be here when you get back. A bunch of us are going to the Ground Control bar for happy hour. Swing by after you land. The first round is on me, Stafford, to celebrate making it through the program. And don't forget to turn out the lights before you leave the building."

"I know, I know, electricity ain't free," Cyndi said. "See you at the bar."

———

Senior Airman Torres was just finishing preparing Cyndi's jet as she walked up. He closed an access panel at the back of the plane then said, "Everything has been checked; your jet is ready to fly, ma'am."

His eyes were swollen and ringed with red again. Sweat dripped from his ashen face. The smell of whiskey preceded Torres as he offered a weak salute. She returned the salute then did her walkaround inspection. Cyndi decided it was time to have a talk with his supervisor after she landed.

Before sitting down in her ejection seat, Cyndi flipped a switch installed on the back of the seat frame. The so-called light switch had been retrofitted to the Martin Baker seat after it was learned that the extreme G forces encountered during an ejection could snap the neck of lighter-weight pilots—like Cyndi.

Flipping the switch altered the ejection sequence slightly, softening it just enough to not kill the pilot.

The Air Force had judged that to be a good thing, worth the added expense of the retrofit.

Another benefit of the F-35 seat was a larger parachute than earlier-generation ejection seats. The leisurely descent rate provided by the chute gave pilots much more time to contemplate their dire predicament before gently returning to earth.

1700 hours, MST

As they were about to roll onto the runway for a formation takeoff, Lance called Cyndi on the radio. "Shadow 12, this is Shadow 37."

"Go for Shadow 12."

"Bad news. When I pushed up the throttle, my engine temperature spiked into the red zone. The damned thing over-temped. I have to abort."

"Roger that."

"Looks like they'll have to change out the engine."

"Well, I'm glad it happened on the ground and not a hundred miles from Luke."

"Yeah, I guess so," Lance grumbled. "See you at Ground Control after you land. Don't die out there."

"That's the plan."

Lance did a U-turn and headed back to the chocks.

When Cyndi called the tower, the controller informed her there would be a fifteen-minute delay due to heavy civilian traffic in the vicinity. Fighters were not built to lug around copious amounts of spare fuel. Burning gas waiting on the ground would have a major impact on the time she could spend on the low-level route.

"Requesting a vertical departure with an unrestricted climb to flight level five-zero-zero to avoid the traffic and delay," Cyndi transmitted.

The rookie controller looked over at his supervisor and said, "Um…can she do that?"

He shook his head at the inexperienced controller. "Give me the mic. I'll handle it. Shadow 12, stand by while I coordinate your request."

The convoluted process of routing her request up the airspace chain began. Each owner of the increasingly higher airspace overlying the base had to give its okay.

The senior controller picked up a handset that connected him directly to Luke Air Force Base departure control. When the controller on the other end picked up, he said, "I've got an APREQ for call sign Shadow 12 for an unrestricted climb after takeoff to flight level five-zero-zero."

The departure controller replied, "Roger, you're looking for an approval request for Shadow 12, unrestricted climb to flight level five-zero-zero. Copy all. Standby."

Then he picked up a separate handset and repeated the process with Phoenix Terminal Radar Approach Control (TRACON), expanding the bubble of protection for Cyndi.

TRACON then called Albuquerque Air Route Traffic Control Center to get permission for her jet to enter their high-altitude airspace.

1710 hours, MST

Once all the necessary approvals had been received, the tower supervisor keyed his mic and said, "Shadow 12, unrestricted climb to flight level five-zero-zero approved, maintain runway heading, cleared for takeoff runway two-one right." Drawing from his long tenure as an Air Force air traffic controller, he understood that things were about to get very busy for Cyndi. To eliminate one distraction as she rocketed skyward, the controller finished his transmission with "Switch to Albuquerque Center now on 126.45."

Cyndi read back his instructions word-for-word

to avoid any misunderstandings then thanked him for his help. With all of the prerequisites squared away, she slammed the throttle into afterburner.

Cyndi got airborne then scooped up the landing gear. She leveled off only ten feet above the pavement. She wasn't trying to impress her fellow fighter jocks. Cyndi had learned during advanced aerodynamics class that staying one wingspan or less above a hard surface reduces the induced drag generated by the wing.

Less drag meant faster acceleration.

And as any jet pilot knows, more acceleration means more fun.

By the time she reached the end of the ten-thousand-foot runway, Cyndi was screaming along at over 350 knots. She yanked back on the stick. Counter-rotating swirls of dust were blasted skyward on each side of the runway. When the horizon was perpendicular to her flight path, Cyndi relaxed the back pressure on the stick. Seconds later, she punched through a thin cloud layer and was rewarded with a bright, clear blue sky.

Passing forty thousand feet, Cyndi gradually pushed the stick forward to prevent overshooting her target altitude. Her arching flight path resulted in a temporary feeling of weightlessness. Despite being strapped in, Cyndi's body levitated up off her ejection seat. Dust on top of the glareshield began to float.

I'm definitely doing that again, Cyndi thought, as she leveled off fifty thousand feet above the mere mortals below who'd never get a chance to experience such unbridled exhilaration.

An upper-level high-pressure area had anchored itself over Southern California, causing a dip in the jet stream over Arizona. Just like she'd been briefed, a one-hundred-knot wind roaring out of the north helped Cyndi arrive at the boundary of the SELLS 1 MOA rapidly.

1720 hours, MST

"Snakeye range control, this is Shadow 12 at flight level five-zero-zero. Requesting clearance to enter the SELLS 1 MOA to begin my low-level on Victor route two-six-three."

"Roger, Shadow 12. I've got you in radar contact. Cleared into the MOA," the range controller said. "Cleared to fly VR-263."

"Copy all," Cyndi transmitted. Once she had double-checked her fuel and engine instruments, Cyndi started down.

"Shadow 12, cancel your clearance," the controller said excitedly. "A Cessna just strayed into the airspace. Execute 360s at your current location until further advised."

"Roger, Snakeye, executing 360s." Cyndi switched on the autopilot and programmed it to fly in circles. If the careless civilian pilot just happened to stray within gun range, Cyndi wasn't entirely sure she could resist popping off a few tracer rounds in his vicinity.

Five minutes later, the Snakeye controller came back on the horn. "Shadow 12, the threat aircraft has exited the MOA. The airspace is clear. Continue with your previous clearance."

Cyndi disengaged the autopilot and pushed the thrust lever up to the go-fast position. At her command, the Pratt & Whitney F135 two-spool afterburning turbofan engine roared. Raw JP-8 fuel was dumped into the scorching-hot exhaust gases in the tailpipe, igniting into a blazing hurricane of extra thrust.

With the help of the biggest engine ever installed in a fighter, her F-35 reached Mach 1.6 in less than ten seconds. Cyndi glanced at her instruments. Combined with the push from the strong tailwind, her speed across the ground was an eye watering 1,325 miles per hour!

A huge grin formed under her oxygen mask. She was

covering almost two thousand feet, or more than the length of six football fields, every *second*. Faster than she'd ever gone in her life. For pilots, speed had always been like a powerful narcotic—no matter how fast they'd gone in the past, they always wanted more. Cyndi was no different.

"Snakeye, Shadow 12 is going ghost." Cyndi turned off her transponder and vanished from the controller's scope.

She was now invisible to the best radars on the planet.

As she headed toward the entry point of the VR-263 low-level route, Cyndi looked down through the floor of her jet. With the help of the onboard space-age tech, she saw the Customs and Border Patrol Ajo Station, just north of Why, Arizona, pass off to her right. Tiny settlements consisting of three or four ramshackle houses were sprinkled among the countryside. Soon, the round white dome of the observatory on top of Kitt Peak rushed by. Off in the distance, the Sierrita copper mine owned by Freeport-McMoRan appeared on the horizon.

Cyndi had planned this mission as a litmus test of her basic piloting skills. She'd configured her screen to only display the most basic flight instruments. Ignoring billions of taxpayer dollars invested in the latest and greatest avionics and a worldwide GPS constellation network, she deselected all navigation data. A paper map, her keen eyesight, and flying techniques perfected during the early airmail days were going to be her only tools today.

Anyone who'd ever stared in frustration at the Blue Screen of Death on their Windows computer understood her reluctancy to fully trust her life to technology.

Fort Huachuca appeared on the horizon at twelve o'clock. A large white balloon was tethered above it at fifteen thousand feet. The balloon supported a ground-scanning radar used to watch for smugglers.

Before reaching the Nogales border crossing, Cyndi turned west and joined VR-263. She slowed to 450 knots and leveled off only five hundred feet above the desert. As Cyndi rocketed along, she realized why the pilot who briefed her before the flight was jealous. The terrain continually challenged her flying skills. One moment she was racing across flatland; the next, she was rolling inverted and pulling when crossing a mountain ridge. Seeing a ridge pass just below her canopy while pulling Gs upside down was an adrenaline rush like no other in the world.

When she rolled upright, San Miguel, a speck of a town, came into view one mile off to her right. The border fence was less than half that distance, off to her left. The most prominent terrain feature south of the border, Horse Peak, soon came into view. The peak was actually two summits with a saddle between them, hence the name. The rocky geological feature was just a stone's throw across the border. When it rushed past her plane, Cyndi had reached her first turn point in the low-level route. She rolled into a crushing eight-G turn. The right wingtip looked like it was going to scrape the ground.

1800 hours, Mountain Standard Time.

After paralleling the border on the VR route for miles, Cyndi checked her watch.

There was more than an hour left before sunset. With plenty of extra fuel, she suddenly opted to exit the low-level route early.

Cyndi turned and slammed the throttle into full afterburner.

CHAPTER 31

2000 hours, MST.

THE SUPERVISOR IN the Luke AFB control tower nervously checked his watch for the tenth time. "Has she checked in with approach yet?"

The rookie controller let out a frustrated sigh. "I'll ask again, sir." He picked up the handset that connected the tower directly to Phoenix approach control. "It's me again. Anything?" After a few moments, he hung up the phone. "Still no contact with Shadow 12."

"This is not good." The supervisor paced the small tower cab with his hands clasped behind his back. "Shit, this is *not* good." He stopped pacing and spun around. "I can't wait any longer. Call the FAA and have them issue an ALNOT."

Air Force Rescue Coordination Center, Tyndall AFB, Florida. 2230 hours, Central Daylight Time (2.5 hours after Cyndi exited low-level route).

The door opened to the darkened room, illuminating rows of empty computer workstations. "It's about damned time, Roosevelt. Shift change was ten minutes ago."

Sweat drenched Tech Sgt. Andre Roosevelt's uniform

after sprinting across the parking lot in the damp Florida heat. "Sorry, man, but it's your fault."

"How the hell is it my fault that you're late?" Airman First Class Dutton demanded, pulling off his headset.

"My old lady wouldn't let me leave the house. She's still pissed about what happened at your bachelor party. Next time you see her, tell her that I didn't touch any of the—"

A chime from one of the workstations had interrupted Roosevelt's plan to get him out of the doghouse.

He bent down and clicked the computer mouse to pull up the message. "Great, it's an alert notice from the FAA. Probably some overdue bug smasher again." Roosevelt pulled out the chair and settled in. The further into the message he read, the bigger his eyes got. "Holy shit! An F-35 from Luke is missing."

A1C Dutton grabbed a headset at the adjacent workstation and jumped into the chair.

Each man opened the checklists for handling an overdue military aircraft.

Roosevelt looked over at Dutton when he got to the last checklist step. "Someone has to notify the boss."

"Screw that. I'm not disturbing a three-star at this time of night," A1C Dutton declared. "For once, being the low man on the totem pole has its advantages. That's on you, Tech Sergeant."

Roosevelt flipped him off. He picked up the phone, took a deep breath, and dialed. "Sir, this is Tech Sgt. Roosevelt in the RCC." He winced at the reply he got. "Yes, sir, I realize what time it is, sir. We just received an ALNOT. It appears an F-35 at Luke is overdue and isn't talking to anyone."

2100 hours MST. (Three hours after Cyndi exited low-level route)

Lance burst through the front door with a big smile on his face. "Honey, I'm home."

"Don't go trying to flirt with me, Junior," Marge said, wagging a scolding finger at him. "I'm old enough to be your…Never mind how old I am. Where is Cyndi?"

"I thought you were Cyndi. I waited at the bar, but she never showed up. So I figured she went straight here after her flight."

"Nope, haven't seen her. You're in luck, though. I just pulled my tuna casserole out of the oven. Grab a seat, and I'll dish up a big helping."

"I'm not hungry. I ate at the bar."

"Nonsense, sit."

The doorbell rang before Lance could be forced to eat again. He rushed to the door, full of excitement and flung it open. "Where have you been, sexy?"

Lieutenant Colonel Tank Abrams was standing on the porch. He was holding a portable radio.

"Excuse me, Lieutenant?"

Lance turned bright red. "Oh, sorry, sir, I thought you were—"

A plump, distraught-looking man stepped out from behind Tank. "Good evening, Lieutenant Garcia, I'm Major Boyd, the base chaplain."

CHAPTER 32

LANCE LEANED FORWARD to get a better look at him. "Wait, weren't you the officiant at Viking's funeral?"

"Yes, I was."

Lance's heart skipped a beat. "Oh my God! What happened? Is Cyndi okay? Did she have an accident?"

"Please, don't be alarmed, my son," the chaplain said in a practiced, serene voice meant to keep Lance from freaking out.

"Don't be alarmed? What the hell are you talking about, Padre! Cyndi should have landed hours ago. Now my commander and the base chaplain, of all people, show up on my front porch. What am I supposed to think? Of course I'm *alarmed.*"

The base chaplain could have used a little more practice.

"Why don't we come inside and sit down before we talk about why we're here? You will be much more comfortable."

The real reason behind the chaplain's suggestion to sit had been learned the hard way when he was new at the job. More than once, loved ones had fainted and injured themselves after hearing bad news he'd delivered.

Lance felt like his head was about to implode. "Sure, whatever, come in." He waved Tank and Major Boyd into the family room. He sat in a chair across from his commander and the chaplain.

Unlike the holy man, Tank wasn't concerned with feelings or mincing words. "Captain Stafford was pronounced missing in action at 2100 this evening. We don't know exactly what happened yet. Did Captain Stafford—"

"Cyndi!"

"Right. Did *Cyndi* contact you this evening? Email? Text? Maybe a phone call?"

"No. I was getting worried. It's not like her to be late."

"Let's talk about your briefing before the flight. Was the prohibition about breaching the ADIZ discussed?"

"Of course. We know we can't enter the air defense identification zone south of the border."

"During the briefing, did she talk about potentially diverting after the low-level flight? Possibly, I don't know, maybe landing at a different airport?"

"The weather was clear and a million this afternoon, why would she divert? What are you getting at, sir?"

"We're just trying to wrap our heads around the situation, Lance," the chaplain said in a compassionate voice. "Cyndi's well-being is our only concern."

The hairs on the back of Lance's neck stood up.

Major Boyd continued his role in the good cop/bad cop routine.

"How has Cyndi's mood been lately?"

"Her mood?"

"Anything seem different about her that you've noticed?"

Lance thought for a moment. After the hectic nine months of training she'd been through, who wouldn't be a little on edge? He looked the padre square in the eyes and said, "Nope."

"How are things going between the two of you?"

"We've been so focused on learning the F-35 we haven't had a lot of time for ourselves lately."

"Any problems paying the bills?"

"You don't get rich fighting for your country."

"Any complaints about the Air Force?"

If there was such a thing as a loaded question, this was it—loaded with career-ending TNT. From getting the shaft during her first try at pilot training, to having a rogue Delta Force team try to assassinate them in the ICBM silo, to being made the scapegoat for a dangerous trainer jet during her second stint at UPT, Captain Cyndi Stafford had a veritable boatload of valid complaints about how the Air Force had treated her.

And there was no way in hell Lance was going to give the officers sitting across from him a single round of ammunition to use against Cyndi.

"Nope. She told me she wants to become a general someday. Cyndi is definitely a lifer."

"So she *didn't* have an ax to grind with the Air Force?" Tank asked with a dubious tone of voice.

Lance had enough. "What the hell is going on here?" he yelled. "Why are you asking all these personal questions? Are you questioning her patriotism?"

"We're just trying to get a feel for Cyndi's state of mind, that's all," the chaplain said in a soothing voice.

"Bull. I see what you're doing. You're trying to build a case against Cyndi so you can hang her out to dry."

Tank slammed his fist on the coffee table. "Lieutenant Garcia, the United States has never had such a highly classified aircraft go missing before. She hasn't made any radio calls, we haven't been able to get any hits on radar, and the SARSAT satellites haven't picked up any ELT beacons on 406 megahertz. Your fiancée has vanished without a trace in one of my F-35s, and I want to know what the hell happened!"

"Let's all take a breath," the chaplain recommended. "There's no need to raise our voices." His smile was replaced with a look of concern. "Lance, you have no idea the political headaches Cyndi's disappearance is already causing. The president isn't waiting until we get more information. He has instructed our ambassador to file a formal inquest with the UN, demanding that China and Russia disclose if they had a hand in the disappearance of her plane."

"Oh crap," Lance said, lowering his head into his hands. "This could get ugly. They're certain to retaliate."

Tank had partially regained his composure and continued his line of questioning. "The briefing officer told me you were scheduled to fly as her wingman on the low-level sortie. Is that correct?"

Lance lifted his head. "Yes, that's right."

"And that you aborted on the runway, claiming that your engine had overheated?"

"Claiming? It did overheat. Check the maintenance log."

Tank sat back and crossed his beefy arms. "I find that coincidence very…concerning."

Lance bolted out of the chair. "Hold on one damned minute, sir. What the hell are you implying? That I had something to do with this?"

Abrams held his radio up to his mouth and said, "Come on in."

Three OSI agents in civilian clothing barged into the house.

He pointed at one of the men and said, "Interrogate Lieutenant Garcia about his involvement in this. Search the house," Abrams said to the others.

Marge had been eavesdropping in the kitchen. She came marching out and planted herself between the armed agents and the stairs. "Hold it right there, Buster." She wielded her cane in their direction like a saber. "Nobody searches my house without my say-so."

The OSI agents held out their faux gold shields and credentials as if they believed Marge would bow and scrape at the mere sight of them.

They might have dealt with some difficult characters in

the line of duty, but they'd never tried to bully a spitfire like Marge Thompson from Bozeman, Montana.

"You fellas in the Air Force?"

"Yes, ma'am, we're with the Air Force Office of Special Investigations."

Marge wasn't the least bit impressed. She sneered at them and scoffed. "You get those nifty suits straight off the rack at Sears before they went out of business?"

"Step aside, ma'am," one of the agents snarled.

"Like hell I will. Have you clowns been deputized by any federal, state, or local law enforcement agencies concerning this matter?"

"Um…well…no, not exactly," he replied.

"Then according to the Posse Comitatus Act of 1878, I can tell you boys to go pound sand. So take your fancy badges, and get your butts off my private property."

The agents looked to Lt. Col. Abrams for help. He just shrugged.

"It's okay, Marge. We've got nothing to hide," Lance said.

While the agents began to ransack the house, the chaplain bowed his head and brought his hands together in prayer. "Lord, be with Captain Stafford during this difficult time. Please protect her and keep her safe."

Rescue Coordination Center, Tyndall AFB.

Every workstation in the room was manned. The air was thick with phone chatter. Lieutenant General Carl Witherspoon, commander of the First Air Force, was presiding over the chaos, barking orders. "Notify the Civil Air Patrol. Have them spin up their radar-analysis team. Start with the SELLS 1 MOA south of Luke. Call the 563rd Rescue Group at Davis-Monthan. Tell them to activate Guardian Angel."

Tech Sgt. Roosevelt spun around in his chair, holding up a phone handset. "Sir, it's the chairman of the Joint Chiefs of Staff. He wants to talk to you."

The three-star general grabbed the phone, not wanting to keep the four-star waiting. "Hello, General VanDorn, this is Carl Witherspoon. I'm afraid I have bad news."

CHAPTER 33

Monday, 1800 hours, MST. (Three hours earlier)

AFTER PARALLELING THE border on the VR route for miles, Cyndi checked her watch.

There was more than an hour left before sunset. She decided to exit the low-level route early, head back to Luke, and meet Lance and the guys at the bar.

Cyndi turned north and slammed the throttle into full afterburner. The jet engine roared to life. She yanked back on the stick and was crushed down in her seat by nine Gs. The aircraft was suddenly enveloped in a silky white shroud of condensation. Cyndi's plane was conducting a Physics 101 lab experiment right before her eyes. The abrupt decrease in air pressure above the wings as they struggled to meet Cyndi's command for maximum lift had instantaneously cooled the air, forcing what little moisture was present to suddenly appear.

With the nose of the fighter pointed straight up, the Gs gradually lightened. She watched the barren desert below drop away. With half her fuel load burned off, Cyndi's jet was easily beyond a one-to-one thrust-to-weight ratio. The altitude readout increased so fast it was just a blur. Passing twenty thousand feet, the Panther shattered through the sound barrier like it was wet tissue paper.

Just as Cyndi was about to switch radio frequencies to contact Snakeye, she heard a tremendous explosion behind her.

Her plane began to gyrate wildly in every axis. Cyndi shrieked as the extreme G forces trapped her in her seat. Like she was caught in a bad dream, time seemed to slow to a crawl as the aircraft disintegrated before her very eyes. The right wing snapped off. The top half of one of the vertical stabilizers bounced off her canopy.

Her jet was rotating so rapidly it was impossible for her vestibular system to keep up with what her eyes were seeing. Cyndi considered closing her eyes to eliminate one input to her brain to prevent getting vertigo.

Instead, she looked down to find the ejection seat handle between her legs. The extreme G forces had pinned her limbs down. Cyndi strained every muscle in her arms until her fingers finally wrapped around the yellow-and-black-stripped ejection handle. Then she pulled up with all her might.

Flexible linear-shaped charge cords that snaked across the inside of the canopy detonated. The two-inch-thick acrylic bubble that had been protecting her from the deadly elements shattered. From the sides of the headrest, airbags shot straight forward milliseconds later, cradling Cyndi's helmet, preventing severe neck injury.

The rocket motor under the Martin Baker US16E seat detonated. The straps surrounding her forearms and calves instantly retracted, restraining her limbs, stopping them from flailing in the supersonic wind.

Thankfully, she'd remembered to flip the lightweight switch before boarding her jet. The additional anthropometric research Martin Baker did when they retested their seat had saved Cyndi from a broken neck.

Frigid air battered her body as she rocketed upward, tumbling out of control. The drogue chute fired from the back of the ejection seat, helping to dampen the tumbling after it inflated. Cyndi looked back and caught sight of a bright orange flash as her jet exploded.

Then everything went black.

CHAPTER 34

Monday, 1930 hours, MST.

CYNDI AWOKE LYING on her back with her eyes closed. The nightmare she'd just had seemed so real that her entire body ached. It felt like there was a jackhammer operating inside her skull. Cyndi yearned for a strong cup of Marge's coffee and an entire bottle of aspirin if there was any hope of surviving the morning. She drew in a deep breath. Her eyes blinked open to the gentle orange glow of the sunrise.

As the world around her came into focus, something was off. Why was she wearing her flight suit and not her pajamas?

Suddenly, she heard an unmistakable noise—the telltale sound of a rattlesnake vibrating its tail. Cyndi rolled onto her left side and saw an eight-foot-long western diamondback coiled up just inches away, glaring at her with its beady, dead eyes. Its forked tongue flicked in its open mouth. Poisonous venom dripped from its razor-sharp fangs. Before she could move, the deadly reptile launched itself at her face.

Its head ricocheted off the clear visor on Cyndi's helmet. Stunned and confused, the snake slithered off and disappeared into a crack in the wall of hard clay that surrounded her.

Despite her pounding headache, the reality of her situation became crystal clear.

Cyndi wasn't at home snuggled against Lance in a warm bed. She was lying in a deep ravine out in the middle of the Sonoran Desert.

She released her parachute harness and took stock of her dire situation. Slowly, all of her senses returned. A gash on her calf was bleeding. She felt a throbbing pain in her ribs. Cyndi gently probed her left side. Her ribs were badly bruised. She assumed she'd been dragged across a rock by her parachute.

The pounding in her head made it difficult to concentrate. Cyndi gingerly pried her helmet off then leaned back against the wall of the ravine. She began to prioritize her next steps, like she'd been taught in SERE school. Although her injuries hurt like hell, she knew none of them were going to kill her. Figuring out where she was and contacting rescue forces was first on her list.

She grabbed the tether attached to the leg of her G suit and reeled it in. A survival kit was stored under the ejection seat and stayed with the pilot after seat separation. When she got to the end of the tether, her survival kit was missing. "What the hell," Cyndi said, tilting her head in disbelief.

The strap had been cleanly cut by a knife. Her dilemma just went from serious to life-threatening. The missing kit was stocked with survival essentials: water, a first aid kit, and an emergency ration. Most importantly, the kit contained the Combat Survivor Evader Locator radio. Without it, Cyndi had no way to determine her precise location or call for help.

Her parachute was hopelessly entangled in thorny bushes and cactuses in the ravine, useless for spreading out as a signal for rescue forces. Cyndi got to her feet and searched for a way out of the ravine. With the crappy day she was having, Cyndi wasn't surprised that her only option was to scale the steep clay walls. She gritted her teeth and began clawing her way up the wall. What should have been an easy climb turned into a painful struggle with each step. By the time she got up to flat land, Cyndi was drenched in sweat. Dirt and sand covered her olive-green flight suit.

In her predicament, appearances were the least of her worries.

Cyndi slowly spun around searching for any sign of civilization. Nothing but desolate, inhospitable desert was visible in every direction. She remembered being instructed to stay at your crash site to make finding you easier. Cyndi scanned the desert again, this time looking for the column of black smoke that would pinpoint the location of her burning F-35. Oddly, there wasn't one.

A quickly receding pale orange light hovered above the horizon. What she had mistakenly thought was a sunrise was actually sunset. All hope was not lost. At least she was able to determine which direction was west. Without any better options, Cyndi fell back on her land navigation training. She looked for the highest natural feature sticking up from the terrain in a southernly direction and used that as her makeshift compass.

Cyndi decided she would head south until reaching the border fence then get the attention of CBP agents by setting off the sensors meant to detect smugglers. She swallowed, took a deep breath of desert air, then started walking.

The arid desert vegetation she navigated through consisted of waist-high scraggly bushes and towering saguaro cactus. Nothing that would supply any shade. Within a few minutes what was left of the sun sank below the horizon, giving Cyndi a welcome respite from the dangerous heat. Unfortunately, it also meant no longer being able to see the terrain feature to the south she'd picked out. There was no way to tell if she was walking in a straight line or in circles.

The night brought its own unique dangers. Howls,

punctuated with staccato yips, yaps, and barks, meant that a pack of coyotes was nearby. The sounds were a warning to any trespassers to stay out of their territory. Cyndi knew that coyotes had much better night vision and sensitivity to movement than humans. That thought sent a chill down her spine. She picked up a softball-size rock from the desert floor for protection.

The darkness that quickly enveloped her was like nothing else she'd ever experienced. The tiny sliver of the crescent moon visible that night reflected next to no light back down to Mother Earth.

Never in her life had Cyndi seen so many stars. Growing up in LA had its advantages, but bountiful opportunities for star gazing wasn't one of them. With no man-made light pollution to obscure her view, the cosmic light show above was awe inspiring. For a fleeting moment, Cyndi's thoughts drifted from surviving to a more existential realm, contemplating humanity's place in the universe. *Are we alone? How could there not be some form of life out there with so many celestial objects to choose from?* Cyndi's heart sank. *Here I am idly speculating about life on other planets while I'll be lucky to make it to the border alive.*

Being alone in the vast desert at night with no weapon, food, or water was practically a death sentence.

But wait, Cyndi thought as she came to a stop. *For millennia, humans have survived in environments as harsh as this, or worse. Somehow they managed to make it through an entire lifetime. Surely I can safely make it a few miles.*

Her dad's inspirational words—if you could call them that—when she doubted her inner strength and started to whine, popped into Cyndi's brain. "So what if it's hard? Suck it up, Buttercup. Time to put on your big girl pants."

Ever the compassionate diplomat, her father.

Bright flashes of light behind Cyndi caught her attention. She spun around. Seconds later, a deep rumble washed over her like a tidal wave. "The bomber strike package!"

CHAPTER 35

CYNDI KNEW IT was next to impossible to judge distance at night, especially across flat terrain. The white flashes from the exploding bombs could be five miles away or less than a mile. Either way, putting as much distance as possible between her and the metal death raining from the sky was the only thing that mattered. She took off at a full sprint through the pitch-black desert. Thorns jutting from the bushes clawed at her flight suit as she weaved through the underbrush.

Suddenly, Cyndi tripped over something and fell face-first into the sand. She spit out a mouthful of sand, dusted herself off, then reached back and picked the object up. It was a large human femur bone. It had been picked clean by animals hungry for a meal. She inspected the ground around her. Other pieces of the hastily buried skeleton were poking up through the windblown sand. Next to it were three small mounds—presumably the rest of the man's family. Cyndi hurled the bone into the darkness and jumped to her feet.

Thirty minutes later, after struggling to make any headway, Cyndi conceded that safely navigating through the desert at night was impossible. She found a large boulder and took cover beside it for the night. She would force herself to stay awake until dawn then set out for the border again.

As the minutes turned into hours, the unfamiliar sounds of the desert that encircled her terrified Cyndi.

Packs of coyotes howled incessantly. Gusts of wind produced eerie noises. She grabbed a small branch lying on the ground to use as a weapon and pressed her back up against the boulder. All Cyndi could think was, *There's probably a thousand ways to die out in the desert. Is there anything in this godforsaken wasteland that wouldn't kill you?*

The bleak, desolate terrain actually had far more life in it than most people believed. If the merciless sun or the violent storms didn't kill you, any number of insects, plants, reptiles, or predatory mammals could do the trick.

If that rogues' gallery of dangerous desert foes wasn't enough to keep Cyndi awake and on guard, knowing that the creepy-looking Gila monster was out there, a venomous lizard native to Arizona and Mexico, sent shivers down her spine.

Then there were the mountain lions. They were skilled nocturnal predators and carnivores.

And Cyndi was bleeding.

If a mountain lion suddenly pounced on her from the cover of darkness, it was sayonara for Cyndi. She wouldn't stand a chance against the big cat. She would die one of the most horrific, painful deaths imaginable—being eaten alive.

So much for being at the top of the food chain.

Not in this desert.

Not at night.

Not all alone.

Cyndi chased those morbid thoughts from her consciousness and focused on how to be seen by the fleet of aircraft that would be searching for her in the morning. Surely, the Air Force would be moving heaven and earth to rescue one of its elite fighter pilots. *Didn't teams of rescuers risk death almost daily during the Vietnam war searching for a solitary pilot shot down in the steamy jungle behind enemy lines? How hard could it be to find me in friendly territory?*

Cyndi was gazing at the constellations when she noticed

a pinpoint of light moving toward her. *Is my mind playing tricks on me? Stars don't move. Oh my God, it's an aircraft!*

The white light slowly arced upward from the horizon as it got closer. Cyndi jumped up and started waving her hands, yelling, "Here! I'm over here!" Grateful that no one was around to witness her futile actions, Cyndi dropped her arms and stopped shouting. She knew all too well that it was impossible for a pilot to hear anyone outside the cockpit.

Then, another white light appeared, not far behind the first. It followed the same path. The lights were lined up to fly directly over her. Cyndi's eyes narrowed. She tilted her head. A third light rose up from the horizon. It too followed the same arc. Less than a minute later, a fourth one appeared.

She stomped her boot into the dirt. "Dammit! Those are satellites!"

The air was so clear, and the night so black, that low-orbiting satellites circling the earth looked close enough to reach out and touch. Cyndi knew that SpaceX had blanketed the heavens with a constellation of four hundred Starlink satellites orbiting the earth at only 550 kilometers.

Cyndi's shoulders slumped. The devastating level of disappointment she felt was palpable. Cyndi was watching a billionaire's brilliant business idea—to bring internet access to the entire world—with her naked eyes, yet she was unable to connect to it and send a simple text message or make a phone call to be rescued.

Dejected, Cyndi slumped back down against the boulder. She pulled the two halves of the pilot wings out of her pocket and clutched them next to her heart for inspiration. She tried to conjure up an image of Lance's handsome face in her mind. Suddenly, his annoying sense of humor didn't seem so bad. She would give anything to have him at her side now.

After her traumatic day, Cyndi's body was beyond exhaustion. Her eyelids became heavy. She couldn't fight sleep any longer. Cyndi closed her eyes and drifted off into a fitful slumber.

CHAPTER 36

The Oval Office.
Tuesday, 0100 hours, Eastern Daylight Time.

"WHY THE HELL haven't you found her yet?" President Ashford demanded, pounding his fist on the Resolute desk.

Staffers scurrying around the Oval Office suddenly clustered together in a far corner, searching for any reason to appear busy and avoid the legendary wrath of the ruthless politician.

"Sir, we are doing everything we can to find that young woman," General Wendall VanDorn croaked weakly, adjusting his suddenly too tight collar. "Our odds will improve greatly once the sun comes up. Even then, it won't be an easy task. The military operations area she was flying in covers over three million acres. That's one and a half times the size of Yellowstone National Park. And we're starting with the assumption that she's somewhere in this one area. At the speeds an F-35 is capable of, she could be almost anywhere. There's another five million acres of restricted areas and bombing ranges surrounding that MOA. It would take a week to conduct a thorough search of all that land."

"That's unacceptable!" Ashford jumped out of his chair and stabbed his finger toward the startled four-star. "Van-Dorn, you obviously don't grasp how important finding this woman is to America. If I don't see results soon, you'll wish you never met me!"

A junior staffer in the room held his hand to his mouth and whispered to the woman next to him. "Translation: I'm behind in the polls, and God help anyone who hurts my chances of getting reelected."

"What assets are you deploying?"

Being used to delivering the rebukes, not receiving them, the blood had drained from the general's face. "At sunrise we'll launch A-10s, HC-130Js, and HH-60Gs from Davis-Monthan Air Force Base. F-16s and F-35s from Luke will join the search as will AV-8Bs and F-35Bs from Marine Corps Air Station Yuma. Teams from each base will also conduct ground searches in vehicles. They'll scour every military range in the Southwest. If she's out there, we'll find her."

Tuesday, 0500 hours, MST.

Abrams, the chaplain, and the OSI agents had left the house empty-handed hours ago. One of the agents was ordered to stay behind. He conspicuously parked in front of the driveway, preventing Lance from leaving.

News of Cyndi's mysterious disappearance had launched the media machine into hyperdrive. The cul-de-sac was overflowing with TV news vans, their roof-mounted telescoping antennas jutting into the sky. Some crews had the audacity to park their heavy vehicles on the neighbors' lawns, lest they get bested by a competitor.

Reporters hungry for a scoop had been knocking on the door incessantly. They finally backed off after Marge read them the riot act and threatened to have them all arrested for trespassing.

Lance had been glued to the TV the entire night, switching channels every few minutes, hoping to learn something—anything—about his fiancée's whereabouts.

Marge offered support to Lance in the best way she knew how: cooking up various dishes to entice him to eat.

For the first time he could recall, Lance had no appetite.

Oval Office.
Tuesday, 0700 hours, EDT.

"Bring me up to date, General VanDorn."

"Certainly, Mr. President. It's almost dawn in Arizona. We have Gray Eagle and Reaper UAVs at Fort Huachuca ready to launch at first light. But there's been an unexpected problem."

"The taxpayers of this fine country don't pay your outrageous salary to bring me problems," President Ashford said, slamming his fist down on his desk. "I expect you to bring me answers!"

"Understood, sir. Our guys have outfitted the UAVs with hyper-spectral imaging cameras for the search mission. The cameras can be programmed to pick up the spectral signatures of the light reflecting off the materials the F–35 is made from."

"Finally, a military system that earns its keep. Then launch the damned drones."

A stickler for accuracy, VanDorn almost torpedoed his multidecade career by correcting the president and informing him that the proper term was unmanned aerial vehicle, not the popular moniker drone. He wisely rejected that idea.

"We can't, Mr. President. Their lawyers are advising the company not to release specifics on the materials used to build their stealth fighter. They're worried they would be held liable if the information is somehow leaked to our enemies."

Ashford went ballistic. "Leave it to the damned lawyers.

Bill Shakespeare had it right when he said how to deal with those weasels. Get Jack Wellington on the phone! Now!"

Less than ten minutes later, claiming it was his patriotic duty, the CEO graciously agreed to provide the material specs. Wellington assured his board that Ashford's threat to kick his company off the DOD-approved contractors list had nothing to do with his decision.

CHAPTER 37

Tuesday, 0600 hours MST.

THE AIRSPACE ABOVE the Southwest United States was teeming with military aircraft. The FAA had to issue a Temporary Flight Restriction notice for the area, prohibiting any gawkers or news choppers from interfering with the search.

Dozens of helicopters, fighters, cargo planes, and UAVs were scouring the desert floor for Cyndi. Two KC-10 Extender tanker aircraft were orbiting, constantly topping off fuel for the other birds so they could stay on station. An E-3 Sentry AWACS from Tinker AFB in Oklahoma had to be called in to manage all the airborne assets. Hundreds of miles above the fray, optical imaging reconnaissance satellites passed over the region every thirty minutes. Even with all those resources, Cyndi was still nowhere to be found.

Despite the billions of dollars of taxpayer's money spent over the years, spy satellites, drones, and surveillance tools weren't everything they're purported to be in the movies. Ten years of false reports of spotting Osama bin Laden had demonstrated that reality. Until he was shot dead in his compound in Abbottabad, Pakistan, the US wasn't entirely sure that bin Laden was even in the building.

Tuesday, 0800 hours, MST.

Frustrated with the lack of progress, the president authorized the mobilization of the Customs and Border Protection agency to help with the search. Every available agent from the CBP Ayo Station was called in. They fanned out across the Sonoran Desert on Yamaha Grizzly ATVs and in the air in Airbus AS350 helicopters. Within an hour, additional CBP personnel from Lukeville, Nogales, San Luis, Gila Bend, and Yuma had volunteered to come in on their day off and join the search.

Tuesday, 0900 hours, MST.

The sun was already well above the horizon when Cyndi was roused from a deep sleep by the call of a nearby coyote. She rubbed her blurry eyes then lifted her arms and stretched them back behind her head. Her bruised ribs screamed in pain.

Cyndi dropped her arms and cradled them against her throbbing side. *Yep*, she said to herself. *Still not dreaming. Still stranded in the damned desert.*

She picked up her boots, turned them upside down, and shook out the sand. She jumped back when scorpions dropped out of each boot.

Cyndi walked south for hours in the blazing heat, careful not to trip and make her dilemma even worse. Three vultures circled overhead wherever Cyndi went, anticipating that a gourmet meal would soon be theirs.

Every mile she covered became more torturous, every minute in the scorching sun more grueling. Exhausted, Cyndi couldn't take another step. She found a small pile of rocks to sit down on and rest. She wiped beads of sweat from her brow with the sleeve of her flight suit, planted her elbows on her legs, and rested her weary head in her hands.

Cyndi contemplated her plan of attack against this formidable adversary. She wasn't about to give up, but her hope of surviving was beginning to dwindle. She looked out at the horizon and began to laugh about her predicament. *Great, I'm so delirious I'm hallucinating,* she thought. The mirage she was seeing in the distance consisted of six sun-bleached, dilapidated shacks.

Cyndi's laughter slowly faded away. She cocked her head and blinked. When the mirage didn't vanish, she sat up straight and rubbed her eyes. It was still there.

With renewed hope and vigor, she jumped up and sprinted toward the mirage, yelling, "Hello! I need help! My airplane crashed last night!" She reached the first house and banged on the door. "Hello! Is anyone home?" No one answered. She rushed over to the second house but got the same result. Cyndi figured the inhabitants must be out working in the local copper mines.

As she approached the next rickety dwelling, a small boy wandered out of it. He stopped and stared up at Cyndi. Fear suddenly flashed across his angelic face as he eyed this stranger to his tiny village. The boy began to tremble and weep.

"No, please don't cry," Cyndi said as she slowly approached the child. "I won't hurt you. I need help. Is your mother or father home?"

The frightened boy backed away from Cyndi.

Cyndi crouched down in front of him and did her best to try to calm the boy. "My name is Cyndi. What's yours?"

The boy's crying lessened somewhat, but he remained wary of the blonde outsider.

Cyndi tried a different approach. Name tags, squadron patches, and the American flag were attached to pilots flight suits with Velcro. If capture was imminent, pilots could easily remove and discard any patches on their flight suit that would tip off the enemy as to their aircraft, base, or mission.

Cyndi removed the colorful 60th Fighter Squadron patch from her right shoulder and held it out. "Here, this is for you. Isn't it pretty?"

Her diversionary tactic worked. The boy's eyes lit up. He stopped crying but refused to get any closer to Cyndi.

She waved the patch to distract the boy while slowly edging closer. "You can have my patch. Go ahead, take it." By the time she was next to the boy, any worries about stranger danger had disappeared. Getting his tiny hands on the colorful patch was his only concern.

Before Cyndi turned over her patch she asked, "Can I use your telephone?"

He looked at her with a blank expression.

"I need to call my base. Luke Air Force Base. Does your mom or dad have a telephone I can use?"

He snatched the patch out of Cyndi's hand, ignoring her question.

The likelihood of a dilapidated shack out in the middle of the Arizona desert having a land line phone seemed remote to Cyndi in this day and age. She patiently waited for the young boy to play with his new toy, knowing the attention span of a child his age was measured in minutes. When he tired of the patch, the boy pointed expectantly at her red name tag.

Before pulling it off her chest, Cyndi said, "I need to get to the border. How far is it to the border?" She pointed to the south.

He just shook his head and shrugged, obviously not comprehending what she was saying.

Cyndi pointed at the flag patch on her left shoulder. "How far to the American border?"

His eyes lit up. This word the boy recognized. "Amer-ica, sí!"

"Right, America," Cyndi said, grateful to be making any headway with the toddler. She kept her request as simple as possible. "I need to get to the border so I can call America." She pointed south.

He shook his head and pointed in the opposite direction. "No, señorita, America there."

She turned and looked in the direction he was pointing. Cyndi clasped her hand to her mouth. "Oh my God! I'm in Mexico!"

CHAPTER 38

CYNDI SUDDENLY FELT lightheaded. She dropped to one knee and supported herself with a hand. The world around her was tumbling out of control worse than her damaged jet had just before she'd ejected. Fearing she might lose consciousness, Cyndi sat on the sand, put her head between her knees, and took slow, deep breaths. Her mind had trouble wrapping itself around this terrifying new reality. With tensions between Mexico and the US at all-time highs, the military and political ramifications of her situation were hard to overstate.

In hopes it would provide some clues as to how she got there, Cyndi tried to recreate the last few moments of her flight in her mind. She remembered turning north, away from the border. Then she pointed the nose of her jet straight up and broken the sound barrier passing twenty thousand feet. That's when things went to hell. Something caused her new stealth fighter to disintegrate before her eyes. At the speed she'd ejected, her momentum must have carried her seat thousands of feet higher before it kicked her out and automatically opened her parachute.

"The jet stream!" she shouted.

The strong jet stream winds coming from the north had carried her across the border and into Mexico as she gradually floated down in her parachute, unconscious.

No matter what came next, she knew she needed to

eat something and rehydrate if there was any hope of overcoming it.

With the boy preoccupied with his new prize, Cyndi quietly slipped away and entered a dilapidated shack. She swatted away annoying flies that were buzzing around her head. Oil-stained coveralls had been carelessly tossed into a corner. A rusty hot plate in the opposite corner of the one-room shack identified the area as the kitchen. Rotting, bloody entrails scooped from a large fish sat in a heap on an old wooden cutting board, next to its severed head. The thick, revolting odors lingering in the air assaulted her nostrils. Cyndi felt a sudden wave of nausea surge upward into her throat. She turned her head to the side and tried to throw up, but nothing came out. It had been more than a day since she'd had anything to eat or drink. And that food had long ago been burned up powering her muscles.

She spotted a muddy, red plastic gas can sitting on the dirt floor. Cyndi picked it up and sniffed the container. It was filled with water, not gasoline. Wherever the family got its water, this was how they transported it back home. Finally, a chance to slake her powerful thirst.

Cyndi put the end of the spout up to her parched lips, tilted the gas can upward, but then suddenly stopped. She lowered the can and poured some water into her cupped hand. Cyndi was thankful she hadn't taken a drink. A dead fly and some type of slimy green growth had been floating in the can.

No matter how desperate she was, what would come next if she drank the contaminated water was indisputable. Throughout the Third World, people without access to clean water regularly suffered from diarrhea, cholera, dysentery, typhoid, and even polio.

Cyndi searched the shack for a better option. A six-pack of Coke occupied the top shelf in a narrow cupboard. She knew the caffeine in the soda was a diuretic, which worsened dehydration. But at least it wasn't contaminated. Thirty seconds later, the first can of Coke was empty. Cyndi stuffed two more cans into empty pockets on her flight suit. She found some tortillas and slipped those into pockets as well.

Cyndi was about to sneak out the back door when her conscience stopped her. She'd just stolen nourishment—in the broadest sense of the word—from the desperately poor family that lived in this ramshackle abode in the middle of a harsh, unforgiving desert. To placate her nagging conscience Cyndi pulled all the money she had out of her billfold and left it on the counter—120 dollars.

Then she stepped out into the blazing sun and began the arduous trek north.

"This just in, a US drone has spotted small pieces of the wreckage, scattered for miles across southern Arizona."

Lance jumped up from the couch he'd been camped out on all night. He grabbed the remote and cranked up the volume.

The buxom blonde reporter from the Washington, DC, affiliate looked into the camera lens like she was flirting with it. "The Pentagon is cautioning the public to not get its hopes up, though. It's saying that the distribution pattern of the wreckage is so random and spread out that it's not providing any clues as to the whereabouts of its pilot, Capt. Cyndi Stafford."

Lance threw the remote down on the floor, shattering it.

"In light of the recent deterioration in diplomatic relations with our neighbor to the south, Mexico has refused to let the US search for any parts of the wreckage that may have landed in its territory. The spokesman for President Ortega has announced that Mexico will do its own investigation. He also said in the likely event that there has been damage to crops or structures from the missing American plane, President Ortega expects its citizens to be fully compensated."

Lance sank back down onto the couch, despondent that he couldn't do anything to help rescue Cyndi.

Marge had been watching from the kitchen door. Her heart ached watching Lance agonize over Cyndi's fate while under virtual house arrest. She came over and placed a comforting hand on his shoulder. "Everything will be okay, Lance. Trust me."

He looked up and forced a smile. "I hope you're right." Lance suddenly cocked his head. "That's the first time you've called me by my real name."

Marge quickly pulled her hand off Lance's shoulder. "Don't go thinking that means I've taken a liking to you."

"No, of course not. Wouldn't dream of it."

"Well good, I'm glad we got that cleared up."

"Me too."

"All right."

"Good."

Marge put a small plate on the coffee table. "Here, I brought you a slice of my famous rhubarb pie. Wouldn't want you to die of starvation. Too much paperwork."

Lance picked up the fork and took a bite. "I'd feel terrible making you fill out a bunch of forms." He put the fork down, stood up, and gave Marge a warm embrace. "Thank you."

"What for?"

Lance cleared his throat. "Um…for your…For the pie, of course."

"Now don't go getting all mushy on me, it's just a piece of pie," Marge replied. Her eyes began to tear up. "They'll find her. We just have to keep the faith." She lifted up the skirt of her apron and dabbed at her eyes. "I better get lunch started." Before she went back into the kitchen,

Marge said, "And turn off the dang TV. The press ain't good for nothing but stirring up fear."

"Isn't that the truth," Lance chuckled as he plopped back down on the couch. He lifted a forkful of hot rhubarb pie up to his mouth. Suddenly, his eyes widened. For the first time in countless hours, a genuine smile crossed his face.

Lance put the fork down and raced out the door. From the front porch he yelled, "Everyone, I'm Lance Garcia, Captain Stafford's fiancé. I know how to find her!"

His pronouncement caused a stampede. Reporters and cameramen nearly trampled each other rushing to the porch. Microphones were shoved in Lance's face. The lights mounted on top of cameras were blinding. Reporters shouted out their usual inane or underinformed questions.

Lance raised his arms. His tired, red-ringed eyes made it look like he'd been crying. "Please, everyone quiet down. I have an announcement to make."

The mob calmed down.

"Like I said, I'm Captain Stafford's fiancé. My heart is breaking knowing that she is missing and that I'm trapped here unable to help find Cyndi. As you wonderful folks know all too well, nobody can survive out in the Arizona heat for long without water. The clock is ticking. If God forbid Cyndi, my one true soulmate, is injured and bleeding, the predators that stalk the desert will zero in on her scent. I know Cyndi better than anyone. I know how she thinks. I can help find her."

"Then why aren't you at your base," a reporter yelled out. "What's stopping you?"

"He is." Lance pointed at the OSI agent munching on a sandwich in his official Air Force sedan parked at the curb.

Like well-trained hunting dogs, the reporters sprinted toward the car, their prey in their sights.

The agent dropped his sandwich and quickly rolled up the window.

Enraged reporters pounded on his window, demanding to know why this sad, brokenhearted man standing alone on the porch wasn't allowed to leave and help the search for his beloved fiancée.

Lance smiled and waved at the frantic OSI agent.

The man whipped out his phone and dialed as fast as his fingers could move. Lance saw him hold the phone up to his ear. His head bobbed up and down, then side to side. By the time he'd hung up, his face was crimson with anger. The agent stabbed a finger at Lance then waved him toward the car.

Lance casually strolled off the porch and across the lawn. The mob of reporters parted as if it was the Red Sea and Moses himself had just commanded it. The OSI man cracked his window open when Lance reached his car. "Get in. I'm taking you to Luke," he snarled.

"Oh, I couldn't possibly inconvenience you like that. Don't you have a long list of patriotic, hardworking airmen you need to harass first?"

The man's beady eyes narrowed as he scanned the battery of cameras and microphones pointed at him. Through clenched teeth, he growled, "Please."

Lance hopped in the back seat.

The agent slowly threaded his vehicle through the mob as reporters chased the car out of the cul-de-sac.

Before turning onto the main road, the agent glared into the rearview mirror and said, "You try anything funny, Garcia, and I won't bring you back here. I'll lock your ass in the brig. Understood?"

Lance ignored his threat and gave a snooty glance out the window at the unchauffeured masses. "To the base, Jeeves."

CHAPTER 39

THE BANK OF monitors behind the briefing counter at the 60th FS were all tuned to different news stations. Anxious pilots were packed shoulder to shoulder in front of the counter, waiting for any good news.

Lance walked in with the OSI agent hot on his heels. The gathering of somber pilots at the counter reminded Lance of his first visit to his new squadron. Viking had died through no fault of his own and had just been interred at the base cemetery. The heart-wrenching uncertainty surrounding Cyndi's fate, combined with the morbid memories from the recent past, proved too much for Lance to bear. The fearsome Air Force fighter pilot broke down.

His squadron mates gathered around Lance and helped him find a vacant office to rest in. The OSI agent followed and tried to force his way into the office. Major Frey—a.k.a. Zombie—the deputy squadron commander, put his hand against the man's chest. "Who the hell are you?"

He whipped out his badge. "OSI. Wherever Lieutenant Garcia goes, I go."

"Not today, Skippy. Your services are no longer needed. Garcia is one of our own. We got this."

Zombie and four other pilots grabbed the agent, roughly escorted him to the front door, and tossed his arrogant ass out of the building.

"Welcome to the jungle, Skippy!" Zombie yelled, as he closed and locked the door.

Tank had been watching the scuffle from the door of his office. He flashed a thumbs-up at Zombie then went back in and closed his door.

Hours later, a CNN anchor was interviewing the US ambassador to Mexico about Cyndi's disappearance.

"Quiet, everybody!" Zombie yelled, pointing at the screen.

The pilots immediately fell silent.

The ambassador wore a silk ascot tucked into his open-collard Brooks Brothers dress shirt. Copious amounts of mousse kept his wavey black mane perfectly coiffed. Despite his refined appearance, the man was just another clueless political hack who'd donated enough money to the president's last campaign to be granted the plum posting.

In answer to a question from the CNN reporter, the ambassador responded, "In what President Ashford feels is an unusually hasty conclusion, the Mexican government has officially declared that our missing pilot is *not* in Mexico. The United States has asked permission for our military to conduct its own search but was turned down. Our hands are tied because it's an act of war to enter a foreign country without permission."

Predictably, the pilots had a few choice words to offer the neighbor to the south.

Hoping that the Mexican government would waste its overextended resources searching for Cyndi was just wishful thinking. Even if it did, the odds of success were doubtful. An increasing percentage of government employees and the police had been corrupted by the drug gangs in Mexico. Any money allocated to a search would have ended up in the wrong pockets.

Relations between the two governments had been spiraling downward ever since US agents had arrested Gen.

Salvador Cienfuegos, a former Mexican defense minister, on drug conspiracy charges in 2020.

Nicknamed *El Padrino*—the Godfather—General Cienfuegos was alleged to have earned millions of dollars in bribes in exchange for protecting the H-2 cartel. Mexico had failed many times to apprehend the well-protected general and was embarrassed when the US easily nabbed him without incident as he stepped off a plane at LAX.

For decades, Mexico had consistently ranked near the bottom of the list for poverty. The systemic failure of Mexico's schools had led to hundreds of thousands of *ninis*, an underclass of school-dropouts who neither worked nor studied. That meant prospective new members of the cartels were in abundant supply and easy to recruit. Without the prospect of a decent future, it wasn't surprising that they ended up as willing combatants on behalf of the cartels.

The economics of the drug trade made it hard to resist. Ever since China cracked down on the production of fentanyl, manufacturing of the highly potent synthetic opioid had shifted to countries like Mexico. It had been flooding onto the streets of First World countries ever since. The low cost to manufacturer was a major driver. Unlike heroin, which had to be cultivated from poppy plants at a cost of around $6,000 a kilogram, fentanyl could be made at the bargain basement price of only $200 a kilogram. This motivated shady entrepreneurs to open illicit opioid labs on nearly every corner.

◆

Later that afternoon, Lance had composed himself enough to join his brothers-in-arms around the briefing counter. It didn't take long for some of his buddies to recommend they go to the squadron bar and drown their sorrows.

After Lance had left the counter, a call came into the front desk. The pilot manning the desk answered, listening intently. After he hung up he said, "They found the engine from Cyndi's jet near Why, Arizona. Well, sort of. It was completely obliterated. Pieces of it were scattered for hundreds of yards. It would have taken a two-thousand-pounder to cause that much destruction."

"The type of bombs dropped last night by the strike package," Zombie murmured.

Every pilot was thinking the same thing. If the explosion could do that much damage to the biggest, toughest part on the F-35, a pilot anywhere nearby would have been vaporized.

Thankfully, none of them spoke up.

"Why the hell would a bomber target the crash site?" one of the pilots asked Zombie.

The deputy squadron commander tapped his pursed lips as he considered the surprisingly astute question. "I'm sure he wasn't aiming for the crash site," Zombie replied without much conviction. "It was probably just a coincidence that a two-thousand-pound bomb landed where the engine did."

CHAPTER 40

Tuesday afternoon.

PHOENIX PD DETECTIVE Mark Barnes had just planted his weary and out-of-shape body at a picnic table next to a row of food trucks parked across the street from the Maryvale station.

Just as he'd sunk his teeth into his fish taco, his radio barked to life. "We found something, Detective. You better just come take a look."

He let out a sigh, covered his taco in the foil wrapper, and chucked it into the trash. "I'm on my way."

———

Barnes flashed his badge to the cop manning the yellow police tape barrier strung up around the crime scene. After being waved through, he lifted the tape and ducked under it.

"What do you have?" he said to the CSI technician standing next to a tricked-out red-and-black Mazda RX-7.

"Suicide," the tech responded matter-of-factly.

Next to a warehouse under construction west of Luke Air Force Base, a man was slumped over the steering wheel. His window was rolled down. Behind the deceased man's left ear was an entry wound. The passenger seat and window were splattered with blood, gray matter, and bits of skull.

Detective Barnes crouched down next to the driver's door, pulled a small flashlight from his shirt pocket, and carefully examined the entry wound. "Powder burns on the scalp," he mumbled absentmindedly.

He slipped on surgical gloves then opened the car door. A .38 special tumbled out. He used his pen to pick up the revolver by the trigger guard. One round in the cylinder had been fired.

He looked up at the forensics agent dressed in a white bunny suit. "Gun landed on the correct side after he dropped it."

"Like I said, suicide," the man repeated, eager to remove his protective suit before suffering heatstroke.

"Was there a note?"

The CSI tech held up a plastic bag with the note inside. "I dusted it for prints. It's clean."

"Why would a guy who's so distraught that he doesn't want to live any longer wipe his prints from his own suicide note?"

"Maybe he was a clean freak." The tech pointed at a small blue sticker on the bottom-left edge of the windshield. "He was military. Stationed at Luke. Those guys are taught to be anal about keeping everything spotless from day one of basic training."

Barnes took the bag, held it up to the sun, and read the contents. "I couldn't take it anymore," he said out loud, reading from the note. "Not the most original final words I've heard," Barnes quipped.

The seasoned detective stood in the space between the open car door and the driver's seat. He faced the same direction as the dead man, arranged the fingers on his left hand in the shape of a gun, and put the tip of his index finger against his skull. Then he simulated pulling the trigger.

"I don't get it," he said, confusion blanketing his face. "Why would a guy who's right-handed shoot himself with the gun in his left hand?"

"What makes you think he was right-handed?" the tech replied.

"Stroke direction."

"Stroke what?"

Barnes pointed at the suicide note and traced his finger along the writing. "The pen strokes of left-handed writers usually make cross-strokes from right to left rather than left to right, like righties. Also, left-handed people write circular letters and numbers with clockwise strokes. If you look closely, you can tell his were written counterclockwise." He handed the note back to the tech. "But I'm sure you noticed that, too."

"Yes, of course I did. I was just about to mention it."

"Of course you were." Barnes let out a sigh. "Do we have a name yet?"

"Benito Torres. We found it on the registration in the glove compartment. Did a background check on him. I was right. He was Air Force."

"What did he do in the Air Force?"

"Crew chief."

The detective jerked back. "Did you say crew chief?"

"Yeah, why?"

He pulled a small notepad from his shirt pocket and started digging through his notes. "I'll bet you a month's pay this guy worked on the plane that's missing. As of now, this is a murder investigation."

Barnes called in instructions to the station on his cell phone as he raced off and ducked back under the yellow tape. "I need an address for Benito Torres. Works at Luke Air Force Base."

The traffic on Interstate 10 was the usual nightmare. Forty-five minutes later, he arrived at a rundown apartment complex in Maryvale. Half a dozen Phoenix PD vehicles were haphazardly parked in the lot with their roof-mounted lightbars flashing.

Detective Barnes bounded up the steps to apartment 329. The door to the cluttered apartment was wide open. Still gasping for air, he went inside and meticulously recorded everything he saw in his notepad.

Moments later, a plump, young Hispanic woman walked into the apartment, propping a crying baby on her left hip and clutching three overflowing Walmart bags in her right hand. She was greeted by officers ransacking the apartment. "Who the hell are you people? How did you get into our apartment?"

Detective Barnes held up his credentials, identified himself as a law enforcement officer, and showed her an official looking piece of paper. "We have a search warrant, ma'am. Your landlord let us in. Are you the wife of Airman Benito Torres?"

"No, we aren't married."

"His girlfriend, then?"

She dropped the grocery bags. "That bastard. What has Benny done now?"

"We need to speak to your boyfriend," Barnes said. "Do you know where he is?" The experienced detective already knew the answer. He was asking to gauge her reaction. Was she somehow connected to all this?

"He's at the base, of course."

"No, ma'am, he never showed up for work today."

"Then check the nearest bar." She covered the child's ears. "Or whorehouse."

It was obvious to Barnes that she wasn't involved. Falling back on a phrase he'd used far too many times in his long career, he said, "I'm afraid I have some terrible news."

Before he could add any more misery to the woman's tragic life, an officer stepped out of a bedroom. "We found something, Detective." He held up a small olive-green kit bag with a cleanly cut leg strap attached to it. The officer opened it up. "It looks like a survival kit."

—◆—

A stone's throw from Chase Field, Chief of Police Bill Miller stepped up on the platform and walked over to the podium at police headquarters. Assistant chiefs and media-savvy members of the city council lined the back of the platform. Members of the press were shouting out questions, badgering the chief for a statement.

He held up his hands to quiet the voracious mob. Miller leaned forward to speak into the jungle of microphones planted on the podium by the media. "As you know, the citizens of our fine city are praying for good news about the brave pilot whose jet went missing from Luke Air Force Base yesterday evening. There has been a new development in our investigation that could possibly be related to the missing pilot. A man was found dead in his car near the base. We have just started our forensic investigation of the crime scene, so there will be no comment about that development at this time."

"Is the person in the car Airman Torres, Captain Stafford's crew chief?" a reporter yelled.

"No comment."

"Do you think his death and the crash of Captain Stafford's jet are somehow connected?"

"No comment."

"Come on, Chief, stop stonewalling. Is there a connection or not?"

"Look, folks, the media has always been a vital and valued partner in our efforts here in the department."

An assistant behind him coughed out loud to prevent a laugh from escaping.

With a straight face, Chief Miller said, "If our investigation leads to any information, be assured that I will notify the press immediately."

———◆———

Used to being stiff-armed by police administration, the Phoenix press coerced its sources on the street and deep in the PD itself into service using whatever tactics they felt were justified to get a scoop on the competition.

Within hours, they'd tracked down the house that Torres grew up in. Their local affiliates near Compton, California, flooded into the neighborhood and trampled the lawn, hounding his family for an interview. Torres's younger sisters supported their grief-stricken mother as she shuffled out onto her porch to speak to the reporters.

Between sniffles, she looked up with bloodshot eyes. "I don't believe a word the cops are saying about my Benny. He would never harm anyone."

Happy to destroy the mother's opinion of her only son to please the ratings gods, a reporter waved her microphone at the woman and yelled, "Mrs. Torres, is it true Benito owed $900 dollars to the notorious Descendientes del Diablo cartel, and that they threatened to kill his family if he didn't pay it back?"

On hearing the scandalous question, the mother's nostrils flared. She wagged an arthritic finger at the reporter. "That's a lie! Benny was a good boy. He just got mixed up with the wrong crowd, that's all."

The girls stepped in front of her, shielding their mother. One of Torres's sisters pulled a small pink Baretta Nano from the waistband on the back of her ripped jeans and fired two rounds into the air. "My brother didn't do shit! This press conference is over. Now get the hell off our lawn before I cap all your asses."

CHAPTER 41

CYNDI STOPPED UNDER an outcropping of rock to take a break and escape the sun. She'd finished off the Coke and tortillas hours ago. Cyndi unzipped a pocket on her flight suit and pulled out the two halves of the pilot wings for much-needed motivation. It did the trick. With renewed determination, Cyndi vowed to not only survive but to do so with her honor intact.

As she was about to resume her hike north, Cyndi heard a noise. She ducked down low against the rock and snuck a peek. A coyote—the human variety—was smuggling a dozen migrants across the desert.

The defenseless travelers looked famished and exhausted after walking a circuitous route through the sweltering desert, avoiding roads, towns, and the extorting *policía*. Most had handed over their life savings to the well-armed, despicable coyote in exchange for the hope of a better life.

Cyndi squinted to get a better look. Each person had something strange strapped to their shoes. A scrap of old carpeting was sown to a piece of black cloth, then attached to the bottom of their shoes with strips of the cloth. The ingenious coyote had provided a pair to each person to prevent them from leaving shoe prints in the sand, making it harder to track the caravan or determine the number of children among the migrants.

To her left, Cyndi heard vehicles approaching. Three beat-up old Toyota pickup trucks with Soviet DShK heavy machine guns mounted on tripods in the beds—technicals in military parlance—roared up to the group. Ten men jumped out of the beds of the trucks and encircled the migrants.

"Drug cartel goons," Cyndi whispered to herself.

They were outfitted with body armor, comm gear, and weapons that would rival any special ops community. They'd stolen the equipment from the Mexican Army. Each man wore a black balaclava to conceal their identity. One difference between cartel members and military members is that they didn't wear camo uniforms. The cartel thugs wore dirty blue jeans and T-shirts. Tattoos covered their necks, arms, and shaved heads, creating a low-class human graffiti mural.

The coyote tossed his rifle to the ground and raised his arms. "Amigos, how can I help you today?"

The apparent leader grabbed the coyote by the front of his shirt. "You must pay a toll to pass through our territory if you expect to make it to the border alive."

"Yes, of course," the trembling smuggler said. "I pay the customary one hundred dollars per head."

The man reared back and viciously slapped the coyote. "That was the toll last week! This week you must pay $1,000 American!"

The coyote didn't bother objecting. He knew the man would pocket the difference before turning over the money to the cartel. In truth, the higher amount would barely make a dent in his profitable business. He pulled out a huge wad of cash and peeled off $12,000.

After the bribe was paid, the armed men distributed fliers to each person. The frightened migrants looked at them and shook their heads.

Just then a glossy new black Cadillac Escalade pulled up. A man chomping on a toothpick stepped out. His enormous potbelly lapped over his oversize silver belt buckle. Alligator cowboy boots and a diamond-studded pinky ring on his left hand suggested the man wasn't an ordinary cartel thug.

The goon who'd demanded the exorbitant bribe rushed up to the man and waved the stack of bills. "El Jefe, I have the toll for you. One thousand dollars each."

He looked dismissively at the money as if he was too good to touch it. "Put it in my car."

"Right away, El Jefe." His underling scurried off to the Escalade and put the money in the glove compartment.

The boss clasped his sweaty hands behind his back and slowly walked among the terrified migrants, stopping at the coyote. "A fine group you have here," he said. "Business must be very good."

"No, El Jefe, business very bad. I no make much money. I only want to help these poor, unfortunate people."

He rested his hand on the butt of the revolver holstered on his right hip. "The toll has just gone up to $2,000."

"Impossible, El Jefe!" the coyote yelled.

"Then turn around and take these wretched scum back to the hellholes they came from."

"I can't do that. They will tear me apart," the coyote whispered.

"That is your problem, not mine." El Jefe turned to the crowd and yelled, "This man refuses to pay his toll! Turn around! Go home!"

After being forced to give the coyote all of their money, the migrants weren't about to let him ruin their hopes of a better life. Their anger began to boil over.

"There has to be another option," the coyote pleaded.

The boss looked over the group, focusing on a cute teenage girl wearing a backpack with faded yellow daisies printed on it. She had been his real objective the whole time. He removed the toothpick from his mouth and pointed. "Bring that one to me."

His men grabbed the girl and dragged her over to him.

El Jefe ran his finger lightly across her smooth cheek.

"After I have my way with this pretty little thing, I could make a fortune trafficking her." He turned to the coyote. "I'm a reasonable man. Give her to me, and that will satisfy the toll for today."

"I am a reasonable man also, El Jefe."

Her mother rushed up and hid the girl behind her. "No, I beg you, don't harm my daughter. Take me instead!"

One of the goons smashed the butt of his rifle into the mother's cheek. She crumpled to the ground, blood gushing from her mouth.

"Take her to my car," El Jefe said.

His men grabbed the teenager. The terrified girl thrashed around trying to free her arms from their grasp but was no match for the men. They tossed her and her backpack into the front seat of the SUV.

Cyndi watched the heart-wrenching scene unfold but was helpless to stop it. If she tried to rush the bandits from one hundred yards away, they would have mowed her down with the truck-mounted machine guns before she made it halfway. Even if she did make it to the men alive, there's no way she could take them all on. With her conscience crying out in pain, Cyndi reluctantly slipped away via a sunken wash, hidden from the view of the bad guys.

Elderly men in the group delicately lifted the injured mother to her feet. The cartel thugs snorted at their display of humanity toward the sobbing woman and fired their guns into the air, howling with laughter. The migrants had come from some of the most lawless and dangerous countries on earth. They knew what their fate would be if they tried to rescue the girl. They grudgingly headed north again and soon disappeared over a small rise.

On the hunt again for the next caravan of migrants, the armed men sped away in their pickup trucks.

El Jefe slid into the driver's seat of his SUV and asked, "What is your name, little one?"

The girl pressed herself against the passenger door. "Maria," she replied, choking back tears.

"How old are you, Maria?"

"Fourteen. Please let me go, I don't have any money to give you."

A filthy smirk formed on his weathered face as he leered at the terrified girl. "It's not money I want." El Jefe slapped Maria then ripped her shirt open.

As he began to molest the girl, there was a loud bang. A large rock cascaded down the shattered windshield and scraped across the hood. The boss whipped out his revolver and rushed to the front of the vehicle to investigate.

Cyndi charged at him from behind, slamming her body into his broad back.

The revolver discharged, blowing a gaping hole in the windshield.

Maria let out a bloodcurdling scream and collapsed to the floor.

Cyndi and the much larger man traded fierce blows in front of the truck. She latched on to his arm with her right hand then slammed her left elbow into his nose. Another gunshot sounded, puncturing the grill.

The boss screeched in agony. His gun dropped to the ground as clutched his badly shattered nose.

Confident in her combat skills, Cyndi kicked the gun out of reach and taunted the man. "Let's see how tough you are against someone who can defend herself."

Enraged, he reached behind his back and pulled out a knife. "You will die for this, *puta!*"

When he lunged at her, Cyndi grabbed his wrist and slammed her closed fist down on his forearm, shattering both his ulna and the radius bones. The knife fell to the ground. "That's all you got?" she said, continuing to taunt the wheezing, obese man.

El Jefe's eyes bulged with rage. He swung his other massive fist at Cyndi.

She ducked then broke his ankle.

The wounded man staggard like a drunken sailor, refusing to give up.

When he lurched toward Cyndi, she grabbed his head with both hands and slammed it into the bumper.

El Jefe lay lifeless at her feet, unable to harm helpless children anymore.

After checking his neck for a pulse, she leaned back against the car and bent over with her hands on her knees, gasping for air. Normally, taking on such a novice wouldn't have even gotten her heart rate up. But in her weakened condition, the fight had taken almost every ounce of strength Cyndi had left.

After recouping some of her energy, Cyndi grabbed the gun, opened the car door, and jumped into the driver's seat.

The girl popped up from the floorboard and began screaming hysterically. "You're one of them! Please don't shoot me."

"It's okay," Cyndi said, laying the gun on the seat. "I'm not one of them. I won't hurt you." Her assurances did nothing to placate the terrified girl. Cyndi tried pointing at her nametag. "My name is Cyndi. What's your name?"

She ignored Cyndi and scanned the barren desert for her family, sobbing uncontrollably.

Cyndi gently guided the girl's face back her way. "Look at me. Focus on my face. What is your name?"

Her sobbing lessened slightly. "Maria."

"You're safe now, Maria. I won't hurt you."

Maria stopped crying and looked down at the gun. "I want my *mamá*."

Cyndi was making little progress calming the girl down.

She needed to find a way to establish trust with her. She tossed the gun into the back seat, thinking it would help. Cyndi gasped when she looked back and saw a stack of fliers with her picture on them. The picture was the same one on her military ID. "What the hell?"

Unfortunately, she didn't read Spanish. Cyndi grabbed a flier and asked Maria to interpret.

Maria wiped her teary eyes and scanned the flier. "It says the evil man is offering many pesos to anyone who turns you in."

"What else?"

"Anyone who tries to help you, the evil man will torture their entire family to death."

"The evil man?"

"Sí, the evil man. El Diablo."

CHAPTER 42

BEFORE SEEING THE flier, Cyndi didn't think her motivation to make it to the border could have been any stronger. She was wrong. The stakes had just changed. The leader of one of the most vicious cartels in Mexico was now hunting her.

If she hoped to make it out of the country alive, there was only one option: Get to the border as quickly as possible. Cyndi started the Escalade and was about to put it into gear when she looked over at Maria. She couldn't imagine the daily trials the distraught teenager must have endured growing up. Now, just as she thought a better life was within her grasp, Maria had suffered unspeakable trauma at the hands of El Jefe.

Cyndi patted Maria's trembling hand. "I will take you back to your family."

"Gracias, Senorita, gracias," Maria shouted, a ray of hope beaming from her innocent, young eyes.

Cyndi had been below ground level in the wash when the caravan left. "Which direction did they walk?"

The girl looked out the damaged windshield, trying to remember the direction the caravan had taken. The shock from all that she'd been through proved too much. Her eyes began to tear up again. "I…don't…I don't know."

"It's okay; I'll find them," Cyndi assured her. The sun had passed overhead hours ago, so Cyndi knew its current position was more westerly. She put the SUV in drive and headed in the direction she assumed was north.

Soon, the radio mounted on the dashboard barked to life. Men were shouting in Spanish. "Maria, what are those men on the radio saying?"

The girl listened for a moment then freaked out. "They call El Jefe! The men, they are coming back!"

Cyndi slammed the gas pedal to the floor. The luxury SUV lurched forward, crashing through bushes and cactuses in its path. Chrome trim pieces on the rocker panel were ripped off as the vehicle repeatedly went airborne then slammed back to earth.

Up ahead, Cyndi saw the outlines of the distinctive Horse Peak rock formation on the northern horizon. Just beyond it was miles of tall rusty steel pipes, stretching east to west, that made up the border fence. Her spirits soared as she realized she was no more than two miles from freedom.

Between herself and the fence, Cyndi noticed the caravan of migrants. She started blaring the horn as she raced across the desert toward the group. The migrants panicked, assuming El Jefe was coming back to kidnap and rape more of the women. They scattered in every direction. The coyote bolted from the group, not wanting any part in what was about to happen.

Cyndi glanced at the rearview mirror. Clouds of dust were billowing up from the desert floor. The trucks were closing in on her fast.

She faced a terrible choice—freedom or valor. Cyndi knew if they caught her anywhere near the migrants, the men would slaughter her and everyone else. But if she kept Maria with her as she dashed to the border, there was no way of telling if the girl would ever be reunited with her mother once the Mexican bureaucracy got involved.

Cyndi slammed on the brakes and slid to a stop. She reached across Maria and pushed her door open. "Go! Go back to your family!"

The frightened girl threw her right leg out of the SUV then suddenly stopped. Maria looked at Cyndi then back at the advancing trucks. Tears gushed down her pretty face. "Bad men, they are coming!" She pointed to the caravan. "You come. You go with me."

Cyndi gently grasped the naïve teenagers hand. "Don't worry; I'll be okay."

Despite her young age, Maria understood what Cyndi was doing and the gruesome fate that awaited her. She grabbed the poster and spit on it. Then she threw it on the floor and stomped on it for good measure. The girl lurched toward Cyndi and wrapped her arms around her neck, hugging Cyndi tightly. "I never forget you."

Cyndi warmly embraced the girl. "I'll never forget you either, Maria." She quietly opened the glove compartment and grabbed the stack of money. Cyndi stuffed it deep down inside Maria's backpack. Then she pulled away and wiped the girl's tears with the sleeve of her flight suit. "Now go, be with your mama."

The girl hopped down from the Escalade and ran off toward the caravan at a full sprint. When the mother caught site of her daughter, she screamed out her name. She rushed up to Maria and scooped the girl up in her arms.

Cyndi spun the truck around to the south. "All right, you sons of bitches, fight's on!" She stomped on the gas pedal. A rooster tail of dust and rock spit out from behind the SUV. Cyndi jerked the steering wheel back and forth as she gained speed, fishtailing across the desert floor and stirring up a huge dust cloud. Her tactic worked. The cloud obscured the view of the fleeing migrants.

The men saw El Jefe's vehicle speeding their way and stopped the trucks to wait for their boss to arrive.

Badly outgunned, Cyndi only had one choice. She blasted right through the middle of the pack and continued south at well over one hundred kilometers per hour.

For a moment, the men stared at each other in stunned silence. The driver of one of the pickups glanced down at a flier. His eyes widened after they'd sent the image on the flier to his drug-addled brain.

The woman they were hunting was escaping.

In their boss's car.

Without El Jefe.

He grabbed the flier and waved it, screaming, "Vámanos! Vámanos!"

CHAPTER 43

THE THREE PICKUPS violently whipped around and gave chase. One of the men was ejected from the bed of a truck as it spun around. The gunners opened up on Cyndi, but keeping their aim was nearly impossible given the rough terrain.

With sand being kicked up by the bullets all around her, Cyndi knew eventually her luck would run out. She noticed a large formation of rocks in her peripheral vision to the left and made a sharp turn toward it to provide some cover.

The pickups did the same. But there was a fatal difference between a heavy SUV and a small pickup with men and a machine gun in the bed. The Escalade had a much lower center of gravity.

The front tire of the lead pickup dug into the sand during the tight turn and caused the top-heavy truck to flip over. It burst into flames, incinerating all of its occupants.

Before she could get to the rocks, the back window shattered, spraying Cyndi with shards of glass. She slid down in her seat, tilted the rearview mirror down, and looked back. It would take a much bigger gap to be out of range of the machine guns, but the Escalade was slowly outrunning the old pickup trucks. The distance between Cyndi and her pursuers continued to widen. The prospect of getting out of this mess alive looked achievable.

Cyndi let out a celebratory yell and pumped her fist into the air.

Murphy's law intervened and ruined her premature celebration. Warning lights on the dashboard began to flash. The engine temperature was pegged. The bullet from El Jefe's gun that had shattered the grill had also pierced the radiator.

"No, no, no!" Cyndi screamed, pounding on the steering wheel.

Steam gushed out from under the hood, mixing with dust and coating the windshield with a tan-colored muck, making it difficult to see. Running the windshield wipers only made it worse. The engine finally surrendered and seized up. The SUV came to a skidding stop.

Cyndi jumped out and raced across the desert toward the formation of rocks. A burst of bullets stitched a line across the sand, two feet in front of her. Cyndi knew the next bursts from the machine guns would cut her in half.

She surrendered, kneeling in the sand with her hands clasped behind her head.

The Descendientes del Diablo goons came rushing up to Cyndi, certain their efforts at bringing in the wanted woman would be amply rewarded by El Diablo.

A black hood was forced over Cyndi's head and cinched tightly around her neck, causing her to gasp for air. The men bound her hands and feet then tossed her into the bed of a pickup.

Despite her desperate situation, Cyndi was determined to use all of her senses to supply clues as to where she was and what was happening. After the truck came to a stop, she estimated the bumpy ride had lasted approximately thirty minutes in a direction that obviously wouldn't have been north.

Cyndi was dragged from the pickup bed by two strong men. She was led forward for a few yards than yanked to a stop.

What sounded like barn doors sliding open was followed by a violent shove, sending Cyndi sprawling down onto a hard, cold surface. Concrete, she assumed. The two men each grabbed an arm and yanked her off the floor. They stood her up and shoved her back against a post.

Cyndi heard more men joining the party. The ropes were cut off. Each of her arms and legs were restrained by a separate man, completely immobilizing her. While painful, their use of that many men had provided a valuable clue. Her reputation preceded her. They were fearful of what she could do to them if given the opportunity for a fair fight.

Cyndi's arms were wrenched behind her, and her wrists bound together by a pair of flex cuffs. The cuffs were cinched up even tighter than the rope. The plastic dug into her flesh, sending jolts of pain up her wrists, through her forearms, and up into her shoulders.

"If you harm one hair on my head, the United States will rain a level of hell down on your gang like you couldn't dream of in your worst nightmare," Cyndi yelled from under the hood with as much bravado as she could muster.

The men laughed like a pack of hyenas at her hollow threat.

One of the thugs decided it was necessary to thoroughly frisk her body for weapons. Considering his appalling choice of careers, it wasn't hard to fathom that his track record with females was abysmal. Without being paid for her time, no woman in Mexico would have ever given the remorseless thug the time of day. Now he had a gorgeous woman in front of him, bound tightly to a post. He wasn't about to waste this rare opportunity.

His meaty hands encircled her neck, squeezing slightly as part of his sick game. Then his hands slowly slid down to her chest. He unzipped her flight suit down to her navel, exposing a lacey pink bra. He began slowly groping Cyndi's firm breasts. The others hooted and jeered like drunks at a strip bar. After he'd gotten his fill of her breasts, his hands slid deliberately down her flat stomach.

Unexpectedly, the man stopped. Her flight suit zipper was hurriedly pulled up. She could sense the group of men backing away.

Someone new had entered the barn.

The sound of heavy footsteps across the concrete floor grew louder as the person approached Cyndi. He was so close that his foul breath penetrated her hood as he stood face to face with her. She felt the man circle behind her. Cyndi tensed up, certain something very painful was about to happen. Suddenly, the hood was ripped off her head.

Cyndi squinted, trying to adjust to the bright light. Once her eyes had adjusted, Cyndi surveyed her surroundings.

She was standing in an immaculate, luxurious barn. The spotless floor was made from smooth concrete and was painted white. A logo made from three capital letter Ds arranged in a triangle, with a viper weaving its way through the letters, was plastered on practically every surface.

Cyndi looked down between her feet then up at the ceiling. She was bound to a massive timber post that extended up to the roof. Horse stalls lined both walls. Champion thoroughbred racehorses occupied the stalls on the left side, while purebred white Arabians occupied the right. The aromatic scent of fresh pinewood shavings that covered the stall floors wafted throughout the space.

The enormous barn was air-conditioned. It felt like she was standing in a refrigerator compared to the broiling Sonoran Desert. Brahms's *Piano Concerto No. 1* played delicately in the background as a disturbingly refined counterpoint to the barbaric abuse she was about to endure.

Most Mexicans live in worse conditions than these pampered horses, Cyndi thought.

Two men were tied to separate posts, one on each side of Cyndi. It was obvious they had been savagely tortured. Before Cyndi looked away from the gruesome sight, she noticed something odd. Although dressed in grubby, cheap clothes, each man wore expensive alligator cowboy boots with sterling silver tips. Cyndi had no way of knowing, but the boots were the signature footwear of the ruthless Omega cartel.

Assuming she was next to be tortured, Cyndi began to tremble. Then just as suddenly, her trembling stopped. Feeling sorry for herself was a luxury Cyndi couldn't afford. Every fiber of her being had to focus on getting out of this—whatever the hell this was—alive. Save the emotions for after the homecoming back at Luke. Cyndi paused in mid-thought. *That's the same strategy the Air Force has been pounding into me since day one of pilot training. And it's certainly the ethos of every fighter pilot I've ever met. Focus only on one thing. Prevail over whatever is thrown your way—surface-to-air missiles, swarms of enemy fighters, mechanical failures—then get your jet safely back on the runway. After that, whatever it takes to fly and fight again the next day is fair game. Get drunk. Start a fight in a bar. Pray. Lock yourself in a room alone. Whatever works for you.*

The man behind Cyndi came around and stood inches from her face. When she saw him, her eyes widened. Cyndi's heart began to beat like a base drum. "Well, this crappy day just got a whole lot worse," she mumbled.

Barbosa, the bodyguard from the alley, stood inches from her face. "Puta, I'm going to fuck you up," he growled. His sadistic grin exposed a mouthful of crooked and stained teeth. His breath smelled like the alley where Cyndi had last seen him.

Not willing to give the thug an ounce of satisfaction, Cyndi stared him down—and smirked.

He reared back and delivered a crushing uppercut to her left side.

Flash bulbs of white light popped off behind Cyndi's closed eyelids as she doubled over. The punch, delivered to her already bruised ribs, felt like a horse had just kicked her. Cyndi coughed violently, trying to regain her breath. She spat the fluid that had forced itself into her mouth onto the floor. It was tinged with blood.

Satisfied, for now, Barbosa spun around and hobbled out the door.

Her surroundings turned foggy. The banter of the guards grew distant and indecipherable. Cyndi's head dropped, and she passed out.

CHAPTER 44

JESUS GALINDO-DIAZ, A.K.A. El Diablo, oversaw his criminal empire from a throne-like chair behind a massive carved walnut desk situated in the middle of his opulent office. He'd gained control of northern Mexico when this ultraviolent upstart had assassinated all the leaders of the much larger criminal organization that had a stranglehold on the area for years. El Diablo's rise was fast and ruthless. The DDD had aggressively expanded ever since.

Illicit areas the cartel focused on had one similar theme—exploiting the most ingrained human vices. Lust was the obvious driver behind the cartel's expansion into sex trafficking. Their money laundering, counterfeiting operation, and takeover of every casino in Sonora were all thriving due to insatiable greed.

It was like some demented fallen angel was dictating their business strategy.

As the sun was setting, one of Diablo's lieutenants, dressed like a hedge fund CEO, nervously entered the office. He was a thin, bookish man wearing half glasses perched on his pointed nose. "I'm here to deliver a progress report on the cartel's business dealings."

Diaz glared at him and waved the man in. "I've been patiently waiting for you, Mateo." He was sipping Old Rip Van Winkle bourbon from a crystal tumbler while he polished one of his prized pistols.

No one had ever accused the drug lord of being subtle.

A Brazilian model was draped across the settee, high on his personal stash of cocaine. Diaz waved the barrel of his gun to signal it was time for her to leave. She manufactured a well-rehearsed pout and trundled out of the room.

"You're here to tell me my operations are doing much better this month. Am I correct, amigo?"

"Si, El Diablo. The dip in last month's take was an unforeseeable anomaly. I have good news. We are ahead of projections this month." Mateo tried to project calm, but he was visibly shaking.

Diablo put down the polishing cloth, pointed the pistol at the man, and sighted down its barrel. "The drop last month—that wouldn't happen to be from you stealing from me, would it?"

"No, Diablo! I would never do such a thing!" The color drained from his lieutenant's face. "The workers at the mine went on strike for a week. The men, they missed a paycheck. That is why. I would never steal from you!"

Diablo closed one eye and straightened the arm holding the pistol.

"I swear it, Diablo!"

He pulled the trigger.

A loud click echoed in the room as the hammer slammed against the empty chamber. A dark, damp patch stained the man's crotch.

"And the union leader who authorized the strike?" Diablo inquired.

"He will be dealt with severely," Mateo said on wobbly knees.

"Not severely. Permanently," Diablo ordered.

"Si, Diablo. I will handle it myself." His eyes searched the floor, unsure about how to proceed.

Diaz got up from his desk and approached the man. "What is it, Mateo?"

Mateo shied away from his mercurial boss.

"You know you can speak freely."

"I…I have an idea on how we can make up last month's shortfall," Mateo said, head bowed down.

"I'm listening."

"We now have a very valuable asset in our possession. One that her country would pay any amount to get back. I could use our back channels in the government to demand a $100 million ransom from the United States."

Diaz's face flushed with anger. "Who do you think I am, just some common criminal trying to make a fast buck!"

The damp spot on his crotch expanded. "Of course not, Diablo. I only thought—"

"Our corrupt and inept government knows that I am impervious to its power! America must now learn that same lesson. They will get their pilot back at a time of my choosing. In a body bag!"

"But Diablo, America is not like our country. If you do this, they will go to war with you."

Diaz stood face to face with his lieutenant. Mateo swallowed hard and looked down in submission. Diaz slapped him, sending Mateo's glasses careening across the plush carpet. "Don't ever question my decisions again."

"Yes, El Diablo."

———◆———

The Federal Ministerial Police, the Mexican equivalent of the FBI, had no intention of losing the long-running fight with the DDD. They'd enlisted the Mexican Army and Air Force to supply the muscle this time. Their divisions based in northern Mexico were armed to the teeth with helicopters, armored personnel carriers, and .50-caliber machine guns mounted on the roofs of Humvees.

After sunset, the formidable force quietly converged a few miles from the DDD cartel's palatial compound near San Francisquito, in the Sonoran Desert.

A massive Tuscan-style villa was situated in the center of the sprawling, highly secure compound. Tall, thin Italian cypress trees lined both sides of the long cobblestone driveway leading to the villa. Behind the main house was an azure infinity-edge pool, a putting green, and a helipad. On it sat a pristine $13-million Sikorsky S-76 helicopter.

A large stable and some smaller outbuildings dotted the grounds. Lush, verdant grass covered the property, in stark contrast to the dusty desert terrain outside the high walls. The cartel had illegally diverted water from the fragile Sonoran aquifer system and didn't care who knew about it.

Out of the darkness, an overwhelming force swooped in. Armored personnel carriers obliterated the ornate wrought iron front gate as they smashed through it. To prevent Diaz from escaping, a UH-60M launched a salvo of rockets at his private helicopter. Its fuel tank exploded in a scorching blaze of orange.

Knowing they were badly outgunned, the mercenary goons who were paid to provide security put up very little resistance. They had no choice but to cordially invite the conquering forces to take a look around.

Two dozen heavily armed men stormed the villa. The front door was unlocked, but a message needed to be sent. A battering ram splintered the custom teak door. They yelled commands for the staff they encountered to get on the floor or be shot.

"Where is Diablo's office!" the commanding officer yelled, jamming the barrel of his Beretta into the skull of one of the staff.

The terrified man pointed to his right.

The team split up on either side of the door, weapons at the ready. The commander silently counted down with his fingers from three. The double doors to Diaz's office burst open. The men swarmed in, ready to slaughter.

Behind the desk, the back of the ornate chair was facing the men. Its occupant was closely watching the battle from a massive window that looked out over the estate.

The commander swiveled the chair around and immediately fired a round into the center of the man's forehead.

The gardener who'd maintained the plantings on the lush grounds tumbled to the marble floor. His muddy work shirt was splattered with his own blood.

The commander swept the contents of the desk onto the floor. He let out a primal yell as he stared down at the dead decoy. "Find that *pendejo!*"

———◆———

Diaz had been tipped off about the raid by informants riddled throughout the government and military. He used them to plant false information about his whereabouts and to get leads on what the government was up to. He wasn't at that compound, and hadn't been for days.

An hour later, video clips from security cameras on the property had been spliced together to create a highlights reel of the debacle. To show the Mexican government that the DDD cartel operated with impunity in their territory, they'd posted the video of the botched raid on their Facebook page to humiliate President Ortega.

To add insult to injury, the cartel would later bill the Mexican government for the damage to the property, including the destroyed helicopter.

CHAPTER 45

Wednesday, 0700 hours.

CYNDI REGAINED CONSCIOUSNESS the next morning with her left side throbbing in pain. She assumed a few ribs were either badly bruised or broken. Her mouth felt parched. Her lips were dry, cracked, and sunburned. It had been over a day since she'd had any fluids.

Cyndi tried to focus on her surroundings to gauge her danger level. No cartel thugs were visible. The air conditioning in the barn had been turned off. Oddly, Brahms still played in the background.

The zipper on Cyndi's flight suit had been pulled down to her navel. Grimy smudges on her bra and torso confirmed that the dirtbags hadn't let her hours of unconsciousness go to waste.

She turned and noticed that only one of the rival gang members was still tied to a timber post.

Cyndi would find out later that the other member of the rival gang had been hung upside down from a bridge in town. With his torso slit open, the man's entrails dangled outside of his body. Swarms of birds had landed on the man and feasted on his exposed entrails—while he was still alive.

As the day wore on without any contact with the enemy, Cyndi drew strength from the times she'd survived life-threatening situations in the past. Using only sheer willpower and clever ploys, she and Lance had survived a heavily armed team of rogue Delta Force mercenaries sent to exterminate them in their launch control center back when they were ICBM missileers. She wasn't about to let a gang of drug-peddling punks have the final say on whether she lived or died today.

Later that afternoon, at the smaller DDD ranch compound twelve miles south of San Francisquito, where Cyndi was really being held, there was a commotion outside the door. A group of people was approaching.

The sliding barn doors parted.

El Diablo strode in. Dressed in a tailored suit, he looked like he'd just stepped out of a fashion shoot.

The warm temperature in the barn suddenly seemed to spike.

His heavily armed protective detail spread out inside the barn.

"We meet again," Diaz said assertively, as if greeting a rival at a business meeting.

His guards ogled Cyndi while making perverted jokes about her in Spanish.

"Amigos, that is no way to treat our guest. A little respect, *por favor*," Diaz chided them. He pointed at Cyndi's exposed torso. "And what is this?" The drug lord acted offended that someone had unzipped her flight suit. Diaz grabbed the zipper tab then stopped. He gazed lustfully at her athletic, sexy body, licking his lips. He looked Cyndi in the eyes and shrugged. "Not that I can blame them. Boys will be boys." He slowly zipped up her flight suit. "*Eso es mucho mejor.*"

"I don't speak Spanish," Cyndi said with contempt.

"How rude of me. What kind of host would I be if I made my guests feel uncomfortable by speaking a language they didn't know? You might get the impression that we were talking about you right in front of your face."

The guards hooted on cue.

Diaz swept his hand across the scene. "Amigos, as a courtesy to our guest, we shall speak English in her presence."

"Thanks for your *hospitality*, but amigo is a Spanish word, Jackass." Cyndi was trying her best to appear unafraid of this dangerous animal dressed in an expensive suit. "Jackass is an English word, by the way."

Diaz just smiled, displaying no anger at her insult. He slipped off his suit jacket, folded it neatly, and handed it to a guard. Diaz put his hand under her chin and lifted Cyndi's head. "It's hotter than…Well, you know the rest. How long has it been since you had a drink?"

Cyndi jerked her head away from his hand.

"Get her some water."

A guard ran into the tack room and grabbed a bottle of water from the refrigerator. He uncapped it and held it up to Cyndi's parched lips. At first, she refused to drink. Then her survival instincts overpowered her stubbornness. Cyndi gulped down as much of the cool, refreshing water as she could. Water that didn't make it into her mouth dribbled down the front of her flight suit. In ten seconds, the bottle was empty.

Skeptical of the kindness she was being shown, Cyndi harbored no illusions about the extreme danger she was in. The next person to enter the barn confirmed that.

Barbosa hobbled into the barn on crutches and planted his massive frame right next to Cyndi. His devious smirk foretold that her luck was about to change.

"I believe you've met my personal bodyguard?" Diaz asked Cyndi.

Cyndi's eyes narrowed. She examined his face for a moment then said, "Yes, I remember now. You're the punk I sent to the hospital."

Barbosa raised his crutch to strike Cyndi.

"Not yet, Barbosa," Diaz commanded. "Your time will come."

The bodyguard lowered his crutch and glared at Cyndi.

Diaz clasped his hands behind his back and began to pace. "I'm a businessman in a very dangerous line of work, Cyndi. My customers count on me to deliver what they want. Despite what you might think of what I do, in my world we live by a set of rules. The most important rule is that nobody embarrasses me and lives. You threatened me in front of my American mistress. You pointed a *gun* at me!" Diaz snapped his fingers at his bodyguard. Barbosa pulled out a huge silver revolver and handed it to Diaz. "A gun just like this." Diaz cocked the hammer and aimed it at Cyndi's temple. "Like I said, nobody embarrasses me and lives. It's bad for business. Say goodbye to this life. I'll see you in hell."

"See you in hell, puta," Barbosa snarled.

Diaz swung the barrel of the miniature cannon a foot to the left and fired. Barbosa's head exploded as the high-powered round passed through his skull and embedded itself in the timber post behind the dead man. He collapsed to the concrete with a thud.

Until Barbosa's heart had gotten the memo that his brain was no longer sending it signals, blood spurted out of his severed arteries for a few seconds, pooling around the dead man.

A stern lesson in the consequences of failure had been unequivocally delivered to Diablo's men.

As if nothing important had just happened, Diaz went back to explaining his motivations for preying on the weak. "Temptation, desire, and greed are not my fault. They've been around as long as mankind has roamed the earth. Every person chooses their path in life. It's called free will. I'm just giving the public what it wants. No different than a travel agent or a used car salesman. I provide a service."

Cyndi had reached her limit. If she was going down, she was going down swinging. "Nice speech, genius. If you were hoping to come across as a legitimate business-man, you blew it. You just paraphrased Al Capone, one of the most ruthless criminals Chicago ever had. I saw what you and your men do to defenseless migrants. To young girls. To your mistress."

Diaz scoffed and waved her comments away. "Don't act so high and mighty. The majority of my customers come from *your* country. Without Americans eager to sample my products, I'd be out of business." He walked over and stood in front of the semiconscious rival gang member. Diaz nodded to a guard. The guard grabbed his chin and held the prisoners head up, facing Diaz. The drug lord bent forward until he was face to face with the prisoner. "A business that you and your Omega filth have been stealing from me."

What was about to happen next was so commonplace in the world of drug cartels that Diaz's henchmen had already placed the tools of the trade next to him. An electric branding iron with the letters DDD on it was glowing red. Next to it was a 24-volt, 400-amp marine battery. Judging from the badly frayed and blood-stained jumper cables attached to it, this method of torture had been regularly used in the past.

Diaz picked up the branding iron and pressed it into the prisoner's bare chest. A bloodcurdling scream escaped from his mouth. The putrid smell of burning flesh filled the barn.

Diaz smirked, having delivered another indisputable message. This one to his rival. He stepped away and let his hand-picked torturer take over. "Finish him off, *Torque-mada.*"

Cyndi recognized the man's nickname. Torquemada had been a Castilian Dominican friar and first Grand Inquisitor of the Tribunal of the Holy Office, and was still known in this modern age for being extremely devoted to his job.

The short, slightly built man was in his late sixties. His shoulders were hunched, his thinning gray hair combed over his blotchy scalp.

The old man picked up the two jumper cable clamps and circled his victim, intentionally ramping up his anxiety before applying the actual jolts.

Cyndi knew firsthand how terrible it felt to be shocked. When she was in elementary school, she inexplicably had thought it would be a good idea to insert the tip of a kitchen knife into a wall socket. To this day, Cyndi still remembered the unbridled intensity of the electricity coursing through her body and the burns it left on her fingertips. Fortunately for her, the shock only lasted one-tenth of a second. The outlet had tripped off almost instantaneously. The grounding she received from her father for that foolish stunt lasted considerably longer, but was infinitely less painful.

Torquemada tapped the metal clamps together, generating a shower of sparks. A demented smile crossed his ugly face. He pressed the ends of the jumper cable clamps into the prisoner's abdomen.

The man howled in agony.

Torquemada pressed harder.

Every muscle in the man's body convulsed uncontrollably. His bowels emptied. His anguished screams intensified.

"Stop!" Diaz grabbed Torquemada's arms and pulled him away from the prisoner. "This isn't right. Witnessing such a thing is bound to be traumatizing."

Cyndi was taken by surprise at his compassion.

Diaz turned and snapped his fingers at his men. "Let the horses out in the exercise pen behind the barn. I don't want them to see what is about to happen. They're very sensitive."

That wasn't the sort of compassion Cyndi had in mind.

Once the coddled horses had been led away, Diaz said, "Continue. I want this to take hours."

The old man gleefully resumed torturing the bound prisoner.

In Spanish, the rival cartel member pleaded for God to help him after every excruciating jolt.

Diablo mocked his calls for divine intervention, which never came. "Amigo, he has more important things to do than save trash like you."

The pristine barn had been transformed into a house of horrors, a medieval dungeon.

The horrific cruelty that flowed so effortlessly from the grinning torturer was Cyndi's first face-to-face encounter with unadulterated evil. The punks, thugs, and drunks she'd dispatched over the years were bad news. But nothing compared with what she was witnessing only a few feet away.

Unable to clasp her hands over her ears to block out the tortured screams of the helpless cartel rival, Cyndi tried to mentally block out the sounds. Nothing she tried worked. The putrid smell of burned flesh assaulted Cyndi's nostrils. Tears flooded down her face as she tightly closed her eyes.

Yes, the man next to her was a heartless killer and a member of a gang of heartless killers. Yes, they'd poisoned the minds and bodies of millions of people. But even he didn't deserve such barbaric treatment.

Even after the man's screams had ceased and his head slumped down until his chin rested on his chest, the electric shocks continued. His heart and brain had given up long ago, but his muscles still twitched with each intense jolt of electric current.

Oddly, the revulsion she was feeling was suddenly replaced with profound admiration for the countless soldiers throughout history who'd looked evil in the eye yet bravely charged toward it anyway, no matter the personal cost. A renewed wave of fortitude washed over Cyndi. *No matter the price I have to pay, there's no way in hell this bastard is going to break me.*

Diaz had to pull Torquemada away from his victim's lifeless corpse. "Give me the clamps," he ordered. The old man reluctantly handed them to Diaz. He walked over in front of Cyndi, dragging the bloody, badly frayed cables.

"Now you will pay for your sins," Diaz said, touching the clamps together in a shower of sparks.

CHAPTER 46

CYNDI'S MUSCLES STRAINED as she recoiled from the smoking jumper cable clamps. Her mouth went dry. Her heartbeat began to pound in her ears. The thought of having every muscle in her body violently convulse when the clamps touched her skin caused the bile churning in her stomach to boil upward into her esophagus. Cyndi struggled to keep from showing any weakness or fear but failed. She dropped her head and involuntarily vomited.

Diaz pulled out a handkerchief. He grabbed Cyndi by the hair, yanked her head back, and wiped her mouth.

Cyndi jerked her face away. "Don't touch me."

"It's okay. Don't be embarrassed, gringa," he said. "Everyone has their limits. I've seen men do the same thing after torture so gruesome you couldn't imagine it in your worst nightmare. Trust me, those men were a lot tougher than pampered bitches like you."

Diaz was a deft student of human nature. He was exploiting the fact that the fear of imminent pain could be much worse than the torture itself.

Diaz glanced down at the $5-million Bao Dai Rolex watch on his wrist. "I apologize, I didn't realize it was so late. I loathe watching my enemies die on an empty stomach. Ruins my appetite. I'll be back soon. Then you will learn what excruciating pain feels like."

"Having to listen to your blather is torture enough."

"That's a very bold thing to say, considering that you

will die a very gruesome death soon." Diaz pulled up a stool and sat in front of Cyndi. "But considering your background, I'm not surprised. A member of the US Olympic tae kwon do team. Studied krav maga in Israel. Youngest Minuteman ICBM crew commander ever. Your father must be very proud of you."

Cyndi cast a suspicious glance at Diaz. "Seems like you've done your homework."

"You'd be surprised what—and who—money can buy."

"So you know that my—"

"Father is dead, yes. Cancer. Four years ago."

"Impressive. I underestimated you, Mr. Diablo. Here I thought you were just another cowardly thug who preys on the weak."

Diaz took great offense at her insult but reigned in his temper.

"I provide a service; that's all."

"A service? So you're like a travel agent."

"Now you're catching on."

"Except in your case, instead of Maui or Paris, you book them a ticket straight to hell."

Diaz shrugged. "What can I say, it was either this or become a lawyer. But enough about me. Let's get back to you. Your brother, Stevie, must be very proud of his little sister and everything you've achieved. It's a shame he hasn't figured out yet what he wants to do with his life. Thirty-two years old and still living with your mother in California. Santa Monica if I remember correctly."

"You bastard!" Cyndi shouted. "You lay a hand on either one of them, I'll—"

"Then there's Lance, your fiancé. Well done, Cyndi. Handsome, charming, comes from a rich family. If his engine hadn't developed a problem on the runway, you wouldn't be my guest this evening, would you? Of all the rotten luck."

Cyndi wrestled against her restraints, her hands clenched into fists. "Cut these cuffs off me, and I'll show you rotten luck."

"Defiance under extreme duress. Now I'm the one who's impressed." Diaz directed his venomous gaze at Cyndi. "You must have learned that resistance technique at SERE school. It can't be easy acting so tough knowing who I am and what is about to happen to you. Most people would have soiled themselves after what you just witnessed. But I'm not buying your act. I can see deep down into your soul. Whether you show it or not, you are terrified."

"You don't know me."

"Oh, but I do, gringa. That look in your eyes—there's something more there than just hatred toward me. No, it's…personal. Something happened in your past, didn't it?" Diablo stood up and paced in front of Cyndi for a few moments, tapping his lips with his finger. "You've been hiding a secret. Something that could destroy the perfect life you've built." He stopped. Diablo's black snake-like eyes zeroed in on Cyndi. "Drugs. You were addicted."

Cyndi looked away. "You don't know what you're talking about."

"I'm guessing you'd gotten injured during a match. The only thing that would deaden the pain was—"

"Opioids." Cyndi's head drooped.

Diaz took a seat on the stool in front of Cyndi and waited.

"After my opponent tore up my shoulder with an armbar, my doctor would only prescribe pain pills for a week before he cut me off. I couldn't sleep. I didn't eat. I had to do something. This lowlife at my high school in LA hooked me up with oxycodone pills from a local gang. It took me six months to kick the habit." She glared at Diablo. "I lost my ranking because of scum just like you!" Cyndi screamed.

Diablo steepled his fingers in front of his mouth. "No, the anger wasn't about your ranking," he calmly replied. "It was about losing control. Not having control is the one thing you can't handle. It shook you to your very core."

"That was years ago. I look at things differently now. You might control everything in this barn, but you can't control how I think or how I feel. Only I can."

"Nice speech, but I don't believe you. Right now, all you want to do is close your eyes, scream, and wake up from this nightmare." Diablo got up and opened barn doors. The sun was sinking below the horizon. He turned back and laid those dead eyes on her. "I'll be back in one hour."

CHAPTER 47

BEFORE HE LEFT, Diaz pointed at one of his henchmen. "Watch her until I get back."

"Yes, Diablo," the man said, quivering in fear.

Diaz and his protective detail left the barn, sliding the doors closed.

The man guarding Cyndi stood in front of her and looked her up and down. A smirk crossed his face as he leered at Cyndi. As he reached out for her breasts, the man remembered Diablo's warning. He pulled his hands back, not foolish enough to risk his boss's ire.

Thirty minutes later another cartel lacky, this one wearing a grungy straw cowboy hat and sporting a bushy beard, walked into the stable with a plate piled with food and a cold bottle of Corona Extra. He handed the guard the platter. "Eat, amigo. I watch her."

The hungry guard didn't bother to thank him. He plopped his considerable backside down on a hay bale, resting his AK-47 against it. He grabbed the plate and the beer and dove in like swine at the trough.

The bearded man wandered over to Cyndi. He nodded, admiring her alluring figure. "*Muy* sexy, chica."

The guard took a swig then looked over at Cyndi. "Sí, muy sexy. I have her next." Like a cow chewing cud, morsels of food fell from the guard's mouth as he hooted about his after-dinner plans. With more important priorities at that moment, he returned to his meal.

With nothing better to do, the newcomer strolled

around the barn, surveying the layout. He eventually ended up behind the guard.

The man reached down and slid a Ka-Bar tactical knife out of a sheath hidden in his boot.

With the silence, precision, and violence of a highly skilled assassin, the man cupped his hand over the guard's mouth then plunged the stainless-steel blade into the base of the guard's neck. His brainstem was instantly severed. The guard dropped the plate, slumped to the floor, and quickly bled out on the pristine white floor.

The killer wiped the blade on the dead guard's sleeve then moved toward Cyndi, brandishing the weapon. He went behind her and cupped his hand over her mouth, exposing her throat.

Cyndi flailed and screamed, but no one outside the barn could hear her.

CHAPTER 48

THE BLADE EASILY sliced through her plastic flex cuffs, but the man kept his hand over Cyndi's mouth. "Shhh," he whispered. "Not a sound."

Something about his voice triggered a recent memory. She nodded, indicating she would oblige.

The man circled in front of Cyndi and slowly removed his hand. She peered into his fierce brown eyes. They were the eyes of a killer. She tilted her head and looked closer. But not the eyes of a murderer.

A fine distinction, but a crucial one at this critical juncture.

Cyndi reached out and removed his cowboy hat. Her eyes widened. "Armando?"

He clamped his hand back over her mouth and held one finger up to his lips. "We don't have much time before Diablo returns. Let's go." He grabbed the guard's AK-47 and ammo belt and handed them to Cyndi. She pulled out the magazine, verified the number of rounds, then slapped it back in place.

Armando cracked the barn door open a few inches then listened. Satisfied they were alone, he retrieved his backpack, pulled out a suppressed Glock 19, and tucked it into his waistband.

He opened the door wider and turned to Cyndi. "Help me."

The pair dragged a lifeless corpse of the unlucky thug

who'd been assigned to bring the guard his meal into the barn.

After locking the barn door, Armando pointed and said, "In there."

They left the body and crept into the tack room, turning off the lights.

Cyndi was dumbfounded. "What the hell are you doing here? I thought you were in Del Rio."

He gave a nonchalant shrug. "I heard you were here, so I thought I'd stop by and say hello. Just in time, it appears."

"Wait, hold on." Cyndi shook her head and held up both hands. "What do you mean, you heard I was here?"

"I've got some connections in this region that go way back." Armando slid over to the window and rose up to take a quick peek. "Turns out the locals don't care much for El Diablo. I put out some feelers after you went missing, and bingo, your name came up." He ducked down and returned to Cyndi, grabbing a bridle off a rack on the wall. "More of his men just arrived at the main house. We need to go. Now."

They silently slipped out the back of the barn into the pen. The high-strung Arabians immediately scattered so Armando cornered a thoroughbred for their getaway.

"Mount up," he told Cyndi, thumbing at the horse.

"But there's no saddle," she shot back, trepidation coloring her voice.

"Not a problem. We couldn't afford a saddle when I was a kid, so I learned to ride bareback." He cupped his hands together and waited for Cyndi to step in for a boost onto the thoroughbred's back.

Cyndi lifted her left foot, hesitated, then put it down. "Wait. I need to set the other horses free."

"That's very kind of you, but we don't have time for that," Armando adamantly whispered.

"I'm not doing it out of kindness. Diablo has people

everywhere. We need to increase our chances of reaching the border. Each horse will serve as a decoy, thinning out his resources."

Armando nodded and smiled. "Make it quick."

"You got it." Cyndi flung the gate open, approached the horses, and flicked her hands outward toward them. "Shoo," she whispered. The horses stared at Cyndi like she was speaking a foreign language. "Go, you stupid horses. You're free. Move toward the gate," she ordered.

Armando couldn't help but chuckle as he slipped the bridle into their horse's mouth and over its ears, cinching it up tight. He mounted the horse, trotted over to the small herd of overpriced equine, and slapped one of them on the rump with the end of the reins. "Vámanos! Vámanos!"

The horses shot out of the open gate and scattered into the night.

Armando laughed as he reached down and gave Cyndi a hand. "City kids."

———————

The highly trained assassin skillfully navigated the prickly obstacles in the desert as the lights from the compound faded away. The farther they traveled, the murkier his view of the arid wasteland became. To safely traverse the rough terrain Armando had no choice but to bring the horse to a slow trot.

"At this speed, it will be daylight before we reach the border," Armando grumbled, clenching his jaw. "Hand me my NODs."

Cyndi had a million questions about how Armando had magically appeared to rescue her but knew he needed to focus all his attention on guiding the horse. She unzipped his backpack and fished a night observation device out, handing it to Armando over his shoulder. He slipped it on and powered it up.

The desert took on a ghostly green glow. Armando spurred the horse with the heels of his boots. It reacted and sped up to a gallop.

The warm temperature and heavy load had caused the animal's coat to become bathed in sweat. Cyndi wrapped her arms around Armando's waist and held on for dear life.

An hour later, without warning, the horse violently shied to the left, throwing Armando and Cyndi off its slick back. What had spooked the animal became immediately clear. The horse had stepped on a slumbering mountain lion.

Injured and enraged, the large cat bared its razor-sharp fangs and pounced on Cyndi.

CHAPTER 49

THE JAWS OF the mountain lion clamped down on Cyndi's forearm, then just as quickly went slack. The beast, with half of its skull missing, rolled off Cyndi with a helpful push from Armando. He tucked the smoking Glock into his waistband and offered Cyndi a hand. "We need to keep moving."

She got up and dusted herself off, too stunned to speak.

When they approached their horse, they found it lying prone on the sand. Foam was frothing from its mouth. Its breathing was labored and shallow.

"Is he going to be okay?" Cyndi asked, biting her lower lip.

Armando examined the thoroughbred and said, "Don't worry; he'll be fine. We just need to give the poor thing a little time to recover from the scare. I'll stay with him. Why don't you go find the backpack and my NODs."

Cyndi smiled and nodded. "Okay, I'm on it." She turned and squinted, searching the sand for their equipment.

Moments later, Cyndi heard the unmistakable sound of two suppressed rounds being discharged from Armando's Glock.

Knowing that the majestic animal would lay in agony for hours with a broken leg before being eaten alive by mountain lions was more than he could stomach. Armando had done the only humane thing possible in this situation.

Cyndi knew he was right but refused to look back.

Without saying a word, Armando rejoined Cyndi to search for his equipment.

"Let's hope there aren't any other mountain lions out here. We won't be able to see them," Cyndi stated. After twenty minutes of searching, she stumbled upon the backpack and the NODs. She shook her head as she held up the mangled night observation device. "So much for these." Cyndi tossed them into the darkness.

"When the cool toys break, fall back on the things that always work." Armando examined the heavens until he found what he was looking for. "There's the North Star," he said, pointing. "Looks like we're walking the rest of the way."

They didn't dare use a flashlight to illuminate a safe path for fear of giving away their location. As they inched along toward the border, the pair struck up a conversation.

"Last time I saw you, you were teaching martial arts to women at your studio in Texas," Cyndi said. "I'm going to go out on a limb here. Teaching amateurs how to kick a guy in the crotch wasn't your real job. Your studio was a front for more clandestine jobs."

Armando shook his head. "Sorry, I can neither confirm nor deny your astute observation, Captain Stafford."

"Understood," she replied—meaning it quite literally. "Why Del Rio?"

"The Middle East isn't the only place we fight wars. Years ago, some gentlemen, who will remain nameless, enlisted the support of a few key politicians to put an end to the threats coming from our own backyard. I liked the idea, so I volunteered. I decided to contribute my unique experience to the cause and moved back closer to home in Del Rio."

"You grew up in this area?"

"Not far."

"What happened? How did you end up working for whatever three-letter agency you're with?"

"When I was a young man, the scumbag before the scumbag before Diablo screwed over my father. My family was driven off our own land. When it happened, not one neighbor or friend would come to his aide. We were destitute, but my father was far too proud to beg for handouts—or worse, join the cartel like the others. Times were different back then. Very old school. He did the only honorable thing a proud Latino man could do. My father showed up at the compound with a pistol, hell-bent on revenge."

A melancholy look washed over Armando's face. "After he was…After that, I became the man of the family. I dropped out of university and came back home. Got a job in the mines and helped my mom raise my siblings. I learned a tough lesson. Some bloke said it best: 'The only thing necessary for evil to triumph in the world is that good men do nothing.' So, I did something. You can probably figure out the rest."

Before Cyndi could respond, what sounded like an angry hive of bees approaching startled the pair.

"A drone!" Cyndi raised her AK and searched for the miniature aircraft.

Armando slapped down the barrel. "Don't shoot. They'll hear it. We need to take cover."

A Chinese DJI Mavic 3 drone outfitted with an IR camera soon hovered overhead. Armando and Cyndi ducked behind a large boulder, hoping the heat signature from the rock would match their body temperatures. The whirring drone slowly circled the boulder. Its camera tracked back and forth, slowly hunting for its prey. After a few minutes, the DJI gave up and disappeared into the night.

Safe from the prying eye of the drone, Cyndi and

Armando came out of hiding. "Keep moving north," he said.

Suddenly, bullets from automatic weapons began to rain down on them. Chips flying from the boulder peppered the pair. They took cover again behind the rock.

Cyndi flicked the safety lever to full auto with her thumb, raised her AK-47, and returned fire in the direction of the muzzle flashes. The thirty-round clip was spent in seconds. While she ducked down to install a fresh clip, Cyndi shouted back over her shoulder. "Reloading! Feel free to join the party any time now!" There was no response. She pivoted toward Armando to question why he wasn't shooting. He lay motionless on the desert floor. A growing circle of crimson fluid was spreading across his chest.

"Hold on! Focus on me!" Cyndi grabbed a first aid kit from the backpack. She ripped open his shirt and pressed large squares of white gauze into the three gaping holes.

"Is it bad?" Armando asked, his face racked with pain.

"Don't worry; you'll be just fine. I promise, you won't end up like our horse."

"You're a terrible liar," he said, wincing. "Always have been." His face suddenly went ghostly white. His breathing became arduous. "And the name is Ángel, by the way. Ángel Mendoza."

Cyndi just nodded and smiled. "I figured as much."

"You knew Armando was a cover name?"

"Who do I look like, Captain Renault at Rick's place? *'I'm shocked, shocked to find that gambling is going on here!'* I might be a terrible liar, but I've been around the block once or twice." She lifted his head and slid the backpack under it.

That small kindness seemed to lessen the pain.

"So tell me, which agency do you work for?"

Ángel shrugged. "Doesn't matter. They're all the same, just different initials. They disavowed me years ago when my agency needed a scapegoat for an op gone bad. In my line of work, you know this day will come eventually. You give them everything you have, then they either hunt you down or leave you out in the desert to die, alone."

Cyndi gently touched his shoulder. "You're not alone, Ángel. You have me."

He reached up and put his hand over hers. "Gracias—" Ángel began to cough uncontrollably. Every jerking motion of his body caused the bullet wounds to gush blood. Cyndi tried to stem the bleeding by pressing the palms of her hands on the bloody gauze. He howled in pain from the pressure. After a few moments, the coughing stopped, and Ángel calmed down. A serene expression filled his weathered and rugged face. His hand went limp and flopped down to the sand.

The sounds of men shouting in Spanish drew closer.

Tears flooded Cyndi's sorrowful eyes. She made the sign of the cross then placed her fingers over his eyelids and gently closed them. "You have my word of honor. You *will* get the recognition you deserve. Gracias, my dear friend."

Cartel goons swept around both sides of the boulder and pounced on Cyndi.

CHAPTER 50

AROUND MIDNIGHT, DIABLO staggered into the barn, carrying a magnum of Dom Perignon champagne. He viciously slapped Cyndi across the face as she stood bound again to the post. "You thought you could escape! With all the resources I have at my disposal?"

The sting from the slap traveled all the way down her spine. Cyndi shook her head to regain her equilibrium then spit out crimson-colored saliva. "You didn't expect me to hang around here and meekly accept my fate, did you? If so, you seriously underestimated who you are up against."

Belligerence was the only remaining weapon at her disposal.

"As have you, gringa." Diablo took another swig then set the bottle on the stool. "I joined the local cartel just like everyone else and clawed my way out of the most violent barrio in Mexico City. Then I watched and learned. I studied the leaders weaknesses. When the time was right, I exploited them. They never saw me coming until it was too late. Now I'm the richest and most feared cartel leader in the entire country!"

"Congratulations, your parents must be very proud of you," Cyndi sneered.

Diablo didn't give a damn what his cruel, abusive stepfather thought of him. But when the SOB had turned his own mother against him, in his warped mind there was no turning back. Diablo took another shot of champagne, seeking to fill the still-gaping, festering emotional wounds of being disowned by his sainted mother.

"Never show any weakness!" he bellowed. "Your enemies will circle you like ravenous sharks. Even your own people will turn on you."

"You would know, wouldn't you."

Diablo's face flushed with anger. "You smug Americans. You think you're better than everyone else, with your money and your spoiled, pampered lives. I'm richer than all of you!"

His braggadocious hyperbole wasn't surprising given his drunken state.

But Cyndi just couldn't resist poking the bear. Considering that she wouldn't see the next sunrise, what did she have to lose?

"You're full of crap. In your line of work, everything you've built could be taken from you in a flash. At least my meager monthly salary is guaranteed by Uncle Sam."

"Like others have before they died, you underestimate me!" Diaz took another swig. "I have $1 billion stashed away in completely untraceable Bitcoin. Only I can get access to it."

"Big deal, so do I," Cyndi bragged, cleverly getting in a small win by mocking the inebriated drug lord.

"Liar!" Too drunk to realize he was being baited, Diablo pulled out his coal black cell phone. It was sheathed in a solid gold phone case that cost more than she made in three years. He opened his crypto wallet app and said his private key. "Heaven." He turned the phone around and showed Cyndi his balance.

He wasn't lying.

"I risk my life for something real. Something I can spend. You risk your life for chump change defending your corrupt country. Where is it now when you need it? Where is your cowardly president? Ashford has abandoned you. He should have moved heaven and earth to rescue you, gringa. Instead, because it served his political interests, he left you to die." Diablo yanked Cyndi's dog tags off her neck and threw them to the ground. "And still, you're willing to die for him!"

Cyndi hated to admit it, but Diablo had scored a direct hit with his criticism. "People like you will never understand," she shot back angrily. "I didn't join the military to protect a politician. I joined to protect an ideal. It's called freedom. The same ideal that's led millions of people to abandon their homeland and seek a better life in America."

Diablo was much too savvy a student of human nature to let this opportunity pass before he killed her. He peered at Cyndi and stroked his chin. "Obviously, your side doesn't care about you. With what you know about military tactics, you could be a valuable top aide in my organization. If you come work for me, I will make it very lucrative for you." He held up his iPhone. "Simply tell me the amount of money you want, and it's yours for the taking." He snapped his fingers. "A million dollars—yours."

Cyndi glared at him. "Take your blood money? Not interested."

"What was I thinking? You are obviously very special." His threatening tone of voice turned friendly and inviting. A genuine smile formed. "Yet you've probably spent your entire life being underestimated. Having to work twice as hard as the guys just to prove you're as good as they are. I'm not going to insult you with such a trivial amount as $1 million. That's a rounding error in my operation. You couldn't even buy a descent prop plane for that. A hotshot fighter pilot like yourself deserves something much more luxurious. The latest Gulfstream, perhaps. Or maybe a Global Express."

Cyndi pulled back. "Are you trying to tempt me?"

"What can I say, I'm a born salesman."

It took a moment while she debated Diablo's offer in her mind, but Cyndi finally came to her senses and spit out the words, "Don't bother; it won't work."

"Then maybe this will." Diaz turned the phone around and tapped on the virtual keyboard, entering his password. When he finished, Diaz showed Cyndi the crypto app. "All this could be yours. Completely untraceable. With one simple tap of this screen, you will have riches beyond your wildest imagination. Just say the word."

Cyndi's eyes widened. An involuntary gasp escaped through her lips. "Oh my God!"

Diablo wagged a scolding finger at Cyndi. "Careful, he has nothing to do with this."

"One hundred *million* dollars if I work for you! You can't be serious!"

"You're worth it, Cyndi. Hell, you're probably worth even more. Only time will tell. Say yes, and I will transfer the money right now to any bank you want."

Diablo tilted his head and searched Cyndi's crystal-blue eyes for any hint she was wavering.

She looked down and drew in a deep breath. The incredibly lavish lifestyle that amount of money could buy was beyond comprehension by a girl raised in a family that had to pinch every penny. And her own top-of-the-line business jet wouldn't be the worst perk for a pilot.

"What makes you think you can trust me?"

"Trust?" Diablo laughed at the very utterance of the word. "I trust no one. But that doesn't mean I can't use you to my advantage."

A look of understanding swashed over Cyndi's face. She slowly nodded her head up and down. "You win. Cut me loose. I'll enter my bank account information into your phone."

"I knew you were a smart woman." Diablo snapped his fingers at his henchman. The thug pulled out a pearl-handled switchblade and snapped it open. He walked behind Cyndi and grabbed one wrist. "Wait," Diablo said, raising one hand. "Once you're free, you'd be tempted to harm me or my men, like you did yesterday. Tell me your account information. Once the money is transferred, there will be no going back. The electronic accounting trail will ensure that."

She looked up and smiled. "You've thought of everything. In other words, in exchange for the money, I sell you my soul—for eternity."

"That's such a crude way to put it. When I frame joining forces with me in a more positive way, people are more likely to come around. I understand human nature and all of its flaws better than anyone. Cunning sales pitches like 'You'll finally get what you deserve,' 'All your problems will magically disappear,' and 'The world will finally admire you,' all work surprisingly well."

"You're insane."

"Am I? Look around, Cyndi. Have you watched the news lately? Ever read a history book? My side is winning. Always has, always will." Diablo flashed a smug, infuriating smile at her.

"Obviously, that's worked out well for you. But you call this living?" She nodded toward the guard. "Never knowing if one of your thugs will put a bullet in the back of your head the next time you turn around? Being relentlessly hunted like a mangy, rabid dog by your own country? I might not have everything figured out, but I know when the devil smiles at you, it's time to hide your soul. The answer is no. Go to hell."

The cartel leader slammed his phone down on the stool. He grabbed the revolver tucked into his guard's waistband. Diablo opened the cylinder and dumped the bullets into the palm of his hand.

"Hell is exactly where you're going!" he screamed in a drunken rage. He inserted one bullet in the cylinder, closed it, then gave it a spin. Diablo pressed the end of the barrel against Cyndi's temple and pulled the trigger.

She flinched at hearing the dull thud of the hammer striking an empty chamber. "Screw you!" she screamed.

Diablo pulled the trigger again.

The hammer struck another empty chamber.

"Screw you!" Cyndi yelled even louder, tears streaming down her cheeks.

Three more times, the hammer struck an empty chamber.

Three more times Cyndi remained defiant, screaming out her final words.

Five of the six chambers had now been dry fired.

Diablo's finger tightened against the trigger for the last time. Just before it reached the point of no return, he let the trigger go slack. "No. Dying this way would be much too quick. I want you to suffer. I want you to regret for eternity not joining forces with me." He snapped his fingers at the guard. "Get me the battery."

CHAPTER 51

DIABLO GRABBED THE jumper cable clamps from his guard and waved them in front of Cyndi's face. "Before I'm finished with you, you'll be begging me to fire the last round into your pathetic little brain."

In her mind, Cyndi relived the barbaric torture she had seen a day ago. She began to violently tremble, knowing what was coming.

Diablo unzipped her flight suit down to her navel. He hovered the clamps over Cyndi's taut stomach. Then he quickly tapped her skin.

Cyndi's nervous system went haywire. The pain was indescribable. "Screw you!" she cried out, her only means of fighting back.

Diablo moved the clamps toward her stomach again. Before they contacted her skin, Cyndi thought she heard an oddly familiar whining sound.

Suddenly, the lights went out.

The guard pulled out a Bic lighter and supplied a microscopic amount of illumination.

A thunderous explosion nearby caused the barn to shift on its foundation. Dust from the loosened rafters floated lazily down on them. Then another tremendous explosion rocked the building.

Diablo was knocked off his feet. "Get out there!" he screamed to his guard. "Find out what's happening!"

The guard dashed out the door, his rifle barking out rounds of ammunition.

He was immediately cut down in a hail of gunfire.

More explosions erupted around the palatial compound.

A pitched battle was raging.

Diablo grabbed the revolver and raced out the door.

Cyndi listened intently to the explosions and gunfire. Gradually, they began to die down. One side in the deadly battle appeared to be victorious. Seizing upon the fleeting opportunity, Cyndi thrashed around in the dark until she felt what she was looking for. She kicked it over.

Moments later, Diablo stumbled into the barn, bleeding and limping. He searched the dark floor for the handles of the jumper cables. When he found them, he grabbed the clamps and dragged the long cables toward Cyndi.

Diablo drew the clamps up near her beautiful face.

She closed her eyes, turned away, and screamed.

A shower of sparks lit up the darkness when he touched them together.

Twenty-four volts of electricity suddenly coursed through his rigid body.

Withering in indescribable pain, Diablo dropped the clamps and collapsed to the ground.

Three men burst through the door and fanned out in a defensive formation. Cyndi squinted to get a better look. The glow from the raging fires outside illuminated them. They were wearing quad-tube night observation devices. Like all the other cartel thugs she'd seen since being taken captive, they were armed with suppressed AK-47s. Black balaclavas concealed their identities.

The men were clad in grimy blue jeans and T-shirts and were covered in tattoos. The expensive boots they wore stood out. Each man sported alligator cowboy boots with sterling silver tips.

Things had just gone from bad to worse.

Cyndi was not only completely defenseless, but she was caught in the crossfire of a raid by the vicious Omega drug cartel seeking revenge.

CHAPTER 52

THE LEADER OF the group keyed a microphone attached to his collar and called for the power to be turned back on.

He spoke perfect English.

The barn was awash in light again. The men removed their NODs and pulled off their balaclavas.

Cyndi looked closely at the invaders. Something was off. The men had full beards and mustaches, but their skin wasn't the deep mocha color common in Central and South America. One was African American. One appeared to be Irish. They all wore earpieces. Black backpacks were slung over their shoulders.

The leader was tan, tall, and athletically built. His penetrating brown eyes were unnerving in their intensity. "Ma'am, we are the United States military. We're here to take you home. Are there any more enemy combatants in the barn?"

"No, he's the only one," Cyndi replied, nodding at the floor.

Diablo lay in a puddle of broken glass and Dom Perignon champagne. The same puddle of liquid that the frayed jumper cables and smoking battery sat in. Next to him was the toppled stool.

"Tell me your rank and full name."

She instinctively looked down at her name tag. "Captain Cynthia Karen Stafford."

He pulled out a photo taken from Cyndi's CAC card

and held it up to her face to verify it was her. On the back of the photo was a question he'd obtained from a highly classified, compartmentalized DOD website. "Ma'am, what is the one thing in this world that would break your heart?"

After all the trauma she'd endured, hearing the question she'd created during SERE school triggered an overwhelming rush of elation, relief, and love. Cyndi could feel the emotional dam inside of her about to rupture. She choked back the tears forming in her beautiful blue eyes and forced herself to hold it together.

Cyndi looked up at the man and said, "If my broken wings were rejoined. If I ever lost Lance."

At hearing Cyndi's answer, the battle-hardened killer swallowed hard before responding to prevent his voice from cracking in front of his men. "That's correct." He gestured to his men. "Cut off her flex cuffs."

One of the men whipped out a Ka-Bar knife and sliced off the cuffs.

After zipping up her flight suit, Cyndi massaged her bruised and lacerated wrists.

Packets of Pedialyte powder were added to a canteen of water for Cyndi to drink. They also gave her three protein bars to eat. She wolfed everything down in less than a minute.

The team leader noticed Diaz curled up in a ball on the concrete, nursing his badly burned hands. "Is he El Diablo?"

"Yes, that's him."

"He's the devil?" the leader asked in amazement.

The man next to him had a freckled face, red hair, and a scruffy red beard to match. The hulking Special Forces operator walked up and towered over Diaz. "This wimpy little bitch is Lucifer?" He turned his head to the side and spit out a mouthful of tar-colored tobacco juice. "More like Lucy, if you ask me."

Despite his attempt at levity, the brawny man radiated an unmistakable aura of aggression that, like a coiled spring, could explode at the least amount of provocation.

"Do you need medical attention, Captain?" the team leader asked.

Cyndi wasn't listening. She had a message to deliver. She walked over to Diaz and said, "I warned you, but your ego wouldn't listen. Never underestimate your enemy."

Diaz refused to look at her.

"Do you need medical attention, Captain?" the team leader repeated.

Cyndi shook her head while continuing to glare at Diaz. "No, I'm fine. Just royally pissed off, that's all." Cyndi hauled off and kicked Diaz in the ass.

"Understood, ma'am. I have just the cure for that." The leader chambered a round then handed Cyndi his rifle. "Let's give the captain a minute alone, boys."

"Boss, you sure you want to do this?" the black operator asked.

"Step outside, gentlemen. That's an order."

They shrugged and reluctantly left the barn.

The leader closed the sliding doors then turned around. He had frighteningly cold, no-nonsense eyes. "I can tell you from experience that mistakes happen during battle. That's my gun and my bullets, ma'am. You'll have no connection to either."

"Are you saying what I think you're saying?"

"Fog of war, ma'am. Things go sideways on every op. Happens all the time." He cracked the doors open and disappeared.

Cyndi had fired an AK many times in the past, but the gun suddenly felt heavier, weightier. Her conscience felt even heavier.

She took a deep breath, put the stock of the rifle against her shoulder, and aimed it at Diaz.

He scampered across the floor on his hands and knees and pressed his back against the wall. Diaz thrust out his charred palms. "Wait! Wait! Five hundred. I'll give you $500 million! Half of everything I have!"

"No deal." Cyndi closed one eye and aimed at the center of Diaz's forehead.

"You can't do this!" Diaz screamed. "You're murdering a defenseless man in cold blood!"

Cyndi stopped. She lowered the rifle slightly and looked down, searching her soul for guidance.

"Admit it, you're a rule follower," Diaz said, grasping for any way to avoid his fate. "You know you can't do this. It will haunt you forever."

Cyndi nodded. "You're right, I am a rule follower."

"See, I knew it. I knew you couldn't do it." Diaz relaxed slightly, sagging back against the wall. "That's why people like me rule the world. Always have, always will."

"Not if I have anything to say about it." A contemplative look formed on her face. "Ironic, isn't it?"

"What is?"

"You've done nothing but bring darkness to the world, and it was darkness that was your undoing. I'd say go to hell"—Cyndi looked around—"but you're already there."

She raised the rifle back up to her shoulder and pulled the trigger.

★★★

The men outside the barn were smoking and trading good-natured insults with each other. Before they had time to finish their cigarettes, they heard the tap, tap, tap sound of suppressed gunshots in rapid succession.

CHAPTER 53

THE TEAM LEADER held back his teammates when they started toward the barn door. "Give her a moment to process what she did. She'll need it." He took a few more drags on his cigarette then flicked it to the ground. "Okay, let's go."

When the men entered the barn, they saw Diaz slumped against the wall with his arms draped over his face.

There were three holes in the side of the barn to his left.

He was alive but whimpering and shaking.

Cyndi had pulled the stool over to Diaz and was sitting on it. The smoking AK was laying across her lap. She hunched over and said, "You'll never understand why I didn't kill you. Never have, never will."

Cyndi stood up and walked over to the leader. "He wasn't worth wasting a bullet on."

"I would've smoked the bastard. But it was your call, Captain Stafford. I respect it."

She handed the rifle back to him. "You know my name. I didn't get yours."

"Where are my manners?" He reached out his large, weathered hand. "I'm Victor." He nodded toward the big Irishman and the tall black man standing guard over Diablo. "These two are Charlie and Oscar."

Cyndi shoved his outstretched hand aside and rolled her eyes. "Not very original, *Victor*. You might want to rethink your ambitions to become a standup comedian.

Or at least don't use the NATO phonetic alphabet for fake names when you're talking to a fighter pilot."

He let out a rowdy laugh. "You got me, ma'am. Nicely done."

"Stick with being a D-boy, Frogman, Bat Boy, or whatever band of door kickers you're with."

"Bat Boy?" Victor appeared genuinely offended as he looked askew at his teammates. "Do I look like some wimpy-ass, beret-wearing Army Ranger to you guys?"

Charlie, the burly Irishman, came to his defense. "I would never dream of wounding your delicate feelings with such an insult, boss."

"Whatever your real name is, thank you for risking your life to rescue me."

"Don't get ahead of things, ma'am. We're not back on friendly soil just yet."

His radio crackled to life. "Boots One, this is Mother."

"Go for Boots One," Victor said into his microphone.

"You have tangos inbound. The Predator flying overwatch just spotted four heavily armed trucks headed your way. They'll arrive at your position in ten mikes."

"Copy that, Mother." Victor's smile disappeared. He instantly morphed back into mission mode. "No time for jawing, ma'am. Time to exfil."

"Roger," Cyndi replied, moving toward the door.

Diaz limped to his feet with renewed energy, no longer whimpering. "Those trucks will be from the Mexican Army. Run away like the pathetic cowards you are. Every general in Sonora is my bitch. You'll never make it to the border alive," he crowed.

Victor just laughed. "Whatever you say, Lucy."

Acting cocky in the face of danger was expected for a seasoned operator, but he didn't seem the least bit concerned that their position was about to be overrun by a platoon of corrupted and heavily armed Mexican soldiers. Or that they were conducting an illegal op in a foreign country.

Diaz enjoyed his newfound tactical advantage. "Go ahead, run. After you're captured, they'll bring you right back here." He glared at Cyndi. "I will personally torture every one of these men in front of you while you watch them die the most barbaric deaths imaginable. Then it will be your turn, *puta*!"

Victor shook his head. "Lucy, you need to learn some manners. That's no way to talk to a lady."

"We need to go, guys," Cyndi said breathlessly. "We can take Diablo with us. Use him as a bargaining chip with the Army."

Victor slowly stroked his chin, considering Cyndi's suggestion. "No…I'm not a big fan of that idea. Let's just hang El Diablo upside down from a beam and leave him here. Seems like a fitting punishment for him."

"How will that help us?" Cyndi asked.

Victor took out a cigarette and casually lit it. He gently blew out a smoke ring. "That's not the Army headed this way. We tipped off the Omega cartel about our little visit this evening. I invited them to crash the party after we split. And guess who their host will be?"

Everyone turned and looked at Diablo.

"No! You can't leave me here!" he screamed. "Please take me with you!" Diaz tugged on Victor's sleeve and looked up at his chiseled face. "I'm not really the devil. I only picked that name because it terrified the deeply religious locals."

Victor shrugged and threw up his hands. "Sorry, amigo, since we were never here, hitching a ride is not an option."

"I'm begging you, take me with you," he whimpered, his charred hands clasped together as if he was praying. "I promise not to fight extradition or get my lawyers involved."

Charlie let out a hardy laugh. "Lawyers? Is this clown serious?"

"Save your begging, Lucy. I think you'll be doing plenty of it very soon," Victor said with obvious relish in his voice.

The three special operators pounced on Diaz. They bound his hands and feet then hung him upside down from a beam. The men left the barn in a hurry, glancing at their watches to gauge the time remaining before the battlefield went hot again.

Before she walked away, Diaz pleaded, "Cyndi, please don't leave me here. You can have it all. One billion dollars!"

Cyndi let out an exasperated sigh. "You just don't get it, do you? There's no amount of money that would make it worth selling my soul. Adios, Lucy."

Cyndi slammed the barn doors closed and never looked back.

CHAPTER 54

WHEN CYNDI EMERGED from the barn, she was stunned by what she saw. Fires raged around the expansive property. There wasn't a single structure left standing, other than the barn that Cyndi had been held captive in.

Cyndi turned to Victor. "You guys did all this?"

"Not us. Four of your buddies from Luke flew down to give us a hand."

"I knew I recognized that noise. Pratt & Whitney F135 two-spool afterburning turbofan engines."

"If you say so, ma'am. I'm not really an airplane guy. Give me the ocean any day." He surveyed the devastation and nodded approvingly. "Still…not bad for a bunch of Air Force pukes. Oh by the way, one of your guys radioed and said to tell you 'Don't die out there.'"

For the first time in two days, Cyndi genuinely smiled.

The rest of the eight-man squad regrouped around their leader. They'd already ditched their cowboy boots and jeans and were suited up for battle. They handed their boss a set of AOR1 desert pattern cammies, body armor, and an OPS Core high-cut helmet with NODs attached.

One of the operators had sustained a gunshot wound to his calf during the fight. The medic in the group had wrapped a bandage around it after he'd cut off the man's pant leg at the knee.

Victor looked at him and frowned. "What happened to you, Mike?"

"One of those assholes shot me," Mike snarled.

"Suck it up, you big baby. It's just a bullet wound," the medic said.

Mike flipped him off.

"I know it's a little slower than what you're used to, ma'am, but it's all we got," Victor said, pointing to his left.

He was referring to the peculiar-looking vehicles they had arrived in. They looked like a Humvee and a dune buggy had gotten drunk during spring break and had a baby. The tan-colored Polaris Defense Dagor A1 ATVs had aggressive off-road tires, tons of ground clearance, and a little insurance mounted to them. Fifty-caliber machine guns poked up above the roof rails.

"Hope you don't get carsick," he said to Cyndi.

"Not if I drive."

"Sorry, Captain, not happening. It's a guy thing." He winked at Cyndi. "I'm sure you understand."

Cyndi chuckled at his overdeveloped sense of machismo. "All too well. Let's get the hell out of here."

They mounted up and headed north for the border.

——◆——

The drivers barreled through the pitch-black desert at insane speeds with their headlights off, using their NODs to scan the treacherous terrain.

Cyndi had a death grip on the grab bar mounted on the back of the driver's seat. With no seatbelt, she felt certain she would be flung to her death out the opening where a door normally hung. Cyndi almost screamed "slow down before you get us all killed!" but held her tongue.

The wide grins on the faces of the adrenaline junkies who'd rescued her indicated either they were in their element and completely comfortable with the speed, or they were enjoying scaring the hell out of Cyndi.

She suspected it was the latter.

Mike was sitting next to Cyndi. He turned and stared at her through his night-vision goggles. "You okay, ma'am? You're looking a little green." He let out a boisterous, obnoxious laugh. "That joke never gets old," he roared.

"One klick to the border, boss," the lead driver yelled.

"Copy." Victor nodded and pointed to his right.

His driver steered the caravan behind a large boulder and stopped. Mike jumped out and limped to the back of the ATV. He released the hold-down straps over the spare tire and gas cans then tossed them out into the desert, puncturing the cans. He pointed at the small bed, held up a canvas tarp, and said, "Ma'am…"

Cyndi swiveled around, confusion evident on her face. "Yes?"

"Climb in."

"You want me to ride in there?"

"You know how the government works, ma'am. Before helping us out tonight, the border patrol demanded total deniability in case the shit hits the fan. CBP cameras recorded eight of us going through the fence earlier on our"—he held up both hands and made air quotes—"training mission, so only eight can return. You'll be riding back here until we get far enough north that the cameras can't see us anymore."

After years in the military, Cyndi was well acquainted with the game. Government organizations had perfected the art of passing the buck to cover their asses. The CBP would be no different. She climbed into the miniature bed and curled up in the fetal position.

The gunner who'd been manning the.50 cal took her seat.

Mike threw the tarp over Cyndi and was about to get back in when a devilish grin crossed his face. He limped over and picked up the gas cans.

When he went to lay the leaking cans on the tarp, Victor growled, "Not cool, dickhead."

"You got no sense of humor, boss." Mike chuckled and threw the wet gas cans back into the desert.

———◆———

Approaching the border fence, the lead ATV driver flashed his headlights three times.

Two border patrol agents and their supervisor stepped out of a weathered and rickety guard shack on the US side of the fence. The agents were kitted up like they were going to war. Each man wore a tactical helmet and body armor and toted an M4 rifle. Guarding the border was obviously not some boring desk job.

A small gate wide enough for Humvees was opened. After they drove through the gate in the pitch black, it closed. Infrared cameras mounted along the fence slowly rotated on their motorized mounts, recording the encounter.

The supervisor shined his flashlight at the lead driver, causing his NODs to bloom out, ruining his night vision. "Welcome back, gentlemen. Your training mission go as planned, *Victor*?"

He just grunted.

"I hear ya. Training sucks. I was a snake eater back in the day. Green Beret at Fort Campbell. Kinda miss being out there where the action is. Now I play catch and release all day long. But I'm home every night, get GS-12 pay, and it's a lot safer now that I'm not hanging around with a bunch of trigger-happy squids."

"You mean safer for us," Victor said rudely.

"All right, smartass, I'm going to need a head count and contraband check." He counted the number of men. Eight. He went to the second vehicle and shined the light in the driver's eyes.

"Get that fucking light out of my eyes before I cram that thing up your ass," Oscar barked.

The CBP supervisor harbored no illusions that the

man's brash bravado and crude threat wouldn't be backed up by violent action in a heartbeat. He lowered the beam from the flashlight and backed away.

He walked to the back of the second vehicle and lifted up the tarp. The glow from his flashlight illuminated enough armament to wage a small-scale war. The former Green Beret went to the lead vehicle, grabbed the edge of the tarp, and began to lift it up.

"Careful, Army. Our equipment can be kinda dangerous," Victor said. "You wouldn't want to see something you'd regret and ruin your pricey GS-12 manicure, if you get my drift."

The two men locked eyes. The CBP supervisor stroked his chin and considered the thinly veiled warning. He'd been around long enough to understand the true meaning of Victor's comment.

He let go of the tarp and said, "Get the hell out of my sector, assholes. And don't come back!"

"Whatever you say, Army."

CHAPTER 55

THE ATVS STOPPED and killed their engines after traveling north for thirty minutes.

Mike threw off the tarp and helped Cyndi climb out of the miniature bed.

On a normal day, Cyndi Stafford could give any beauty queen in the country a run for her money. But by the end of this ordeal, her flight suit was stained with blood and saturated with sweat and dust. Winning a beauty contest or posing for the cover of a fashion magazine were the least of her concerns. Getting back alive, with her honor intact, was her only goal.

She stretched out her sore muscles and surveyed her surroundings. There was just enough light from the heavens to see they had stopped out in the middle of nowhere, at the edge of a ravine. An MH-60M Black Hawk helicopter, flown by pilots from the Night Stalkers 160th Special Operations Aviation Regiment, waited quietly in the distance.

Mike handed Cyndi water and more protein bars. Two men jumped out of the helicopter carrying a parachute from an F-35 ejection seat and a survival kit. They tossed them down into the ravine.

"Make sure it is well hidden," Victor directed.

"What the hell is going on?" she asked.

"Ask him," Victor replied, pointing behind her.

Cyndi spun around.

President Horatio Ashford walked up.

Everyone on the team but Victor stepped away.

Cyndi snapped to attention and saluted.

Ashford smirked and didn't return the salute. "At ease, Captain. You are lucky to be alive, young woman."

"Yes, sir, I am. Thank you for coming to get me, sir."

He planted his hands on his hips and glared at Cyndi. "You caused one hell of a mess for me when your plane went down. Our diplomats at the UN haven't slept since you disappeared. China and Russia are demanding a formal apology for being accused of conducting cyber warfare to down your plane. I told them where they could stick their damned apology. Then I find out a few hours ago that you parachuted into Mexico. I could hardly declare war on our neighbor to the south to get you back. If I had, I could kiss the Hispanic vote goodbye." He thumbed toward Victor. "A more surgical approach was in order."

"Sorry to *inconvenience* you sir, but my plane just came apart. I had nothing to do with the crash. Next thing I knew, I woke up in Mexico."

"I know that. The brainiacs in our intelligence services put their oversized, Ivy League heads together and have a theory about what happened. They think Diablo put a contract out on you for embarrassing him that day in Maryvale. Your crew chief, Airman…?" The President looked back at Victor for some help, snapping his fingers impatiently.

"Torres, sir."

"Right. We learned Airman Torres owed $900 to the cartel. Diablo threatened to kill his entire family if he didn't do the job. We found traces of bomb-making chemicals in his apartment. He must have planted an IED in the ELT compartment in the back of your plane. That's why we never got a signal from the emergency beacon when you went down."

"Nine hundred dollars?" Cyndi was horrified at the

trivial amount of money that her life was worth to her crew chief. "I nearly died because of him. I saw things I'll never be able to unsee. I hope the bastard rots away in a cell in Leavenworth."

"That's not going to happen. The official version of the story is that he drove out to an industrial park near Luke and committed suicide when we began to suspect him."

"And the truth?"

"As you well know, those cartels can be vicious. Either way, justice was served." Ashford looked at the special ops team leader. "Where's Diaz?"

"Unfortunately, he didn't make it, Mr. President. Took his own life before we could stop him."

The look on Ashford's face signaled his skepticism. He pointed at Cyndi. "Is that true, Captain? El Diablo is dead?"

Cyndi thought very carefully before answering. Lying to the commander in chief meant a guaranteed court-martial. "Fog of war, sir. Things go sideways on every op."

"I've been in this game a long time, Stafford. You really expect me to believe that?"

Cyndi swallowed hard. Her palms began to sweat. She drew in a deep breath and said, "Actually, sir—"

Ashford held up a hand. "It was a rhetorical question, Captain. I didn't expect an answer. That cartel scum got what he deserved."

"Yes, sir." Cyndi exhaled loudly. "Um…about the cartel. After what happened, I assume they'll put a massive bounty on my head."

"With their leadership decapitated, it's the low-level thugs who'll have bounties on their heads. The police, the Army, and every cartel in Mexico will be hunting them. Karma can be a real bitch. The Descendientes del Diablo cartel is out of business in Sonora. But like Medusa, another one always pops up to take its place. That would be the Omega cartel."

"Oh great," Cyndi moaned.

"Rest easy. Our comm intercepts show they sent word to their members that they owe you one. When the leadership of the DDD cartel was taken out during your rescue, we basically did their dirty work for them. They get the territory and the illegal proceeds that go with it without a war with El Diablo because of you."

"What about the Mexican government? Won't they lodge a protest at the UN for our F-35s violating their national sovereignty and airspace?"

Ashford jabbed a finger at Cyndi and raised his voice. "Our aircraft were never in Mexican territory! If President Ortega can show any proof from their antiquated air traffic control radars that our fifth-generation stealth planes were in his country, I'd be happy to create a committee to investigate his baseless accusations.

"And even if a few planes did accidentally stray across the border, the Justice Department has assured me that our legal bases are covered. If a country is given the opportunity to rescue a US military member and they don't do it, under international law our military has the authority and the right to enter a foreign country and rescue our member."

Cyndi nodded in admiration. "I'll be honest, I underestimated you, sir. You do know how to play the game. You've thought of everything."

Ashford's eyes narrowed. "I'll take that as a compliment, Captain."

Cyndi glanced at the MH-60M Black Hawk helicopter. "Mind if I hitch a ride back to Luke, sir?"

"Sorry, Captain Stafford, I'm afraid that's not going to happen."

The muscles in Cyndi's neck stiffened up. "Sir?"

"As you so impolitely stated, I've been at this game a long time."

CHAPTER 56

"WHAT DO YOU mean, sir?"

"Here's the deal, Stafford. You got amnesia when you landed and hit your head." Ashford snapped his fingers.

A carbon fiber F-35 flight helmet with Cyndi's name on it was brought up by Charlie and given to his team leader.

Victor threw it on the ground and slammed the butt of his rifle into the side of the helmet. He picked it up and tossed the $450,000 helmet into the ravine.

"When you snapped out of it later tonight," Ashford continued, "you pulled your parachute out of the ravine and spread it out. The surveillance satellites will spot it when the sun comes up tomorrow morning, and you will be rescued. Make sure you do it before 4 a.m. I want the story to make the morning news programs on the East Coast. I'll get credit for following through with my pledge to never leave a missing soldier behind, my poll numbers will soar, and you get to go back to your unit."

Cyndi began to shiver, despite the warm temperature. "But sir, that's not what happened."

Ashford let out an exasperated breath. "I'm sorry to hear you say that. Look around, Captain. We're in the middle of millions of acres of a military restricted area that is off-limits to civilians. Who knows what kind of dangerous animals are roaming around this place at night?" The President looked to his right.

Victor, the SEAL team leader, standing next to his commander in chief, pulled his Ka-Bar knife out of the sheath strapped to the side of his leg.

Ashford looked back at Cyndi. Any hint of humanity was gone from his expression. "A smart gal like yourself surely understands there is another option besides going home if you decide to challenge my official explanation this close to my reelection. If not, let me spell it out for you. In a few weeks, after an exhaustive search, this team of knuckle draggers you see here…" he pointed at Victor and his team.

The highly trained killer took great offense but held his temper in check.

"They will find what's left of your badly decomposed body after it's been picked clean by the animals. The nation will mourn your loss, but I'll still get credit for bringing you home. You'll get full military honors at your funeral, of course. Hell, I'll even take time out of my busy campaign schedule to deliver the eulogy."

Cyndi clenched her jaw. "Your sick plan won't work, Mr. President. Too many people know I'm here. Someone will vouch for me. You won't get away with this."

The president turned to the SEAL team leader. "What's your name, son?"

"Victor, sir."

The president shook his head. "Sure, whatever. I've been meaning to review the budget for your fine outfit. Right now it could go either way. What do you say, Vic? Do you and your team recall finding our attractive but politically naïve pilot during your mission?"

"You mean us knuckle draggers, sir?"

Ashford's face turned crimson with anger. "Just answer the damned question."

Victor turned back and looked at his team, his brothers-in-arms. The men he'd gone to war with. The men who would die for him. The men he'd die for. "That would be a no, sir."

Cyndi glared at Victor. "I wasn't talking about your errand boys." She pointed out the empty patch of Velcro on the chest of her flight suit. "Notice anything that's missing? I tossed my name tag out from under the tarp when we stopped at the border gate. The CBP agents will surely recognize my name when they find it. The clue I left will have spread throughout the entire CBP Ajo Station by now. And these eight men are on camera, shown driving through the gate tonight. From what I overheard, they didn't leave a very good impression with them."

Ashford snapped his fingers at Victor. "Take care of that. I don't want any loose ends."

"Take care of it yourself, *sir*." Victor stomped off toward the helicopter.

Cyndi crossed her arms and gave Ashford a smug smirk.

The President of the United States cleared his throat. "My compliments, Captain Stafford. You're not as naïve as I thought. Looks like we have some horse trading to do."

"Looks like we do."

"Before we get down to business, I'll warn you, I make a much better ally than enemy."

Cyndi looked him straight in the eye. "Ditto."

"What do you want? A cushy job at the Pentagon? I know, an ambassadorship. I'm guessing from your last name you'd probably prefer Ireland."

"None of the above. I want the record corrected for Ángel Mendoza. He was a patriot, not some nut who went rogue like the BS story the government is selling. I want him posthumously awarded the highest honors and a star on the wall in the building of whatever three-letter agency he worked for."

"I don't condone disavowed agents going around pulling off their own rescue missions. It shows a disrespect for the chain of command. But his little escapade did cause a spike in comm traffic between the cartel and their flunkies in the military when you escaped. That confirmed your location. I'll see that Mendoza's record reflects what a valuable asset he was to this country."

An opportunity like this didn't come along every day. Cyndi wasn't about to waste it. "While I'm on the subject, where did you find the amateurs who sanitized my record after what happened in the Minuteman silo? It's been completely wiped. What do I look like, a nun? Find some spook with an imagination this time and have them sprinkle in a parking ticket or two. Like a normal person would have." Cyndi thrust out her hand. "Do we have a deal?"

Ashford rolled his eyes. "Jesus, the *cojones* on this one." The president reluctantly shook her hand. With the deal done, he switched gears. "All the money and influence in the world couldn't buy the positive PR you're going to get when you return. You'll be a damn national hero. You know that, right?" He regarded Cyndi while he slowly stroked his chin. "If you play your cards right, who knows where it might lead? With my help, you'd be a shoo-in for the Arizona governor's office. Then a few years later, a senator. After paying your dues, I could see you as the first female—"

"Not interested. Selling my soul is not really my thing," Cyndi said, shaking her head.

Ashford gave her a jaded, inside-the-Beltway reply. "That's what they all say. Until they get a whiff of real power within their grasp."

When the devil smiles at you..., Cyndi thought to herself. She lifted both hands and said, "I'm afraid it's a hard pass, sir."

Ashford shook his head. "And my wife thinks *I'm* stubborn. Okay, Stafford, time to climb down into the ravine.

Don't forget to spread out your parachute before the sun comes up."

The SEAL team collected water bottles and protein bar wrappers so there wouldn't be any evidence they were there.

"You are dismissed, Captain."

Cyndi turned to hunker down in the ravine for a long, chilly night.

"Stafford! I expect you to show me proper military courtesy before you walk away," Ashford yelled, fed up with her obstinance.

Cyndi stopped. Her back was turned on the President of the United States. Although he was technically correct, Ashford's blatant power play did not sit well with her. Especially after the day she'd just had. Her defiant, stubborn persona began to boil up inside of her like an overheated pressure cooker.

Cyndi turned around and glowered at Ashford. She clenched her teeth and raised her hand to her forehead, forming a perfectly rigid salute.

"Your understanding of military protocol in the presence of higher-ranking officers could use a refresher, captain." The President of the United States and commander in chief ignored her salute and walked away.

The pressure cooker exploded.

Before Ashford got far, Cyndi yelled, "Wait! I have one more demand."

CHAPTER 57

THE SEALS CLIMBED aboard their ATVs and lowered their NODs. They headed north at a leisurely pace and disappeared into the night.

Or at least they appeared to leave the area.

The helicopter lifted off then deliberately circled the area a few feet off the desert floor, obliterating any evidence of tire tracks and footprints with the hurricane-force downwash from its rotors.

Alone again in enemy territory, Cyndi gathered rocks and a long stick to defend herself against the predators that roamed about—whatever variety that might turn out to be. She leaned back against the ravine wall, wrapped herself in the parachute, and willed herself to stay awake.

Thursday, 0700 hours, MST.

The alarm on her Casio G-Shock watch went off, jerking Cyndi out of a sound sleep. She was greeted with a beautiful azure sky, well after the morning news shows on the East Coast had finished broadcasting.

She gathered up the parachute and tossed it up onto the desert floor. Cyndi bent down to pick up the smashed flight helmet with her name emblazoned across it. She decided taking the prop with her that was meant to validate President Ashford's bogus story wasn't happening. She kicked it across the ravine and said, "Maybe you were right, Bruno. Maybe I am a testa dura."

———◆———

Cyndi spread out the parachute and weighed down the perimeter with rocks. Then she sat back and waited. Thirty minutes later, an HC-130J Combat King II from the 79th Rescue Squadron at Davis-Monthan AFB roared over her, two hundred feet off the deck. Its nose lurched skyward, then the modified SAR version of the venerable Hercules went into a wide orbit at one thousand feet.

Fifteen minutes later, two HH-60G Pave Hawks from the 55th Rescue Squadron appeared. They landed far enough from the parachute to prevent it from fouling their rotors in case the downwash sent it airborne.

Cyndi stood with her back to the helicopters to keep the blowing sand and dust from blinding her. "Oh yeah, can't forget this," she mumbled. Cyndi unzipped a pocket on the sleeve of her flight suit. She pulled out the two halves of the broken wings. Then she reached back in and pulled out her bright red name tag. Cyndi reattached it to the empty patch of Velcro on the chest of her flight suit.

A self-satisfied smile formed on her face.

———◆———

Seated next to the door, in the back of the Pave Hawk as it cruised toward Luke AFB, Cyndi looked down on the desert terrain. The morning sun had bathed it in a peaceful, tranquil light. *Appearances can be deceiving*, she thought.

———◆———

The expansive tarmac at Luke came into view as the helicopter gently touched down. Two pararescuemen jumped out and helped Cyndi toward the waiting ambulance. She climbed in and had a seat on the side bench.

The base flight surgeon was waiting for her. "Welcome home, Captain Stafford. How are you feeling?"

"Thanks, Doc. I'm fine, I don't need any help."

The doctor flashed a warm smile. "Why don't we head over to the clinic anyway. I can do a quick exam just to be sure. It sure would make me feel a whole lot better knowing you were okay."

The doctor was a shrewd practitioner who'd dealt with challenging pilot personalities for many years. How was she supposed to say no after such a seemingly caring and compassionate statement?

He leaned in, pinched his nose, and pretended to cough. "You might want to take a hot shower first, though."

Healing talents and a sense of humor, both skillfully delivered.

———◆———

After a shower and donning a fresh flight suit, the doctor wrapped Cyndi's bruised ribs and bandaged her cuts and scrapes. "Overall I'd say you came through your…um…situation in pretty good shape. Stay off any mechanical bulls to let those bruised ribs heal, and you should be good to go back on flight status in just a few days." He draped his stethoscope around his neck and said, "There's one more person I'd like you to see before I discharge you." The doctor excused himself and left the exam room.

Cyndi sat up straight, anticipating the arrival of her fiancé.

A few minutes later the base chaplain, Major Boyd, walked in. "Hi, Cyndi. I'm so glad to see you. The doctor tells me that physically you're in good shape, all things considered."

After years in the military, Cyndi knew how the game

was played—anything she said could and would be used against her if it came to that. Her shoulders sagged. "Why do I get the feeling you're not here to talk about my blood pressure?"

"No, no, I'm not. You've been through quite a lot in the last few days."

"That's one way to put it," Cyndi replied dryly.

The chaplain took a breath and smiled. "I'm just here to help. Speaking of helping, a team of experts from the Joint Personnel Recovery Agency have been flown in from Fairchild to help with your reintegration."

"Reintegration? Sounds like military jargon for intelligence debriefings to me."

"No, not at all," he assured Cyndi. "Specialists on the team will work with you to help ease your transition from captivity to freedom. They've been trained to address the psychological trauma that you've experienced, and any long-term effects that you might wrestle with."

Cyndi jumped down from the exam table. "All you people are acting like I'm made of glass. As I told the doc, I'm fine. I don't need any help."

"It's just us, Captain Stafford. Anything you say in this room will be held in the strictest of confidence. You don't have to pretend you're okay."

"Give me a friggin' break. I'm in the military, not running a ride at Disneyland. Sometimes bad things happen. It comes with the job. You just put it behind you and move on. It was barely more than forty-eight hours, not seven years like some Vietnam POWs. The bottom line is I'm alive, Diablo isn't. I won, he lost. It's as simple as that. Tell the JPRA folks thanks but no thanks."

The chaplain could tell he was getting nowhere with Cyndi. He forced a smile and said, "If you change your mind, let me know."

"Sure, I'll do that," Cyndi said just to placate the man.

As the chaplain reached for the doorknob, Cyndi said,

"Hang on, there is one person I need to talk to." She wrote a name on a sticky note and handed it to the chaplain. "You shouldn't have any problem tracking this person down."

He looked at the name. "I'll see what I can do."

"I'll need a phone."

Major Boyd shook his head. "Please wait here."

Ten minutes later, the chaplain returned with the phone number. He handed it to Cyndi then unlocked his iPhone and gave it to her. "I'll be right outside if you need me."

After he left, Cyndi took a deep breath then dialed the number. After six rings an irritated voice said, "This better be important."

"Hello, this is Captain Stafford."

Her salutation was met with silence on the other end. After a few moments Cyndi thought the line had disconnected.

"Are you still there?"

"Yes ma'am, I'm here. I have to be honest; I'm surprised to hear from you. All things considered."

"I'm sorry to bother you at work but..." Cyndi stopped to compose herself before continuing. She grabbed a tissue and dabbed at her moist eyes. "I assume you heard about what happened."

"Yes, ma'am."

"Okay, good. I um…I called to say…I called to apologize for—"

"Not necessary, ma'am. I understand. But, since you so rudely interrupted me, I might as well listen to whatever you have to say. That is if you're up to it."

For the next ten minutes, Cyndi shared every terrifying, painful, and triumphant detail about her captivity by the brutal drug cartel. By the time she'd finished, Cyndi felt a powerful cathartic release wash over her.

"A lot of good people will benefit from what you've

told me, ma'am." In a gruff voice he grumbled, "Now, if you don't mind, I need to get back to work."

"Wait, there's one more thing. If you ever want me to come and speak to your students about my experience, don't hesitate to call me. Goodbye, Master Sergeant Gagliardi."

CHAPTER 58

THE FLIGHT SURGEON returned to the exam room. "Before I release you, is there anything else for the record you need to get off your chest? Anything that didn't sit well with you during your captivity or rescue?"

Cyndi did a quick mental analysis of the pros and cons of exposing the frightful, self-serving behavior of President Ashford.

The advice drilled into her at SERE school popped into Cyndi's mind. *Learn how to pick your battles.* According to the myth, David had prevailed over Goliath. In the real world, he'd get his butt handed to him.

President Horatio Ashford wasn't some hard-ass enlisted instructor in the Air Force, he was the commander of the world's most powerful military and intelligence apparatus on earth. Taking him on would result in a hell of a lot more pain than getting waterboarded.

"Nope, I'm good. Nothing else to talk about."

The doctor handed Cyndi a form. "In that case, would you mind signing this? It's a DD Form 2810, Personnel Recovery Debriefing Statement."

"What's it for?"

"It's just routine paperwork. Nothing to be concerned about."

Cyndi slowly scanned the confusing legal document. "Whose interests does it protect, mine or the government's?"

"Like I said, it's just routine paperwork."

Cyndi folded up the form and stuffed it into a pocket. "I'll get back to you about it."

———◆———

When she stepped out of the clinic, Cyndi couldn't believe her eyes. Both sides of the road leading away from the clinic were packed with people. Everyone on base had turned out for a parade in her honor. They'd come to celebrate Cyndi's return.

Lance rushed up and grabbed Cyndi in his arms. He picked her up and twirled her around. Her ribs hurt like hell, but being in his warm embrace again felt like heaven. When he put Cyndi down, he gave her the most heartfelt kiss he'd ever delivered. Lance took her by the hand and led her to his sandblasted pickup truck. He opened the driver's door and held out his keys. "Here."

"You're letting me drive?"

"Takes a *real* Texas man to let someone drive his pickup truck."

As she cruised down the street waving to the crowd, Cyndi couldn't believe the reception she was getting. Yellow ribbons were tied to every fixed object possible. School kids were holding up handmade signs. The Luke AFB band was playing. It was as if she had suddenly become royalty.

In the Air Force, such extraordinary treatment was reserved exclusively for its pilots. Die and the whole base showed up for your funeral. Don't die and the whole base threw you a parade.

When they pulled into the parking lot of the 60th Fighter Squadron, every pilot stationed at Luke Air Force Base was waiting. They hoisted Cyndi up on their shoulders and paraded her into the building.

Armed security policemen were stationed at the door. Tank stood toe to toe with one of them and growled,

"No one without silver wings on their chest gets in my building. Do I make myself clear?"

"Yes, sir. Understood, sir."

The pilots crammed into the bar, a.k.a. Heritage Room, to celebrate Cyndi's return. "Welcome to the Jungle" by Guns N' Roses, was blaring from the speakers. Crud games between rival squadrons broke out at once. Trips to the clinic to patch up the ensuing injuries soon followed.

Toilet walked up holding a beer. "Welcome back, Stafford. The guys and I talked about it, and we came up with your official call sign. It's Gringa."

True to form, her call sign was a mixture of humor, insult, and a reference to an unpleasant or embarrassing event.

Cyndi knew that contesting her new call sign would only result in a worse one. She smiled and said, "Lance told me you were one of the pilots that bombed the compound they were holding me at."

"I volunteered to go on the mission."

Cyndi's eyes began to mist over. "You risked your life to help rescue me."

"I know I haven't always been a perfect gentleman, but that prick messed with one of our own. Once you start the B-course, you're family. Sometimes a dysfunctional one. Always a competitive one. But still family. And no one messes with my family without paying a severe price." He raised his bottle. "Welcome to hell, Diablo."

"Thanks, Toilet, I owe you one."

"Damn straight you do, Gringa. Bring it in." Toilet opened his arms wide. "Let's hug it out and I'll call it even."

The lascivious expression on his face revealed that he had more than a platonic embrace on his mind.

"Don't press your luck, Toilet." Cyndi stuck out her hand. "A handshake will have to do."

Toilet held a mischievous grin. "Hey, you can't blame a guy for trying."

After shaking her hand, Toilet said, "The rental period on all these beers has run out." He burped loudly and announced, "I need to hit the head."

After the festivities had ended, Tank escorted Cyndi to the door. "Take the rest of the week off, Stafford. Get some rest, get some food in you, and come back Monday morning ready to fly."

She vigorously shook his hand. "Will do, sir."

———◆———

Cyndi snuggled up next to Lance in their bed.

Lance had no idea how to handle Cyndi's return from captivity. He didn't want to push her to relive her ordeal, but he wanted to be supportive and provide a shoulder to cry on.

"Do you feel like talking about it?" he probed gently.

Cyndi blew out a long breath. "A lot happened in the last two days. I just need time to process it."

"Sounds like you're still in mission mode. You don't have to hide anything from me."

"I'm not ready to talk about it yet." Cyndi swallowed hard and began to tear up. "I'm sorry."

"Don't be." He softly cradled her face in his hands. "You're not a superhero. It's okay to admit you're human."

The emotional dam that she'd been bravely holding back for days finally ruptured. She laid her head against his muscular chest. Cyndi's toned body began to shake. She broke down crying. "It was bad. Really bad."

CHAPTER 59

Monday morning.

LANCE AND CYNDI walked up to the brief counter in the squadron building. Their comrades greeted Cyndi with open arms and heartfelt handshakes.

Tank came up and slapped Cyndi on the back. "You ready to get back on the horse, Stafford?"

"Absolutely, sir. Send me up; I'm ready."

"Good to hear it. Before we get to that, I've got something for you. Given the extraordinary circumstances, I decided to sign off your final sortie as complete. You are now a graduate of the F-35 B-Course." Tank peeled his 60th Fighter Squadron patch off his left shoulder and slapped it on the blank Velcro on Cyndi's left shoulder. "Welcome to the jungle."

The room erupted in cheers.

Cyndi snapped to attention and saluted. "Thank you, sir."

Before the celebration could get started, the wing commander, Brig. Gen. Kirby Wallace, suddenly walked in with two aides trailing him. The left breast of his crisp blue uniform was brimming with multicolored ribbons and medals.

"Atten hut!" Tank shouted.

"Captain Stafford, front and center," the short, stout one-star barked.

She rushed up and stood at attention, confusion blanketing her face.

"You almost started World War III with our neighbor to the south because of your little stunt, Captain," Wallace growled. "Because of that, I am grounding you."

"What?" Cyndi's shoulders slumped. Her eyes began to moisten.

Grumbling immediately spread among the pilots.

Tank stepped forward. "But sir, Captain—"

"If you value your career, you will stand down, Abrams," Wallace snapped.

Tank glared at the general then backed away.

An aide fished a piece of paper from a dark leather satchel and handed it to Wallace. "I've been ordered by someone in the chain of command who significantly outranks me to transfer you and Lieutenant Garcia immediately."

"And who might that be, sir?" Cyndi asked.

"I'm not at liberty to say."

The man was obviously a savvy politician. A bona fide bureaucrat in an Air Force officer's uniform.

Whether talking about Washington politics or military politics, the end result was always the same: the shit rolled downhill until it came to rest on the lowest-ranking person. They would hang while the top dogs/brass got promoted or reelected.

The general handed Cyndi the orders.

Cyndi scanned the page. "I'll be damned."

"What's it say?" Lance asked nervously.

"We're being given three weeks of leave. Then we're being transferred to Edwards. You're going to test upgrades to the F-35." A huge smile crossed her face. "And I'm going to *test pilot school!*" Cyndi grabbed Lance and hugged him.

The fabricated scowl on Wallace's face reversed to a broad, genuine smile. "Congratulations, Captain Stafford.

I can't think of a more courageous and deserving pilot to get a crack at test pilot school." The one-star general surprised Cyndi once more. He snapped to attention and saluted.

The room erupted in cheers again.

It seemed like David had actually won this round with Goliath.

<hr>

President Ashford's prediction during their tense encounter in the desert had been spot-on. The media turned Cyndi into a national hero overnight. Everyone from the governor to late-night talk show hosts wanted to exploit the spotlight focused on Cyndi for their own benefit.

The Air Force didn't waste any time cashing in on her newfound stardom. A film crew from the 2nd Audiovisual Squadron at Hill AFB was rushed to Luke. It hurriedly shot footage for a new recruiting commercial featuring Cyndi confidently strutting across the tarmac up to an F-35 before her transfer to Edwards.

The deluge of requests for her time had grown so over-whelming that Cyndi had to change her phone number to get the calls to stop. Autograph hounds badgered her wherever she went. Even pilots in her own squadron surreptitiously obtained her autograph by claiming she needed to sign a random form or document before leav-ing.

During the chaos, Lance scrambled to arrange the move while Cyndi hastily planned a small, intimate wed-ding. Her mother was practically hysterical about the prospect of hosting a wedding in her backyard on such short notice. So they tied the knot at the historic White Chapel on base.

Lance wore the formal Air Force mess dress uniform, the equivalent of civilian black-tie attire. He stood at the altar, nervously fiddling with his bowtie, as he waited for his soul mate. Cyndi looked radiant as she glided down the aisle in a flowing white wedding dress, escorted by her mother.

With patient prompting from the priest, the couple exchanged their vows with only a few minor glitches.

News choppers hovered just outside the airspace boundary of the base hoping to get video of the nuptials. Gyro-stabilized cameras with 44x magnification capability captured closeup shots of Lance and Cyndi emerging hand-in-hand after the ceremony.

As the newlyweds darted through the tunnel of well-wishers showering them with birdseed, a four-ship of F-35s flew low over the chapel just below the speed of sound.

Eager to start off on the right foot with her new in-laws, Cyndi had agreed to a lavish wedding reception at the legendary Biltmore hotel in Phoenix, paid for by them.

The hotel exuded an Old Hollywood glamour, Arizona style. Nestled among palm trees and mountain ranges, the Frank Lloyd Wright masterpiece formed a magical oasis at the base of the Phoenix Mountains Preserve. Lance's parents sprang for the diamond dinner package at $250 per person, on top of the $6,000 wedding package. Of course that didn't include any hotel rooms. Those were extra.

In a deviation from tradition, and at Cyndi's request, the figurines of a couple that normally adorned the top of a wedding cake were replaced by two broken halves of Air Force pilot wings. Given everything that Cyndi and Lance had endured during their time together, the symbolism behind the fondant creation held a much greater significance for them.

During the couple's first dance, Lance bopped himself on the forehead. "Between packing for our move to Edwards, the media badgering us, and arranging all the details for our wedding, we forgot to plan our honeymoon!" He thought for a moment then said, "How about Cancun?"

Cyndi looked at him askew. "Mexico? Really?"

Lance flashed a sheepish grin and said, "Oh, I see your point."

"I thought New York City would be nice this time of year. I booked a room at the Motel 6 in Brooklyn for a week. It's all we could afford on our salaries."

Before he could respond to her announcement, members of their squadron pulled Cyndi away and battled each other for a dance.

Later that evening, as Cyndi came out of the ladies room, Lance's four older sisters surrounded her.

The oldest, Gabriela, smiled and said, "Welcome to the Garcia family. We're so happy for you two. Our baby brother can be a little cocky sometimes, but he's a wonderful guy. I don't know if he mentioned it to you, but he was sort of an oops child. My sisters and I helped raise him." Her smile vanished. "We're sure you understand how important it is to us that Lance is happy."

This wasn't just a simple case of female rivalry. Gabriela was warning Cyndi not to break her baby brother's heart.

Cyndi faked a warm smile. "Oh, that's so sweet. I'm sure he appreciates all the things his much older sisters did for him, now that he's a big boy and all grown up. I'll be sure and tell him about our little talk. Well, back to the party." Cyndi brushed by the ring of sisters. Before getting very far, she turned back. "I forgot to mention, welcome to the Stafford family."

CHAPTER 60

"YOU WANT ANYTHING from the gift shop?" Lance asked as they waited for their flight to LaGuardia from the Sky Harbor airport.

"A bottle of water would be great."

He boosted himself out of the black vinyl seat and started to walk away.

"And a magazine!" Cyndi called out before he disappeared into the crowd.

Moments later a tall, broad-shouldered passenger planted himself in Lance's seat. He had closely cropped hair and wore dark sunglasses that masked his identity.

"Sorry," Cyndi said, "that seat is taken."

The passenger ignored her and pulled a slip of paper out of his pocket.

"Hey, pal, I said the seat's taken."

He passed her the slip of paper.

"What's this?"

"Open it," he replied, scanning the waiting area. When he turned his head, Cyndi caught a glimpse of a small, coiled wire leading up from under his collar to an earpiece in his right ear.

Cyndi's eyes narrowed as she scanned the gate area to see if anyone was watching the odd encounter. The other passengers were oblivious to what was going on. She unfolded the slip of paper. On it was written *Confirmation # P378-923*.

"It's a confirmation number."

"I can see that. For what?" she asked.

"When you get to New York City, give it to the front desk at the Waldorf Astoria hotel. They'll know what to do with it. Consider it a wedding present."

"From whom?"

"It comes from someone who hopes you consider him an ally. Other than that, I'm not at liberty to say." The stranger leaned in close to Cyndi. "I'm sure he can count on your full discretion concerning this matter." The grossly overqualified messenger stood up. "Enjoy your honeymoon. I hear the presidential suite at the Waldorf is quite luxurious."

As the stranger walked away, four other randomly situated passengers suddenly got up and followed him. Each of them had earpieces in their ears and wore dark shades.

Lance strolled back from the gift shop with a bag of peanut M&Ms and the current edition of the *Arizona Republic* newspaper. He sat in the newly vacated seat next to Cyndi and handed her a bottle of water and the latest *Plane & Pilot* magazine.

Cyndi discreetly folded up the note and slipped it into her pocket.

Lance opened his paper and scanned the front page. Suddenly, he shot up straight in his seat. "You're not going to believe this." He tapped on the startling headline. "Anonymous Donor Gives Astronomical Amount to Fight Cartels."

Lance turned to Cyndi and read the first sentence of the article. "An anonymous donor gave the staggering sum of $1,000,000,000 in Bitcoin to the Mexican government with the stipulation that it must be used to fight the drug cartels that are ravaging the country."

Cyndi gave an indifferent shrug. "That's interesting." She opened up her magazine and pretended to read.

Lance folded up his paper and stared at Cyndi, his mouth agape.

Before he could say what he was obviously thinking, she lifted a hand and said, "Don't ask."

Lance just shook his head and chuckled. He got up and went over to the window to watch airplanes take off and land.

Cyndi peered over the top of her magazine, checking to see that Lance's back was to her. She picked up her backpack and quietly slipped away to the ladies room. Cyndi carefully checked each stall to make sure she was alone. Then she put her pack on the counter and pulled out a black iPhone in a solid gold phone case.

Under her breath she mumbled, "You did say I could have it all." She popped the phone out of the extravagant case and placed it on the colorful terrazzo floor. Then Cyndi stomped on the iPhone, cracking it in half. For good measure, she stomped on it a second time then tossed the destroyed phone into the trash can next to the sink. With a triumphant smirk she said, "Never underestimate your enemy, Lucy."

When she pulled open the door to leave, Cyndi had to step aside for a cleaning cart being pushed into the bathroom by a janitor. Cyndi reached out and handed the phone case to the woman. "Merry Christmas," she said with a broad smile.

The woman just shrugged at the gringa who didn't even know what month it was. Assuming it was a cheap knockoff, she dropped the case into the front pocket of her apron and began scrubbing the toilets.

Cyndi retraced her steps back to the gate and casually leafed through her magazine, pretending to read while secretly scanning the crowd for any more covert messengers.

AUTHOR'S NOTES

WANT MORE? Be the first to know about upcoming book releases, events Dan will be at, and more. Sign up for his email list at: https://danstratmanauthor.com/

Check out Dan's YouTube channel for book trailer videos and his series **Practical Tips for Writers** - *http://bit.ly/YTChannel-AuthorDanStratman*

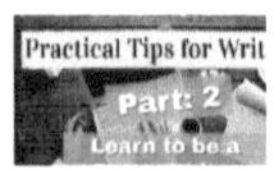

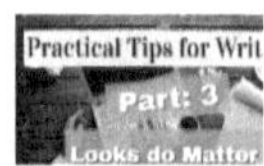

Follow the Dan Stratman Facebook page: *facebook.com/DanStratmanAuthor*

Please consider leaving a review. Honest reviews are immensely helpful for self-published authors.

ALSO BY DAN STRATMAN

WANT TO GO behind the scenes on Dan's research trips without needing a Top Secret background check? Check out these cool videos:

Air Force Pilot Training Behind the Scenes:
A Guided Tour
https://bit.ly/AFPilotTrainingBehindTheScenes

The F-35 and Luke AFB:
Rare Behind the Scenes Access
https://bit.ly/TheF-35-BehindTheScenes

ACKNOWLEDGEMENTS

The acknowledgements section of my books is where I get to express my thanks to all the wonderful people who help make them possible. It never fails to amaze me how generous people are with their time, expertise, and knowledge. I thoroughly enjoy the research process that precedes crafting my stories. The friends I make, the cool places I get to go to, and the knowledge I gain are just as important to me as writing my stories. The least I can do for these people is to thank them by name. And yes, those of you who asked not to be named, I thank you as well.

Captain Brandon "Crime" Maxson. My go-to guy for all things fighter pilot and a good friend.

Major Kristin "Beo" Wolfe, USAF F-35 Demonstration Pilot.

Staff Sgt. Codie Trimble, NCOIC, Public Affairs, F-35 Demonstration Team.

Sean Clements, Chief of Media Relations-Luke AFB Public Affairs. Instrumental in coordinating my visit to Luke AFB.

Anne Sittmann, Television and Motion Picture Division, Office of Public Affairs, US Customs and Border Protection, Washington, DC.

Jodie Underwood, Group Supervisor/PIO, US Drug Enforcement Administration, Phoenix Field Division.

David Holtzman, Writer, Technologist, Cybersecurity, and Privacy Expert.

Steve Stratton, former Green Beret who deployed with 20th Special Forces on counter-drug missions back in the day. He also served on the White House Communications Agency supporting presidents and vice-presidents.

Steve was very helpful providing insights into the tactics used by special forces hostage rescue teams.

First Lt. Analise "Miss" Howard and 1st Lt. Kelsey "Goomba" Flannery, F-35 Students at Luke AFB. I interviewed them on day one of my visit. They provided invaluable perspectives on life as a female fighter pilot.

Staff Sgt. Jorge Aparicio-Aguilar and Senior Airman Bryce Evans, Weapons Load Crew, 56th WSS. They introduced me to the weapons carried on the F-35, showed me where they are stowed, how to attach them, and most importantly, how they are released. Whoever said researching the details before writing a novel is boring!

Tech Sgt. Shawn Layou, F-35 Ejection Seat FTD Instructor. The first person a pilot would thank upon safely returning to base after an ejection!

Lieutenant Col. Hunter "Cain" Powell, F-35 Instructor Pilot.

Major Drew "Apollo" Taylor, F-16 Instructor Pilot.

Chas Buchanan, Director, 56th Range Management Office. Chas was very generous with his time, educating me about the immense amount of land in southern Arizona set aside for military training, and the dangers (both human and animal) that await anyone who finds themselves stranded in the unforgiving environment of the Sonoran Desert.

Charles Gutierrez, Director of Operations, 56th Range Management Office

Lieutenant Col. Raymond "John" Boyer, 56th Fighter Wing Chaplain. Chaplain Boyer provided exceptionally valuable information on how the Air Force respectfully and compassionately deals with loved ones when pilots die on duty or go missing in action.

Sergeant Kent Battmer, KCPD, retired. Walked me through each step a police officer goes through when arriving on the scene of an active shooting situation—so that they can go home that night to their family.

Officers Nate Anderson and Carlos Mena, both with the KCPD. Thanks for sharing your expertise and your endless patience with all my questions about police work during my ride-along. Above all else, thank you for your bravery and courage for being willing to put your safety at risk to protect the rest of us.

Paul Hansen, KMCI Senior Air traffic Controller, retired.

Doctor Cameron C. Lindsey, Professor in Chair, Division of Pharmacy and Administration, UMKC School of Pharmacy. Thank you for taking time out of your busy schedule to educate me on the complicated world of pharmacology.

Kathy Day-Faulkner, An accomplished author in her own right and an expert in all things equine.

Staff Sgt. Nichoson and Airman 1st Class Jones, SERE Specialists, 336th Training Group, USAF Survival School. Thank you for bringing me up to speed on SERE school and the incredibly valuable survival skills you teach personnel who are "at risk of isolation" (the baffling official term for aircrew).

Danny Conley, Air Force Rescue Coordination Center SAR Program Manager, Tyndall AFB. Thanks for walking me through each step of the process of activating the search-and-rescue capabilities of the Air Force. The impressive hardware and the assortment of highly trained professionals that the military unleashes to search for downed aircrew is beyond amazing.

My beta readers voluntarily perform the unpleasant job of reading the first drafts of my manuscripts. Your patience and editing skills are greatly appreciated: Paul Stratman, Phil Heffley, Rob Perschau, and Anita Marra Rogers.

My editor, Jason Whited, makes my ramblings appear much more professional than I could ever achieve without him.

And last but certainly not least, I thank my dear sweet
wife. I love you with all my heart.
Sincerely,

Dan Stratman

ABOUT THE AUTHOR

Dan Stratman is a # 1 bestselling author and retired major airline Captain with over 42 years of experience in the aviation industry. Before flying for the airlines he was a decorated Air Force pilot. In addition, Captain Stratman is a highly sought-after aviation consultant and a popular aviation spokesperson with the media. He is also a World traveler, having been to 43 countries so far.

Dan has an entrepreneurial side that stretches back many years. He developed the popular air travel app, Airport Life. In addition, he created an eCommerce website, ran an aviation consulting company he founded, and has filed numerous patents for consumer products.

Dan is a volunteer pilot with the Civil Air Patrol, performing search and rescue missions and disaster response flights when called on. In his spare time he enjoys mentoring budding entrepreneurs and volunteering weekly with Habitat for Humanity.

The two things he is most proud of are his long marriage to his lovely wife and his three wonderful kids.